MURDER
ON THE
GREEN

a Modern Midwife Mystery

Christine Knapp

To Nora Eliza
Solas réalta, réalta geal, is tú an mian is mian linn anocht

To Laura
Is tusa an spéir a choinníonn na réaltaí

Modern Midwife Mysteries

"And I'd give the world if I could hear that song of hers today"
—"Too-Ra-Loo-Ra-Loo-Ra (That's an Irish Lullaby),"
James Royce Shannon, 1913

CHAPTER ONE

———

Approximately 5 percent of babies are born on their "due date."

August had arrived with a string of ninety-degree days in the seaside town of Langford. The population swelled with the usual vacationers and day trippers. Mike's Lobster Shack drew a steady stream of customers who lined up around the pier, and in-town parking suddenly became a rare find.

As I looked out at the harbor from the large glass window at the end of the labor and delivery unit, I could barely believe that I would be winging my way across the Atlantic tomorrow night. That's when Mom, her three closest friends, Meg, and I would be off on a long-awaited holiday to Ireland courtesy of the Massachusetts State Lottery. Mom had hit the jackpot on a scratcher last fall and had immediately started planning this trip. Schedules were coordinated, flights were booked, and a host of Irish relatives were joyfully awaiting our arrival. We would have a three-week visit, and then my husband Will, my girls Rowan and Sloane, and the rest of the family would join us for our final ten days.

Merely contemplating this journey made me think of the many supplies I needed to add to my packing list. But as I took out my phone to add a few notes to my ever-growing travel file, I received a text from Trinity, the recently hired nurse midwife I was orienting today.

Camille is ready to start pushing.

I returned the phone to the pocket of my scrubs and walked down the corridor. Pausing at the second door just long enough to knock, I opened it to find Camille Owens, who was not just a patient but a fellow rower, and her partner, Louis. They both had crewed at the University of Washington in their undergraduate days. Camille and I often spent the first few moments of her prenatal appointments reliving memorable races and discussing our favorite places to scull around Langford.

"Camille felt a lot of pressure, so I checked her cervix. She's fully dilated," Trinity said, looking to me for acknowledgement.

"Excellent," I said and gave her an encouraging smile. "Camille, we'll get everything ready. I remember you said your first baby was born quickly."

"Yes, Maeve. I pushed for about twenty minutes with Austin. My obstetrician in Atlanta barely made it in time. She said to be sure to tell my next provider how fast his birth was."

Robin, one of Creighton Memorial's most experienced labor nurses, had already opened a birth pack and checked the fetal heartbeat. We had worked together so often that no words needed to be exchanged.

Trinity looked my way and gave me a nod. She was fresh out of a nurse-midwifery program but had been a labor and delivery RN for a few years before that. When she applied for the midwife position at Creighton, there had been some reluctance within the group about taking a new graduate into the practice. However, Trinity's experience and personality proved to be a strong argument in her favor, and outstanding recommendations pushed her to the top of everyone's list. Finally, the last concerns were overcome when it was pointed out that our practice was firmly established and we could spend extended time on one-on-one orientation.

"Contraction starting," Camille announced quietly, reaching for Louis's hand.

"You're doing great. Time to push again," Trinity said in a reassuring tone.

Camille was fully engaged on birthing her baby, and as I watched, I noticed her shoulders seemed tense. After the contraction subsided, she took a deep breath and lay back on the pillows.

"Camille, is your upper back bothering you?" I asked.

"It is, Maeve. I think I wedged a pillow behind me during the night, and now it's a bit sore."

I moved toward the bed and gently rubbed her shoulders.

"Let me get a warm blanket. The heat might help," Robin commented as she left the room.

"How about pushing on your side?" I suggested.

Camille nodded her assent, and Trinity and I moved her into position.

Louis was at her side as the next contraction began. As it peaked, Camille bore down with everything she had and held it until the contraction let up. As it receded, she rotated each shoulder. Then she smiled and said, "Much better, Maeve."

"I can see your baby's head, Camille. It won't be long," Trinity said.

I could hear the excitement in her voice and smiled at her enthusiasm. Even after years of birth experiences, this never got old.

Robin returned carrying a standard-issue white hospital blanket taken fresh from the warming cabinet. "Guess we can save this until after the birth," she chuckled.

Seeing that the birth was near, I stepped back to let Trinity take charge.

"Camille, with the next push or two, you'll have your baby." Trinity moved closer to the birthing bed. "I want you to have a gentle birth. Please blow out when I tell you."

With the next contraction, I saw the baby's head begin to crown. I folded my arms to keep them still. Orienting was hard for me. I wanted to reach out and guide the baby's head, but I had to remind myself that I was not Camille's midwife today. Doing was my strong suit, not watching. Although now that I taught nursing students during the school year, I was learning to be a patient observer, inch by inch.

The baby's head emerged slowly, and Trinity was calm and collected. After the baby's head rotated to the right, she applied slight traction to help deliver the anterior shoulder. It was a lovely birth, with the baby letting out a vigorous cry as it emerged.

"It's a girl," Trinity exclaimed, lifting the baby into Camille's arms.

"You have a big brother named Austin," Louis said, gently touching the newborn's face.

"Hello, beautiful," Camille crooned.

Louis leaned over and kissed his wife's forehead as Robin placed the warm blanket over Camille and the baby.

"This is Jocelyn Rose," Camille said, beaming.

Moving to her side, I admired the baby while unobtrusively watching Trinity expertly deliver the placenta and check Camille for lacerations.

"You were so strong," I said to Camille.

"Thanks, Maeve. I have to say that during transition, I felt like I was competing in a 6K race in very choppy water, but no rowing medal compares to this prize." She kissed Jocelyn and snuggled her closer.

Trinity finished her post-birth checklist, and I left her talking to Camille and Louis. Walking to the main desk, I felt a text arrive on my Apple watch. It was from my sister, Meg.

Mom is up or rather down to three suitcases. Gonna need help.

Stifling a giggle, I headed to the midwifery call room for a cup of coffee and to wait for Trinity to finish up and join me.

Heaven help Meg, I thought. Mom somehow had the idea that she needed to take her entire wardrobe overseas. It was going to be difficult to convince her otherwise.

When I opened the door to the midwifery sanctuary, I was greeted by a sea of green. Green balloons and emerald streamers filled the room. Behind all the decorations, Maddie, Winnie, and Bev, the women who made up the rest of the original midwife foursome at Creighton, were sitting on the couch smiling.

Winnie was a Montserrat native who had studied midwifery in London. She was highly skilled and experienced and was always calm in any storm. Bev was our Haitian-via-Flatbush sophisticated style queen. The two of us were like sisters and were thrilled to be raising our children together. The chief midwife, Maddie, had four young children and lived in a rambling, constantly under-construction farmhouse with her wife, Joy. She was a phenomenal leader, full of both vision and kindness.

"Bon voyage," Winnie, the unofficial mother of the midwifery practice, said. "Come and have a scone or maybe a shamrock cupcake."

That's when I noticed the small table held tea, goodies, green plates, and napkins. "I can't believe the three of you," I said as I thanked them one by one.

"Maeve, we want you to have a wonderful trip. The timing couldn't be better. With Trinity and the other recent hires, the midwifery staffing is fine. Plus, you'll be back before the fall term at Rosemont College starts. So, stop worrying," Maddie said as she nibbled on some green icing.

Last year, I started a dual appointment between Rosemont College and Creighton Memorial Hospital. Somehow, that led me to uncover a multiple murder scheme, but all the excitement and distractions had finally settled down. Now, I was back for another, hopefully, more normal, foray into academia.

"Yes, Maeve, just be sure to return in time to help me birth Adelaide Marie's brother," Bev laughed as she rubbed her baby bump. I had been at her first birth and fully intended to be at the next one. After all, I was her midwife.

"Considering that you're not due until the end of November, of course I'll be back. I'm not emigrating!"

"Now, I don't want to hear any talk of emigration, and I also don't want to hear about any police involvement." Bev wagged her finger at me in a pretend scold.

I laughed. "Even sleuths deserve a vacation."

"And remember, Maeve, Montserrat's history includes a fair number of Irish settlers. So, I have roots in Eire, too," Winnie said with a proud nod.

"I know you've been to Ireland. What's your favorite place?"

"Aah, let me see…" She gazed off into the distance as if visualizing her past travel. "There are so many phenomenal sights, but I think the Dingle Peninsula and the Wild Atlantic Way are must-see places. However, every part of Ireland has its charm. You'll see. We'll compare notes when you return. Where are you going first?"

"The first three weeks we'll be based in Ballymoor, which is part of County Galway. My mother's relatives are there. We will do some sightseeing, especially in Dublin. When the rest of the family arrives, we'll visit Cork, where my dad was born, and then Killarney, Dingle, and the Cliffs of Moher, of course. Trust me, there is an extensive list. My sister has a comprehensive itinerary ready to go."

As we sipped tea and ate pastry, I reflected on how lucky I was to have this awesome hospital group. We were there for each other through thick and thin, and nothing would change that in the future. It felt odd to be leaving Creighton Memorial for such an extended period. I would miss my colleagues, but I was excited to be visiting Ireland. Other than a week in Paris for my honeymoon, I had not traveled out of the country. As magical as that experience had been, I had a feeling that discovering Ireland with my entire family would be the trip of a lifetime for all of us.

After what seemed like a speedy five minutes, phones pinged with texts as my fellow midwives were called back to their respective clinical areas. We exchanged quick goodbyes, and the room was suddenly empty. Well, except for a myriad of green balloons and streamers.

I was on cupcake number two when Trinity entered the midwifery call room.

"Well, this is a surprise," she said, eyeing the balloon bouquet.

"Maddie, Winnie, and Bev had a little send-off for me. I'm going to Ireland for vacation."

"That's wonderful. I saw on the schedule that you're going to be on holiday. Take lots of photos. That's one of the many places I'd like to visit."

We sat down and reviewed Camille's birth. I checked Trinity's charting and found it to be concise and complete.

"That was a beautiful birth, Trinity. I'm very impressed. Are you feeling comfortable at Creighton Memorial?"

"I am, Maeve. The midwifery group is so supportive. I'm finally off orientation next week, and I feel confident."

"And you have every reason to. But always remember that advice or help is only a stone's throw away, and that's been the group's strength from the beginning. Please have a treat, and then we'll see what awaits us next."

Our shift continued to be busy, and I was happy to see that Trinity handled each situation deftly. She would be a great addition to our staff.

At the end of the day, as I was changing out of my scrubs, I received a text from MJ, a delightful RN in the emergency room with whom I had become friends over the past year.

Before you cross the pond, stop by if you can.

Checking the time, I saw that I could fit in a quick visit. Saying goodbye even briefly to my colleagues made me realize again that I was so lucky to have two families, one at the hospital and one at home.

CHAPTER TWO

———

Hibernia is the ancient name for Ireland.

"Hey, Maeve, I hear you're off to uncover your roots." Troy, the ED administrative assistant and jack-of-all-trades, greeted me as I approached the front desk. Since the tragic events of last year, when one of the staff nurse's siblings had been murdered, I had become friendly with most of the ED staff and stopped in occasionally.

"We'll visit some relatives. Who knows what I'll discover?" I countered, laughing.

As I looked around, I quickly noticed that the ED was eerily quiet. I looked at Troy and put my hands up questioningly.

"The bus apparently hasn't arrived yet." Troy put his finger to his lips.

Hospital staff are very superstitious about patient census. We never directly address a low one, afraid of causing bad karma and opening the floodgates.

"Last week, one of the new orthopedic fellows was called down for a consult, and he went on and on about how lucky we were because it was so empty," he said, frowning. "The ED was in overflow one hour later." Troy shook his head and laughed. "Let's just say, he won't be on the top of the holiday party list. Speaking of parties—go check out the scene in the staff lounge."

Since it was shift change and the ED was so vacant, the lounge was full of arriving and departing staff. MJ was seated at a packed table where Anthony, one of the physician assistants, was cutting into a birthday cake.

"Maeve, come and grab a plate. Anthony is twenty-nine today. His favorite flavor is chocolate fudge with vanilla buttercream icing—a classic."

"Happy birthday, Anthony," I said.

"Thank you, thank you all. This looks delicious."

As he passed slices around, MJ came to stand next to me. "I wanted to tell you to have a great time, and I have a small parting gift."

"MJ, you are too much. You shouldn't have," I said as she handed me a box wrapped in green glittery paper with a large gold bow. I opened the rectangular package. Nestled in white tissue paper was a beautiful soft green silk scarf. I gently lifted it out and held it up admiringly.

"Oh, MJ, it's lovely. Thank you so much," I said, reaching out to hug her.

"I found it in a little shop in Norberg and immediately thought of you and your trip."

"I love it. I'll be very fashionable on my journey."

We turned back to the table as a loud rendition of "Happy Birthday" was being sung to Anthony.

As we ate cake, Jean-Pierre, an ED physician and the one who was always the last to leave a party, called out, "And now an Irish tune for Maeve."

The room hushed as Jean-Pierre and Anthony stepped forward. The two began singing "Danny Boy" to shouts of approval and encouragement from the staff.

As they finished, I gave them a bow of thanks. But MJ, with hands on her hips and a scowl on her face, said, "That's a song for funerals. Let's hear an upbeat tune."

The words were barely out of MJ's mouth when Jean-Pierre saluted her. Without missing a beat, he and Anthony belted out "The Wild Rover" to cheers from the staff. At this, MJ nodded and grinned her approval as she joined in on the chorus.

When the merriment settled down, I gathered my scarf and walked to the door. As I did, I thanked MJ again.

"Just one thing, Maeve," she replied. "No dead bodies in Ireland, please."

I held up my little finger. "Pinky promise. I am so done with murders."

I left the hospital and went straight to my car. As I pulled out of the employee lot, Meg called. My older sister could have been a model but instead had opted for a stellar career as a premier real estate agent. She was always composed and routinely handled complicated, multimillion-dollar transactions without breaking a sweat.

Today, though, hadn't shaped up to be a banner day for her.

"Maeve, I officially give up. I take no responsibility for whatever Mom brings to the airport."

I bit my lip so I would not laugh. Don't poke the bear. After a couple of deep breaths, I finally asked, "Does she know she can only check two bags?"

But it was as if Meg never heard the question. "I left after I counted thirty sequined scarves. She's on her own."

I knew exactly what Meg was getting at. Our mother firmly believed that more was more. Mary Margaret Callahan O'Reilly was a force of nature, often on the order of hurricanes, tsunamis, or devastating floods. The oldest of fourteen, she loved family, friends, animals, the oppressed, all things Irish, Saint Jude, the Red Sox, and a good party, or as she called it, a time. She had been widowed young and now used a wheelchair full-time because of debilitating arthritis. In her signature style, sequins were necessary for daily wear, and I had no trouble believing she would insist on taking most of her wardrobe to Ireland.

"Gaby will probably talk some sense into her," I pointed out. Gaby was a Jamaican transplant and Mom's neighbor at Hanville Grove Senior Residence. She was also Mom's best friend. Along with Ethel and Louella, the other members of the 'Ladies of the Lobby,' they made a formidable foursome. Together, they patrolled the lobby at Hanville Grove and had recently shown considerable ingenuity and resilience under extreme pressure. On our last adventure, they had even put their lives on the line for me and my daughter, Sloane. I owed them so much and was so happy that they were coming with us to Ireland.

"We can only hope," Meg grudgingly allowed. "If she doesn't, the plane may be too heavy to fly. Anyway, I'll see you at Olivia and Patrick's in a few minutes. It's so nice they are hosting family dinner before we leave."

Will had texted me that he, Rowan, and Sloane would meet me at my brother's house. Checking the time, I decided to stop at my favorite flower shop, A Bloom of One's Own, to pick up a bouquet for Olivia. As I pulled the front door open, a tall figure in a long purple velvet cape trimmed with fur emerged carrying a massive armful of bright yellow sunflowers. As she looked up, I gave a small gasp.

Zeena! She was the local mystic whom Mom adored and I was still cautious around. She had seemingly foretold so many events in the lives of the O'Reilly women. Or had she? Deep down, I truly believed she was a charlatan, but I must admit a very accurate one. Her predictions were uncanny.

"Mrave," she said in her distinct raspy voice as she nodded at me.

That was what Zeena had called me from the start. I guess her magical powers did not include spellcheck.

"Hello, Zeena, it's nice to see you," I stammered. Was it nice? I certainly didn't want her to predict some gruesome event in my future.

Zeena stopped short and stared at me with her heavily mascaraed eyes. Gee, I didn't know orange glitter eyeshadow was even a thing.

"Find your roots. Be a good midwife." With that declaration, she was gone with her telltale scent of patchouli and lavender wafting behind.

My head was spinning. How did Zeena know I was leaving for Ireland? Did she think I was going there for work? I tried to shake off her words as I went into the flower shop.

Arriving at Olivia and Patrick's home, I saw tricolor Irish flags lining the driveway. In typical fashion, my sister-in-law was all in on the theme. Glittering white and green lights were strung around the front door, and a sign read, *Céad Míle Fáilte*. A hundred thousand welcomes. An O'Reilly leave-taking for the ages. What could be better?

CHAPTER THREE

In 1921, per the Anglo-Irish Treaty, Ireland was partitioned, and southern Ireland became the Republic of Ireland while the six counties that remained with the United Kingdom were called Northern Ireland.

"Aunt Maeve, we're going to Ireland!" Abigail, Patrick and Olivia's oldest, sang out as she kissed me hello when I entered the front hallway. Her long blonde braids were entwined with green and white ribbons.

"I know, Abigail. It's going to be so much fun," I said, returning her kiss.

Making the rounds, I handed the multicolored dahlia bouquet to Olivia, who was dressed in a forest green turtleneck and a red plaid County Galway tartan kilt. As she arranged the flowers, I saw that her fingernails were painted in a green and white pattern. She was the complete package. I kissed Patrick and his other children, Penelope, Cassie, and Becca. The girls were clad in white sweaters with tiny shamrocks and Patrick sported a dark green crew neck sweater. Olivia loved a color-coordinated family.

My brother Aidan and his husband, Sebi, were settling their daughters, Chloe and Louisa, at the table, which was set with a snowy white damask tablecloth and gleaming Waterford crystal.

Mom, in her wheelchair, sparkled from head to toe in an emerald sequined ensemble and her smile spread from ear to ear. She dearly loved her family and taking them to Ireland was an answer to a lifelong prayer. Meg was sitting to her right and saluted me with her glass of Chablis. Our eyes met, and she gave me a familiar sisterly look. It held the unspoken promise that we would rehash every aspect of this gathering later. Henry, Meg's teenage son, was helping Will with Rowan and Sloane. There were seventeen of us now. We certainly filled a room!

"Hi, honey," I said, kissing Will and my girls, one by one. Rowan and Sloane were dressed in identical Kelly green overalls and jerseys, gifts from our Irish nanny, Kate. They were my one-and-two-year-old daughters and the heart of our family. After infertility struggles, Will and I knew how lucky we were.

"Hi, Maeve—everyone is so excited tonight. I know that Olivia must have cooked up some Irish delicacies," Will said, smiling.

As soon as everyone was seated, Patrick said grace. "Dear Lord, thanks for bringing us all together for this wonderful family gathering. Thank you and my beautiful Olivia for the meal we are about to enjoy together. Please keep this family safe in their travels." He hesitated for a moment before continuing, "Oh, and Lord, please do not let me read about my lovely sisters in the papers. Amen."

Patrick was the deputy chief of the Langford Police Department, and Meg and I had been involved in a few of his murder investigations—a few too many for his taste. I could see both relief and concern on his face as he offered up his prayer. Relief that we wouldn't find any more bodies in his jurisdiction for a while…and concern that we might not be able to help ourselves once we were overseas.

As he finished, Aidan raised his glass for a toast. "I'll second that." A chorus of "*Sláinte*" echoed around the table.

"Are you all packed, Mom?" Patrick inquired as he helped his younger daughters unfold their napkins.

"Oh, I've been ready for days."

"Mom, I was just at your apartment this afternoon. You ran out of room for your tremendous collection of scarves!" Meg exclaimed with an exaggerated eyeroll.

Mom took a long sip of her Manhattan, looked piercingly at Meg, and said, "This is intercontinental travel, dear. I intend to have all my outfits tastefully coordinated. The girls had room in their suitcases for my extras."

"I bet we'll end up buying an extra suitcase for souvenirs," Meg said sotto voce.

Just as Mom opened her mouth to respond, Olivia announced, "Dinner is served," as she and Henry brought platters of corned beef, cabbage, potatoes, and carrots to the table.

Meg one, Mom zero.

As the food was passed around, the conversation centered on what sites to visit in Ireland, what movies to watch on the flight, and the time difference.

"You know, Olivia, corned beef is not traditionally served in Ireland—it's more of an American dish. I mean, I love it, but I don't think we'll see it on the menu on our holiday," Mom remarked.

Before Olivia could respond, Will chimed in. "This feels like a Saint Patrick's Day banquet, Olivia—I hope you'll share your fantastic recipes with me."

"Of course." Olivia beamed with pride. Will's café was extremely successful, and I could tell that she was very flattered. Meg gave me a quick, relieved nod. Will had artfully deflected Mom's well-meaning but off-putting comment.

"So, Mom, tell us the story again of how you met Dad," Aidan said while carefully wiping Chloe's mouth.

Mom looked around the table, then folded her hands under her chin and gave a little chuckle of delight.

"Oh, how your father would love to be here. He was so proud of all of you." She paused before continuing. "Our story begins with my own family. My mother and father were raised in Ireland and, after they married, decided to settle in Boston. There was not much opportunity for work in Ireland in those days, and people arrived weekly from various counties. When I was growing up, we lived in a predominately Irish neighborhood. I believe that people tried to create a sense of home by living near their compatriots. Most families were very involved with the local Catholic parish. When I was in high school, there were weekly dances and socials. The newly arrived were always welcomed." She got a faraway look in her eyes and her mouth curved in a smile. "At the end of my senior year, I met my Declan. He had recently arrived from Cork and was working as a plumber's apprentice."

"Why did he decide to come to America, Grandma?" Henry asked.

Mom pursed her lips. "Well, Henry, in those days, in rural Ireland, the family farm was left to the first-born son. Both my father and my husband were second-born sons. Generations apart, they ultimately decided to come here to seek their fortune.

It was the same for so many Irish." She rubbed her hands together as she related the past.

"Was it love at first sight?" Olivia, the Hallmark movie aficionado, asked dreamily.

"Well, once we met, there was never anyone else for either of us. Even though we wed young, we had too short a time together, but it was a wonderful marriage." She wiped a tear away from her cheek. "And look at the family we created."

"Will we meet some of his relatives, Mom?" Aidan asked.

"Yes, his older brother and younger sister are still in Cork, and they want us to come for a visit. You know that I keep in regular touch with my father's family in Galway. Meg, Maeve, and I will stay near them until all of you arrive. You'll meet both sides of the family. My mother had an older brother who passed a few years ago, but we'll hopefully meet his remaining kin."

"That's wonderful, Mom. Thanks for arranging everything," Patrick said, gently patting her shoulder.

Mom smiled and continued, "Declan described Ireland in detail to me. I can't wait to see it. He never got back there but would be so happy to know his children and grandchildren will see his native country."

We were all quiet. Well, as quiet as the Ò'Reilly clan got with a table full of young children.

This trip meant so much to Mom. It meant so much to all of us.

Sebi broke the silence and brought us back to the present. "What time do you leave tomorrow?"

"The limo will pick us up at five p.m. sharp. The Aer Lingus Premier Lounge has a nice buffet. Hopefully, we'll be able to sleep on the flight," Meg answered.

Somehow, I doubted the group would settle down quickly, even with premium seats.

"Are you ready for your first flight, Mom? It's a long time in the air," Aidan asked.

"I read a wonderful article about how to prepare for long-distance travel in *The New York Times*. So, I'm all set."

If it was in print and originated in the Big Apple, it was gospel to Mom.

"Remember, you can check two bags but only take a small carry-on, Mom. It must fit under the seat or in the overhead compartment," Meg said, looking exasperated. Helping Mom pack today had clearly tried her patience.

"Not to worry. I bought a great bag from QVC. That lovely brunette Kathy Dean was selling them last month. She's so personable and swears by it. I watch her all the time. Mine is fuchsia, has tons of pockets, and even expands. Kathy Dean's is fuchsia, also. Too bad that you prefer leather, Meg. All the seasoned travelers use these." Mom's smile was worthy of the Cheshire cat.

Okay, Meg one, Mom one.

Hopefully, once the trip started, the little barbs would stop. I knew it was just pre-trip anxiety.

For dessert, Olivia served a vanilla layer cake decorated with green sprinkles and leprechaun gingerbread cookies. But the pièce de résistance was a combination of vanilla and pistachio ice cream with a dollop of orange sherbet, the colors of the Irish flag. Why was I even surprised? Olivia always hit the mark. She served Mom a special Irish coffee.

"Mom, maybe Dad's family are Irish road bowlers. We know it's a big sport in Cork," Meg said, pulling her right arm back and pantomiming a throw.

Road bowling involves hurling a metal ball down country lanes. The team that throws the farthest is the winner. We had seen this sport up close not long ago.

Patrick put his head in his hands and shook it from side to side. The rest of the adults suppressed giggles.

"The Irish never let you down, Meg. Maybe you and Maeve should take a lesson," Mom said proudly.

Time to change the subject. "Henry, I heard that you and your father are taking a trip to California before you meet us in Galway," I said, smiling at my tall, handsome nephew.

Henry's dad, Artie, was Meg's uber-wealthy ex. He was a financial titan who unfortunately had not spent prolonged periods with his only child. He was a wonderful father but only when time allowed. Meg had done the lion's share of raising Henry, and their bond was very close.

"Yes, I'm very excited. Dad got us a tee time at Pebble Beach. We'll tour Stanford, too."

Meg smiled, but I could see tension in her eyes. I knew she hoped Henry would choose a college on the East Coast.

"Henry is such a good student that his school is letting him take time off," Mom said, raising her fancy glass coffee cup proudly.

Blushing to his dark roots, Henry said, "Thanks, Grandma, but I do have to keep up with my work remotely."

"All my grandchildren are brilliant. They follow your lead, Henry."

The adults all gave a silent toast to the children of the family. Who could disagree with a proud grandmother?

As we packed up, there was a lengthy traditional Irish goodbye. No one in this crowd left without hugs and kisses.

Meg leaned toward me and whispered, "Maeve, don't forget to bring that periwinkle cashmere travel wrap I gave you. It will class up any outfit."

Meg never missed an opportunity to impart fashion advice. My sister could give Anna Wintour a run for her money.

CHAPTER FOUR

———

Belfast is the capital of Northern Ireland.

Waking early the following day, I reached across our bed and held Will tightly. I would miss him so much. Since we met, the longest we had been apart was a week at a time, here and there, for various conferences. My husband had come from a rather frosty, upper-class family, yet he was the most loving, down-to-earth person one could ever meet. After deciding not to join his father's financial empire, causing a lot of family consternation, he followed his heart. He was now the owner of A Thyme for All Seasons, a prime Langford catering company.

"Will, I can't believe I'm leaving today. Are you sure you'll be fine with the girls?"

Kissing me on the neck, he said, "Honey, Kate will be here, and Grand and the crew will be over all the time. Plus, I know the midwives will be dropping by. Stop worrying, please."

Kate, our wonderful nanny, was from Galway. She would be with us one more year before she returned to Ireland to study law. Mom had found Kate through her extensive Irish network, and now they enjoyed long talks over tea about their common acquaintances and Galway gossip. Mom had always dreamed of going to Ireland, but since Kate's arrival, her desire to visit surfaced daily.

Kate would be backed up by Grand, who was Will's loving grandmother, and her household staff.

"I know you and the girls have a cadre of support, but a large piece of my heart will remain at Primrose Cottage."

"Woof."

"Well, good morning, Fenway. Come on up," Will said as he lifted our short-haired dachshund onto our bed. We had found her at a shelter when she was five months old, and she had rescued us.

I scratched her around the ears. "And Fenway…what will you think with your pack gone?"

"We'll only all be gone for ten days," Will reminded me. "And trust me, Fenway will be living in the lap of luxury with Grand."

I smiled at that, knowing Grand routinely spoiled Fenway with tasty bacon treats, soft pillows to sleep on, and walks in her oceanfront flower garden. "True," I allowed. "After days of that treatment, she may never come home."

"Mama," came the sweet voice of Rowan, our oldest, through the baby monitor.

After giving me one more kiss, Will pulled away. "I'll get the girls. You shower first, Maeve. This day will fly by."

Will was right, of course. Checking passports, making lists of clothes for Kate to pack for the girls, and answering numerous texts from Meg and Mom filled the day. It left me feeling somewhat exhausted by late afternoon.

Finally, it was time to go. Trying hard not to cry, I kissed the girls and Will goodbye and headed to Hanville Grove with Meg. Since Rowan and Sloane were so young, they had no idea that their Mama would be away from them for three weeks. Will and I had decided to keep our farewell very low-key so the girls would hopefully take my absence in stride. Fenway, on the other hand, had been crying, off and on, since she saw my suitcase appear in the foyer. She knew exactly what it meant and sobbed piteously in my arms as I kissed her goodbye. The Oscars should have a category for best farewell performance by a dachshund!

"Well, you certainly look comfy," Meg said, eyeing my navy jersey pants and top.

"It's an overnight flight, Meg. I thought this outfit was perfect."

Meg was niftily attired in a jet-black Eileen Fisher crepe ensemble. As usual, she would look cover-ready on arrival in Dublin.

By means of defending my wardrobe choice, I said, "I do hope we get a few hours of shut-eye. Can you imagine clearing customs with our group after no sleep?"

We pulled up to Hanville Grove and saw a large crowd at the entrance. Mom, Gaby, Louella, and Ethel were front and center, surrounded by green balloons. All of them were adorned in long sequined emerald scarves.

"Ireland may never recover," Meg said as we exited the Uber. "Come to think of it, *we* may never recover."

Laughing, we rolled our suitcases over to the gathering. A few minutes later, the limo pulled up. As we got in, goodbyes were called out by the large group.

"Have a wonderful time."

"Don't forget we need photos."

"Kiss the Blarney Stone, but don't break a hip."

"Drink a pint of Guinness for me. Actually, drink two."

"*Erin go Bragh.*"

Finally, we were fully loaded, wheels up, and rolling for Logan Airport. Champagne popped, and Mom and her friends chatted excitedly nonstop. I put my head back into the deep leather seat. We were on our way!

The Aer Lingus lounge was heavenly. Sitting in a comfy chair, I feasted on scones and tea to get myself in an Irish state of mind. It was a delightful new experience with a lounge to wait in and plane seats that converted to beds. No wonder passengers disembarking from the front of the aircraft always looked so well-rested.

Once seated on the aircraft, our group took up a large portion of the business class cabin. Meg had placed Mom and her friends in front of us so we would know if they needed any assistance. From our vantage point, we could see Mom, Gaby, and Ethel chatting nonstop to the cabin crew. Although Louella was silent as usual, she was listening intently to every word. They undoubtedly were relaying every minute detail of our trip.

"That gab fest could be considered a 'friendly' hostage situation," Meg muttered as she leaned back and shut her eyes.

"Welcome. May I get you a beverage?" asked a deeply dimpled, middle-aged female flight attendant.

"A gin and tonic, thanks," Meg said.

"A glass of Chardonnay, please."

"I hope the ladies don't keep you on your feet all night," Meg commented.

"They are so excited. I love to see their joy. I've already heard about the amazing lotto win and every one of the relatives they will visit."

As she moved to the fiftyish chestnut-haired guy sitting across the aisle, I heard her ask, "Going home or on holiday?"

"I'm a first-timer. I'm going to a work conference in Dublin."

He ordered a whiskey neat and settled back in his seat. Hopefully, our group would not disturb his trip.

Once in the air and over Canada, Meg and I were served a delicious roast chicken meal. After dessert, we both got up to stretch and visit the restroom before trying to sleep.

"What are you girls doing? Why are you both up at the same time?" Mom cried out as we passed her row.

Mom was seated beside Gaby. On her pull-down table was a small wooden statue of Saint Christopher, the patron saint of travelers. Even though he had been slightly demoted and his feast day removed from Catholic calendars, Mom never gave up on him. Along with the saint, a large bronze crucifix, vials of holy water, colorful prayer cards, and an oversized, white, glow-in-the-dark rosary made a tableau of divine protection. Her collection could easily rival a Vatican Museum display. For an extra safeguard, Mom had adorned Gaby's seat with rose-scented rosary beads and a lacy black mantilla often worn at Catholic masses years ago.

"We're going to the restroom, Mom," Meg said.

"Only one of you at a time! The plane must be balanced. Maeve, you can go when someone from across the aisle gets up." Even though Meg and I were seated behind her, Mom kept an eagle eye on us.

Mouth agape, I went back to my seat. There was no sense arguing aerodynamics on an international flight with Mom.

As I buckled my seatbelt, the man across the aisle spoke, "When you're ready, I can get up with you, so the plane won't go down."

"Thank you for understanding. It's my mother's first flight."

As we talked, I discovered his name was Rob Larson from Portsmouth, New Hampshire. He was an IT professional and planned to stay in Dublin for the week. Amazingly, during the entire flight, he always got up when I did and kept Mom appeased.

When I returned to my seat, I started watching *Waking Ned Devine* in honor of Mom's lottery win. Although I grew up listening to my father's Irish brogue, I wanted to prepare to hear the accent full-time. About halfway through, I fell asleep dreaming of cozy peat fires, rocky coasts, and colorful characters.

"Maeve, look," Meg said, touching my arm and startling me awake.

A patchwork quilt of green appeared out the plane window and stretched for miles. It was magnificent! Who knew green came in so many shades?

Applause broke out in the rows ahead of us. Mom, Gaby, Ethel, and Louella had the window shades up and were applauding the view.

Ireland, here we come. Rest, relaxation, family, new sights, and no sleuthing!

I couldn't wait.

CHAPTER FIVE

The official name of the country is The Republic of Ireland or Poblacht na hÉireann.

The plane landed safely on the ground, much to Mom's relief. Once at the gate, Meg and I settled Mom comfortably into her wheelchair, successfully rescued all the group's belongings from the plane's seat pockets, and trooped everyone to the customs hall at Dublin International Airport. By the time we got there, I somehow had gotten my second wind.

Still, it was eight a.m. local time, and I desperately craved a large Dunkin' iced coffee—or the Irish equivalent. That would be a while off because the entire plane had made it to the hall ahead of us.

As the line snaked along, I noticed that Meg looked totally fresh and unwrinkled, while I resembled an unmade bed. That was par for the course, even though it was a total mystery to me how she accomplished this time after time. My musing was interrupted when the tall, lean customs officer motioned Mom and me to come forward.

Mom jumped right in. "We're here to see my cousins. It's my first time visiting this beautiful land. My parents were born in Ballinasloe." Mom was on a roll. Without cracking a smile, the customs guard examined our passports and asked various questions regarding our length of stay and the contents of our luggage. After a few minutes, our documents were stamped, and the officer gave Mom a toothy smile. "Welcome home, Mrs. O'Reilly."

Mom wiped away a few tears while a slight chill ran up my spine. This, indeed, was our homeland. All our ancestors were from this amazing island. We were home.

Our group moved along, finally arriving at the curb outside the terminal. A six-passenger van soon pulled up, and the driver got out to find six women, twelve suitcases, plus assorted carry-on baggage lined up, ready, and waiting.

"Good morning, I'm Finn Walsh, your driver. You're going to Ballymoor, right? It's a beautiful town."

Finn was a solid six feet three inches, appeared to be in his late thirties, and had a ruddy complexion.

He gave Meg and me an anxious look. "Gosh, you have a lot of luggage. I'm not sure it will all fit."

"Not to worry. The two of us are renting a car," Meg replied, gesturing to me. "You're only responsible for these ladies, Finn."

He broke into a relieved grin. "I'll treat them like my own Nan." He continued, "Nan's what many of us call our grandmothers here. I know they are precious cargo."

He quickly stowed the luggage and lifted Mom into the back seat with ease. Pulling out a heavy blanket, he wrapped it around Mom's wheelchair with extraordinary care.

Meg and I watched and waved as the white passenger van pulled off.

At the car rental, Meg went straight to the desk. "Ma'am, your car is ready," a female employee said, handing Meg a key fob. "Are you sure that you don't want the extra insurance?"

Meg pulled out her oversized black Chanel sunglasses. "I'm a great driver. I have no need of it."

Try to reason with a tired, cranky Meg? Nope. What could possibly go wrong?

Outside, Meg promptly walked over to a shiny red Peugeot 5008. A *big*, shiny red Peugeot 5008.

"An SUV, Meg?"

"I wanted us to be comfy. We're too tall to be stuffed into a compact."

Since we were both six feet, Meg had a point.

"But the roads here are small," I said while eyeing the car's dimensions.

"Oh please, Maeve. Get a grip. What could possibly happen?"

I decided to hold my tongue. Meg driving a large car on the left side of the road in a foreign country held a world of possibilities. Not all of them promising.

As we left the parking lot, I noticed Rob Larson getting into a carbon blue Hyundai.

"Look, there's the guy from the plane. I wonder why he's renting a car. He said he would be so busy at his conference that he doubted he would venture out of Dublin."

"Who knows? Maeve, could you please put our guesthouse address into the GPS? We need to catch up to Mom and her posse."

"Okay, okay. Here we go. Let's see. It's a little over two hours. Are you sure you're good to drive?"

"Reach into my tote."

I pulled out a white plastic bag containing six king-size Cadbury chocolate bars and two large water bottles—breakfast of champions.

"I picked them up in the Dublin terminal. Candy is so much better here. I think it's the cream, or maybe it's the chocolate. Whatever it is, I intend to eat a lot of it," Meg said happily, munching away.

We were absorbed in the sights as we left the city's environs behind and began to see farms, rolling hills of green, and fields and fields of sheep.

"This is like a dream. I've looked at a lot of photos and films, but Ireland is even more beautiful than I imagined."

"We've got a lot of exploring to do, Maeve. I'm so glad we rented a car."

"It will be terrific. Can you believe we are going to watch Mom meet her relatives? I can't wait."

Following the voice commands, which came in a delightful Irish brogue, we pulled off at the ramp to Ballymoor. Amazingly, Meg was handling the left-sided driving without a hitch so far.

"Take the third exit off the next roundabout," the GPS sang out.

Traffic was heavy and Meg drove very close to the side of the road.

As she turned to exit, I said, "Meg, I think this is the second exit, not the third."

"What? No, I counted."

"Recalculating," came the robotic feminine voice.

Meg followed the directions, and we reentered the roundabout.

"Take the third exit," the GPS commanded.

"Got it, Colleen," Meg retorted.

Great, Meg was naming the GPS. Now to convince her that Colleen was a friend.

"Meg, it's the next exit."

"What? This roundabout is different than the rotaries back home."

"Recalculating," Colleen said as Meg once again backtracked.

Finally, we were on the right path.

"Happy now, Colleen?" Meg asked in a sharp tone.

Oh, Colleen, you're in for a workout.

Numerous cattle farms eventually gave way to a glimpse of a magnificent bay and the bustling town center beyond. Delivery trucks were depositing fresh produce, early shoppers were filling the sidewalks, and traffic was slow. Ballymoor looked enchanting, Similar in size, it reminded me of Langford although with a different view of the mighty Atlantic. Reaching the end of the town green, I had counted three groceries, at least four pubs, a dental office, a veterinarian, and an ancient stone church, Saint Columbkille's.

"Maeve, I'm going to pull over at the flower shop. I know we brought gifts for the family, but I want to get a bouquet for Cousin Catherine. Pick out something tasteful."

I guess I was getting out. I held back from saluting Meg. I didn't want to cause a disturbance in the force this early in our trip. Glancing in the mirror, I took my hair tie out, shook my head, and hoped I did not look too jet-lagged. Stretching as I stepped out of the SUV, I smoothed my top down and looked carefully for crumbs or spots. I would pass.

Soft chimes rang out as I opened the heavy glass door to enter 'Blooms by Rose.' Immediately, my senses were assaulted in the most wonderful and inviting way. The shop was painted spring green and crisp white. Orchids, cacti, and jade plants of every size were lined up at the front bow window. Two rocking chairs fronted a pink mosaic table, which held albums of various floral arrangements. Fresh scents of roses, gardenias, lavender, and lilies filled the air. An older woman with white hair pulled into a tight bun occupied one of the rockers. She was knitting something in a soft shade of pale yellow.

"Hello," I said and smiled at her. She stared at me intently, and her needles stopped clicking immediately, but she did not speak.

I wasn't very presentable, but I didn't think I was shock-worthy.

I moved a little closer. Maybe she was a bit hard of hearing.

Steel blue eyes locked on mine. My breath caught. Could she look into my soul?

"Babies," she said in a chilling hiss. "Take care of the babies."

What was going on? Had I stumbled upon the Irish Zeena? I mean, there was no pink-streaked hair, heavy makeup, or velvet robes, but I knew a soothsayer when I saw one. Were there Zeenas in every country or did I attract them? The Langford Zeena had admonished me to be a midwife on my trip, and now the Irish Zeena was telling me to look after babies! What was going on?

"May I help you?" asked a cheery voice. I turned to see a raven-haired beauty carrying an armful of white hydrangeas.

"Hello, I'm looking for a bouquet for a family member."

"I'm Rose. And I can tell that you're from the States." She eyed my outfit in a friendly way. "Just landed?"

"Yes, I'm from south of Boston. My mother, sister, and I are here to visit family. We want to bring an arrangement to our cousin."

"That's so nice. We get a lot of visitors from Boston. I see that you've met my Nan."

I nodded. I wouldn't say met. I would say Nan received a message from the beyond and passed it along to me.

"Now, what type of flowers were you thinking of?"

"Those hydrangeas look lovely."

"How about some white hydrangeas and pink peonies?"

"That sounds like a perfect combination."

As Rose began preparing my flowers, Nan happily returned to her knitting.

Maybe I had imagined her shrill outburst. I was overtired. Rose and I chatted about Ballymoor and the sights not to miss.

As I was finishing up the transaction and turned to leave, Nan again pierced me with her eyes.

"Say goodbye, Nan. Our guest is leaving," Rose encouraged her.

"Babies, gone everywhere."

"Oh, Nan." Rose looked at me. "I don't know if you have wee ones, but Nan says what she sees nowadays. Mom used to say she had the gift of second sight. She sees you with babies."

"I…I'm a midwife," I said hesitantly.

"That's it then. See, Nan, you still have it."

Taking the beautiful stems, I waved goodbye and opened the door to the bustling street.

Babies? What did Nan see in me? Wouldn't this just be a peaceful vacation? Before opening the door of the SUV, I took another look around the captivating town. I doubted a murder had ever even occurred here.

But then I shook my head. I was fatigued. I was overthinking. It was time to get myself off to the guesthouse.

"What's up, Maeve? You look troubled."

"Meg, before we left Langford, I ran into Zeena. She told me to find my roots and be a good midwife."

"How did she know you were going on a trip to Ireland?"

I shrugged. "There was an older woman in the flower shop just now who told me to take care of the babies."

"What? Did you tell her you were a midwife?"

"No, I only said hello."

Meg looked me up and down. She took a bite of chocolate, chewed it thoughtfully, and finally said, "Zeena could have heard about our trip. Mom basically told the world. Zeena knows you're a midwife. Maybe she was just being friendly."

"Meg, Zeena has foretold some of our toughest crime-solving situations. She also predicted our travel and Mom's lottery win."

Meg finished the candy bar and wiped her hands.

"Zeena could have gotten lucky. The woman in the flower shop probably had you confused with someone she knew."

She started the car.

"Maeve, nothing will go wrong on this holiday. We are tourists. Relax."

Meg was right. I was overthinking the words of two women who hardly knew me.

"But maybe while you're here, steer clear of pregnant women," she said as she pulled onto the main thoroughfare.

"Recalculating," Colleen sang out in her charming brogue.

Not a bad idea, I thought.

CHAPTER SIX

———

Dublin is the capital of Ireland.

Farrell's Garden Estates were precisely as the brochure depicted. Ten-foot hedges hid a large brick two-story guesthouse with bountiful gardens from the main road. Climbing roses adorned white arches, and a fountain was in the middle of the large courtyard. Meg had rented the entire bed-and-breakfast for Mom and her friends. It had an attached two-bedroom cottage for the two of us and, conveniently, was right on the edge of the Ballymoor business district. We would be based here for three weeks. When the rest of the tribe arrived for our final ten days, Mom had insisted that after the families met we would move to the stately Elkford Castle on the southwest coast in County Kerry, where she had booked two floors. What could we say? She might be the happiest lottery winner ever. She certainly was among the most generous.

Briar Cottage exceeded all my expectations. Velvet overstuffed couches, padded rockers, and chenille ottomans filled the sunroom overlooking the back garden and pond. The two bedrooms held queen beds with fluffy white comforters. There was a small kitchenette stocked with all the essentials. Unlike American guest suites which carried coffeemakers, an electric teakettle with tea of every description took pride of place. Best of all, the bathroom featured a large rainfall shower and a long clawfoot tub, complete with various scented bubble bath concoctions and shea butter body lotion. What a sublime refuge.

After checking to ensure Mom, Gaby, Ethel, and Louella were settled, Meg and I showered and took long naps. We were due at Catherine's for dinner, and it would surely be a long night.

Promptly at five p.m., Finn had the passenger van ready for Mom and the ladies. As I walked over to greet Molly and

Owen Farrell, the property owners, I heard Finn say, "Right this way, please."

Gaby was wheeling Mom. She was decked out in another new green outfit, topping her ensemble off with her emerald sequined scarf—a true Irish vision. Gaby was in a persimmon check skirt and an electric blue blouse complemented by a silver sequined scarf. Clearly, Mom's taste had rubbed off on her. Ethel, always the most conservative dresser of the bunch, was in maroon striped slacks and a pale pink houndstooth jacket, and bringing up the rear was Louella in a vibrant shade of yellow as usual. It was like watching a moving kaleidoscope. The ladies always dressed to impress. Who knew what Catherine would think?

"Oh, don't they look festive," Molly Farrell exclaimed. She and Owen had bought the property seven years ago and had lovingly updated it. They even had a room fitted for wheelchair access.

Festive was one word. Not the one I would have chosen.

"They are such lively ladies. I love to see them enjoying life," Owen said, beaming.

Finn looked a bit overwhelmed as he saw multiple beribboned shopping bags lining the drive.

"Are these for Molly and Owen?" he asked.

"No, Finn, they go with the ladies. My mother brought a few presents," Meg chuckled.

"Right, so," Finn said as we all helped him load the precious cargo.

As we saw them off, Meg and I settled into the SUV. Catherine's home was only two miles away.

"Do you think Mom brought enough gifts?" I asked sarcastically.

"I honestly don't know how she fit everything. She must have asked Gaby, Ethel, and Louella to pack a lot of her loot." Meg was decked out in chic dark khaki trousers and a white denim jacket. "Did you remember the flowers?"

"Yes, they're in the back seat."

"This should be fun. I can't wait to meet the Callahan clan. I had photos of our entire family printed out. I made Catherine a small album."

"What a great idea, Meg."

"Well, I know Mom will want to go over all the weddings and show photos of Dad and all the grandkids. Who knows? Maybe someday Catherine will be able to visit us."

We drove along the rambling road, passing farmhouses and glimpses of the rocky coastline. After a short rain, the sun was still high in the sky, and a rainbow was off to the left—just a spectacular sight.

"Turn left in one kilometer," Colleen directed.

"Kilometers it is, Colleen," Meg responded.

We turned down a very pretty lane and saw Finn's van in the driveway of a tall brick home. After Meg parked, I grabbed the bouquet and started up the walkway.

"Have a lovely evening. Mary knows to call me when they're ready to go back," Finn said as he approached us.

"Where will you wait, Finn?" I asked.

"Your mum was so sweet. She invited me to stay, but I'm going to visit a lad I met at uni. He lives in the next village and might be interested in starting a car touring service, too."

"All right, Finn, have a nice visit," I said.

As Meg went to knock, the door opened, and she was quickly enveloped in a hug.

"Oh my, aren't you the very picture of Aunt Nora? I'm your Cousin Catherine. Welcome, welcome."

A beaming, salt-and-pepper-haired woman, about Mom's age, ushered Meg into the house and then turned to me. "Oh, love, you must be Maeve. With that height, you're definitely an O'Reilly, but I think you have some Callahan too," she said, holding my chin and studying my face.

Suddenly, we were introduced to numerous cousins, in-laws, children, and babies. Everyone was talking at once and laughing. I saw Mom holding a tiny infant in the center of the spacious sitting room. She wore a massive smile—this is what she had dreamt of for so long. After a welcoming drink and a toast of "*Sláinte*," Catherine took the floor and introduced everyone formally. She assigned seats for the meal, and we all settled in. A buttery fish chowder and brown bread were served. Then, a piping hot, delectable shepherd's pie was set before us. The fresh, mouthwatering food was so tasty. I found myself readily accepting a second helping.

"How grand to have you here," Catherine said, looking around the table. "I've dreamt of this day."

"Me too," Mom said. "I can't believe I've finally met you in person and I'll also get to see my parents' childhood homes."

"My nephew James lives on the family farm now. He can't wait to meet you and your family. Your mother's home was sold years ago after her brother died, but his son and family are anxious to get acquainted. Also, I know the Coughlins who bought the farm. I'm sure they'll be happy to have you take a look, Mary."

Elisabeth Devlin, Catherine's daughter, placed some more brown bread on the table and said, "Isn't it interesting to think about how birth order influenced people's lives?" She was of medium height and had vibrant shoulder-length ginger hair and sapphire blue eyes. It was an arresting combination. Cousin Catherine had said she taught at Ballymoor Primary School.

"Are you referring to how property was passed down?" Meg asked, reaching for another slice.

"Yes, it's the reason so many of our people emigrated. Well, that and the Great Famine," Elisabeth said.

The Great Famine, also known as the Irish Potato Famine, lasted from 1845 to 1852 and was caused by a blight on potato crops. About one million people died and over two million emigrated to other countries.

"I only have one son, but it's hard for me to envision leaving a home to the oldest child and nothing to younger siblings," Elisabeth said, twisting her napkin while she spoke.

"To the oldest son," Mom said softly.

Was she thinking of her father and her husband? It made me wonder what they thought of being excluded from inheriting property. Was her father fearful, setting off with his young bride for an unfamiliar land? What about her husband? As he left, did Dad wonder if he would ever see his family and Ireland again? Sailing off into the unknown took a special kind of courage.

"Things are changing now," Catherine said. "By the way, Elisabeth, did you know that Meg is an estate agent? You might want to ask her thoughts about a home purchase."

Did Catherine change the subject because her father had inherited the Callahan family home and Mom's parents left Ireland? Perhaps Catherine was imagining herself being born out of the country she clearly loved.

Elisabeth and Meg started a lively conversation about homes that ended with Meg promising to review Galway properties currently for sale.

I turned to talk to Aisling Doyle, one of Catherine's many nieces, who was also a midwife. After a few minutes of comparing notes, she asked, "Maeve, would you like to visit my practice and get a closer look at midwifery in Ireland?"

"I'd love it," I said.

Even as I said yes, the twin Zeena warnings flickered in my mind. Should I stay away because of the obscure references to my profession?

Of course not, that was ridiculous. I was only a visiting midwife. What harm could that cause?

"Great, my practice is in town. I'll call you to arrange a time. I know the midwifery group would love to meet you."

As the table was cleared, Catherine placed a chocolate Guinness cake with creamy white icing in the center. It looked mouthwatering.

"Now, Catherine, before we start on dessert, we need to pass out some presents from the States. Gaby, can you help me, please?" Mom asked.

Gaby brought out two massive bags from the foyer. It looked like Santa had arrived early. Soon, the room was filled with scraps of wrapping paper as sounds of delight filled the air. There were Boston Red Sox caps and New England Patriots T-shirts for everyone. All the children got books with Boston themes and, of course, bubbles, marbles, and jump ropes. Lobster lollipops and individually wrapped Harbor Sweets chocolates were handed out. The women received silver Swan Boat pins and nasturtium jewelry from the Isabella Stuart Gardener Museum. Mom had shopped well.

Next, Catherine and Elisabeth proudly distributed Irish linen lace handkerchiefs embroidered and initialed in deep green to the six of us.

"These are works of art," Ethel said, holding hers up for the guests to admire.

Gaby smiled broadly. "Thank you so much. They are lovely."

Louella did not speak but timidly nodded in agreement. Her gift was probably already stowed in her large ever-present black patent leather purse. Who could blame her? That carryall and its many treasures had been a godsend in a previous murder case.

As we nibbled cake, Meg's photo album was passed around and proved to be a colossal hit.

"Look at your daughter, Rowan, and her gorgeous red locks, just like her cousin, Elisabeth. Can't deny her Irish background," Catherine exclaimed.

I smiled. I didn't know if Catherine knew that Rowan was adopted, but she was my daughter, so of course, she shared my Irish heritage.

As the hours slipped by, I could see that Mom and the ladies were discreetly yawning. It had been a very long day, and jet lag was setting in. Meg and I nodded at each other. No words were necessary. Meg got up to arrange for Finn to return for his charges.

Lining up to say goodbye and with plans to meet tomorrow for tours and dinner, we finally made our way outside. True to his word, Finn was right on time and assisted the ladies into the van.

"We'll follow you," Meg called out.

"What a warm welcome. I love seeing Mom so happy," I said.

"She is. But it saddened me to hear how property was handed down," Meg replied.

"So many lives affected."

"So interesting how profoundly birth order affected lives. And women, as usual, got the short end of everything. Thank goodness, that's beginning to change."

"Let's hope so," I said, thinking of Rowan and Sloane.

"The Red Sox and Patriots gained a few fans in Ballymoor," Meg commented with a laugh.

"Mom should work for the Boston tourist board," I agreed. "I need to get Will to put that chocolate Guinness cake on the café selections. Maybe a special Saint Patrick's Day tasting menu."

"And that brown bread is to die for," Meg said.

"No bodies, no murders, no dying, only vacation."

"Your destination is ahead on the left," Colleen eventually announced.

Meg smirked. "See, you need a woman to tell you where to go."

CHAPTER SEVEN

———

The official languages of Ireland are Irish and English.

Where was I? Had our bedroom been wallpapered in a shell pink trellis pattern while I slept? As I peered around at the white wicker dresser, it came to me. I was in Galway! Snuggling under the fluffy comforter, I realized that even after the long trip, I felt very rested. Grabbing my phone, I checked the World Clock setting and smiled, knowing that my family would all currently be in dreamland. Well, hopefully. Just as my thoughts were about to go down a dark road of worry about them, Meg appeared at my bedroom door.

"Hey, Maeve, are you awake?" she whispered loudly.

"Yes. I slept great. What about you?"

"I've had better nights. I finally got up a few hours ago. Do you want to take a quick walk before breakfast?"

Walk? My sister was suggesting a walk? Her usual idea of exercise was strolling to her Jaguar.

"Sure."

I brushed my teeth, washed my face, and pulled my hair into a large tortoiseshell clip. As I pulled on my UMASS Amherst sweatshirt and entered the sunroom, I saw that Meg was fully made up, hair blown out, and dressed in neatly pressed jeans and an aqua cotton sweater.

"What is this, Beauty and the Beast?"

"Oh, stop, I got up early. I thought we could maybe grab a beverage and some scones before breakfast."

This was the story of my life. My sister could eat five meals a day, never exercise, and stay razor-thin. I, on the other hand, watched my carbs and rowed on a regular schedule, but as an old nemesis had once remarked, was a bit fuller than Meg.

Starting out the gravel pathway, we headed right toward the shops. Down the road to the left was a small footbridge that crossed a fast-running brook and led to the bay and ocean beyond. Ballymoor Green fronted the water and held a large field for sports, a playground, and a Victorian-looking gazebo. The whole area was dotted with benches for sitting and gazing.

"Let's find some food and eat outside," Meg said.

We stopped at the Morningside Cafe, picked up two large Barry's Gold hot teas and four buttermilk scones with jam and butter, and returned to Ballymoor Green. Since tea was the national drink and iced coffee was not readily available on every corner, Meg and I were going to have to adapt. The morning was beautiful, and the lawn and walkway were pristine. As we sat down, I noticed something waving in the breeze. Was it a piece of paper? It was stuck to the bottom rail of the park bench. Taking a clean napkin, I picked up the trash to put it in the bin. It was a napkin stamped with a logo from an establishment called Delaney's Pub. Someone must have had a late-night snack and dropped it.

"That's my Girl Scout," Meg commented as I sat beside her.

"Just doing my part," I countered.

Leaning back, I sipped the golden tea and bit into a flaky scone. Delicious.

"Can Will please get this recipe, too?" Meg asked.

We appeared to be the first visitors to the Ballymoor Green this morning. Our bench was set on a small outcrop overlooking a tall, weedy patch of the brook close to the footbridge.

"Imagine if we had grown up here, Meg."

"I doubt that Mom and Dad would have ever met each other if he didn't ship out to Boston."

"True, but you know what I mean," I said, thinking about our childhood.

"I hear you. It would have been different. I wonder if we would have ever left?"

We ate our scones, lost in thoughts of what might have been

"Do you think Catherine feels some guilt that her father inherited the farm?" I asked.

"Oh, I think that's water under the bridge now. It happened so long ago," Meg said.

"Old hurts are never truly buried."

"Oh, come on, Maeve. You are starting to sound like a young Zeena."

I shrugged. It was interesting that this trip had already brought up some 'what ifs.'

"What did you think of Elisabeth?"

"She was very welcoming, and I saw her going out of her way to include Louella in the conversation. Elisabeth's students must appreciate her warm manner. She did seem a bit stressed about her property search though. She really wants the benefit of your house-hunting expertise, Meg," I commented.

"I get the feeling affordable housing is hard to come by in Ballymoor, especially for young families."

"That seems to be a worldwide problem."

"True." Swallowing another bite, she said, "Well, I can't wait to see more of Ballymoor and meet more of our relatives."

"You know Mom and the ladies will want to tour the entire town today. I wonder how long it will take them to adapt to the time change?" I pondered.

"Ha, I doubt it will bother them much. This is the trip of their lives. They don't want to miss anything."

As I surveyed the coastline, I saw the bay was choppy today. It appeared to have a fast current. Would I ever look at any body of water and not assess its suitability for rowing? Probably not.

"Hey, Maeve, looks like some more rubbish got stuck in the tall grass. You might become the Ballymoor cleanup patrol."

I glanced over at the bank to see what Meg was talking about. There appeared to be a small pile of paper or some type of material caught at the base of the weeds. More trash? A mislaid book? Had someone lost a hat? I stood to get a closer look, although I had no intention of dredging the brook. Standing on a large rock, I used a long stick I found to move the top of the weeds and peered into the clear water. My right foot slipped a bit, and my arms windmilled as I tried to steady myself.

"Hey, Maeve, are you dizzy? Has jet lag got you?"

Meg pulled me back onto the grass. "What is it? You're very pale."

Turning to her, I slowly shook my head. "Not rubbish," I blurted.

"Are you ill?"

"A body. There's a body in the weeds, Meg."

Eyes wide, mouth in a perfect *O*, Meg leaned over and studied the water under the footbridge.

She turned and faced me, hands on her hips. "No, no, no! Another dead body? In a foreign country? Maeve, seriously, you are a magnet for corpses."

Once she calmed down, I said, "We need to call the authorities."

Shaking her head, she pulled out her phone.

"The emergency number here is 9-9-9, and the police are called the Gardaí or the Garda, or the Guards or something," Meg said, furiously pressing her phone screen.

Glancing around, I could see that some dog walkers and joggers were beginning to fill the Green. We needed to protect the crime scene and not cause panic. I knew that Mom and her group would wonder why we were late for breakfast.

Meg walked down the path as she relayed our findings on her phone. Within a few minutes, we heard a siren and saw two official vehicles approaching.

Meg looked at me sternly. "Now remember, Nancy Drew, be concise—only the facts. Please don't overshare. Let's try not to have an international incident."

CHAPTER EIGHT

———

The national symbol of Ireland is the harp.

Meg and I gave statements together and separately. The officers were totally professional, efficient, and much gentler than our brother Patrick would have been. As usual, Meg looked newspaper-ready, while I looked like I'd spent the night on one of the park benches. The situation was quickly under tight control. Ballymoor Green was shut down, and privacy fences were erected to shield the victim from public view. We were ushered to a nearby bench within the police barrier. Because of my vantage point, I did see that the deceased was an older woman. Her long white hair had loosened from its tortoiseshell clasp. Now I could see that Meg had mistaken clumps of hair for trash. As the body was laid on the tarp, I felt a deep sadness. The rocks were slippery. Maybe she fell and hit her head? Was her family distraught looking for her?

"Oh," I gasped and put my head between my knees.

"Maeve, talk to me. Are you feeling faint?" Meg asked, looking horrified. Illness was not her forte.

The female Garda put her hand on my shoulder.

Lifting my head, I pointed toward the opening in the privacy fence.

Meg gasped. The officer quickly moved to block our view. But we could not unsee the horror. A large kitchen knife protruded from the victim's back.

After being told not to share any details of the incident, the authorities recorded our names, passport numbers, and phone numbers, and we were finally allowed to leave. A small crowd had gathered at the entrance to the Green, and as we passed, I heard a woman call out, "Maeve, Meg, over here."

Scanning the faces, I saw Elisabeth Devlin motioning to us.

"I was walking to school, and I heard that a body's been found. How terrible for the two of you. What a horrible welcome to our town."

"The Garda were here in an instant and are very efficient," Meg said, removing her oversized tortoiseshell sunglasses. She no doubt had packed multiple pairs to match her outfits. Hmm, dozens of sequined scarves for Mom and numerous designer sunglasses for Meg…the apple didn't fall far from the tree.

In a gentle voice, Elisabeth said, "The word Garda is similar to your word police. The official name is the Garda Siochána or the Irish police force. The term Garda refers to the physical station or a single guard. Gardaí refers to more than one officer." She scanned our faces to make sure we understood. One could see that she was a teacher to her roots.

Suddenly, Dennis, Elisabeth's four-year-old ginger-haired son, broke into the conversation. Clearly, I was still in a bit of a fog because I hadn't even seen him.

"Mum, I need to go potty," he said, looking distressed.

"One minute, please, Dennis. I need to talk to Maeve and Meg."

"Mum, I need to go now."

Elisabeth looked at Dennis and then at us. "Fine then, I'll catch you later. If you need anything, please call me." As she turned to go, she said, "This isn't typical of Ballymoor. It's usually a very peaceful town."

Meg and I quickly made our way to our cottage, where I took a long, hot shower. Changing and then doing my hair and putting on makeup made me feel more alive. When I was ready, I met Meg in the sitting room.

"Well, here we are. Another day, another murder."

"Meg, we're not involved in this in any way. We are tourists."

"Why don't I feel reassured?"

"We must be careful not to share any information. We can't interfere in the investigation."

"Try telling that to Mom. I feel a grilling coming on. She could give the CIA lessons in inquisition techniques. We should head over to the guesthouse, Maeve. The group will be wondering where we are."

Meg and I squared our shoulders and walked over to breakfast. We knew Ballymoor was a small town and that news of the morning's activity had probably spread fast. Molly met us at the door with a look of dismay and ushered us into the large dining room. The word was definitely out. Mom and the ladies were gathered around a large, round oak table and had obviously enjoyed a lavish breakfast. Meg and I took our seats and said good morning to the group.

"How did everyone sleep?" Meg asked with a big smile. I knew she was hoping they had not heard of the murder yet.

"Let's just quit the small talk, girls. Fill us in on your activities."

Meg and I just stared at Mom. She was indeed one of a kind.

"Come on now, Meg and Maeve, start from the beginning and tell us all about finding the body. Don't leave out any of the gory details."

I shrugged as I took some sausage and scrambled eggs. I saw that Meg took two pieces of brown bread and began to butter them. There was absolutely no hiding anything from our mother, so we might as well have breakfast while we were questioned.

"Tell us how you heard," Meg said.

"Cousin Catherine called me this morning. She heard that two young women tourists from Boston found a body. I mean, who else could it be but my M&M's?"

Mom had called us her M&M's since we were very young.

As we ate, we told Mom, Gaby, Ethel, and Louella everything that had happened except for seeing the knife in the woman's back. I saw Molly and Owen standing by the buffet table, listening to every word. Meg and I had to be very discreet about what information we relayed.

When we finished speaking, Mom gave us a long, hard look.

"Is that all?"

"Yes, Mom, that's everything."

"What about the knife?"

Gaby, Louella, and Ethel suddenly found their plates very interesting.

Clink. Meg accidentally dropped her spoon onto her stoneware dish.

"How did you hear about that, Mom?"

"Oh please, Catherine and her family have lived in this town for years. The news spread like wildfire. People were very concerned, but I told them not to worry. I said my girls, the famous detectives of Boston, would be right on the case."

Finally breaking away with the excuse that I needed to check in with Will, I made my escape. My thoughts kept going back to the scene of the crime. Somewhere in Ballymoor, there was a murderer.

Back in the room, I checked my watch. It was 5:30 in the morning in Boston. Will would be up. Sitting on the mulberry velvet sofa, I called his phone. He picked up instantly.

"Hello, my beautiful wife. I miss you so much already."

"Will, how are you? How are the girls?" A small sob escaped as I spoke. I rapidly coughed to hide it. The morning's events must have shaken me up more than I realized.

"We're all doing well. Probably overfed from the multitude of treats being dropped off. There are a few tears for Mama, but so far I have been able to keep Rowan and Sloane happy. Fenway is bereft, however. She's sleeping with one of your socks," he said, chuckling. "Come on now, tell me your first impressions of Ireland."

Oh, Will, you really don't want to know.

"It's so beautiful Will. Wait until you see it. And Cousin Catherine and her family could not be any nicer."

"Maeve, what's wrong?"

I was silent. There was no use denying anything. Will was my soulmate. He knew me way too well. Although I thought I had hidden it, he was obviously picking up on my anxiety.

"Ah, Will, please don't worry. Meg and I are fine. Mom and the ladies are doing so well."

The line went silent. Will patiently waited for me to speak.

"All right, I'll tell you the whole story, but please know that Meg and I are fine. Totally fine." I paused a moment before continuing. "This morning, Meg and I woke up early and got some tea and scones. We sat by the river and…and I found a body in the weeds. Seriously, Will, we were just having breakfast on the Ballymoor Green."

"What? That is unbelievable. A body? Maeve, are you both doing all right?"

"We're fine, Will, just fine. The Gardaí were wonderful, just like Patrick's team."

"Do the police think it was an accident?"

"Umm, I don't think so." Will did not need to know about the kitchen knife right now.

Again, silence.

"Will, are you there?"

"Yes. Honey, I know that you and Meg are great sleuths. But please try not to get involved. Remember, you're in unfamiliar territory."

"Will, trust me. We just want to enjoy our vacation."

"I know, Maeve. I'm sorry this happened to the two of you."

"I know, honey. I love you so much. Kiss the girls for me, and please don't tell Patrick we've already met the authorities here."

"I won't. Love you, Maeve. Please be careful. I know that you and Meg won't be able to resist helping, but caution is the word of the day. Call me anytime, day or night."

Five minutes later, I was still holding my phone in my hand and staring into space, rethinking the M&M's past cases. We had brought criminals to justice but had a few narrow escapes. From our conversation, I knew that Will was worried about Meg and me but was somewhat accepting of our Hercule Poirot ambitions. How time had changed things.

I looked at the photo on my lock screen. It was of Will, Rowan, Sloane, and Fenway at Langford Harbor—my beautiful family. A wave of homesickness washed over me, but I quickly shook it off. I would see them soon. I needed to regroup. Maybe, just maybe, Meg and I could help the Gardaí in their investigation. All right, that was crazy. A foreign country, a new town, and an unknown victim would make it almost impossible for us to get involved. Or would it?

CHAPTER NINE

———

The shamrock is the national flower of Ireland.

After Finn had given Mom and the ladies an extensive tour of Ballymoor and its environs, we had a date for late afternoon tea with Catherine at Dolly's Tea and Pastry Shoppe.

Meg and I were apprehensive since we had been strictly instructed not to share any information. We knew we would be put to the test during tea with Mom. She had earned her detective badge by religiously watching *NCIS* and *CSI* and had probably spent the day formulating questions for us. What could possibly go wrong?

Dolly's tea shop was done up in shades of lilac, pink, and ivory, with white lace curtains gracing the windows. Six round white tables filled the dining area. In the center of each, pink and purple tulips were in round glass vases, further enhancing the color pallet.

As our large contingent entered, Dolly greeted us warmly. She was dressed in a plum, high-collared blouse and deep purple slacks and appeared to be in her mid-forties with light brown curly hair.

"I'm so happy to have you here. I know you're from Boston. Catherine filled me in on your travels. Please have a seat, and Sarah will arrange for your tea. I hope you're hungry. I have quite the selection of sandwiches and desserts prepared."

Catherine, her daughter Elisabeth, and their good friend and neighbor Helen Lyons stood to greet our group.

"This is so special, Catherine," Gaby exclaimed. "I can't believe we're having afternoon tea in Ireland. At home, you need to book a reservation at a ritzy hotel. That is if they even offer the service. It's just not part of American life."

As usual, Mom and the ladies were decked out in every color combination imaginable. They added considerably to the décor.

Dolly quickly decided to push several tables together so we could talk more easily. Once this was done, Sarah, an enthusiastic teenager, brought out teas of every description. The dinnerware featured exotic floral varieties. The flatware was pale lilac, and the napkins were a pastel pink. It was a feast for the eyes.

Once the tea was poured, Dolly rolled out a cart with a wide variety of finger sandwiches. There was olive and cream cheese, curried chicken salad, ham and cheddar, and smoked salmon with goat cheese. The tiered dessert cart contained mini berry tartlets, rosemary shortbread cookies, lemon curd squares, chocolate mousse cups, and a myriad of bite-size cupcakes.

This was tea? I swiftly decided I loved Irish afternoon tea. I wanted to try this at home. Okay, perhaps I was getting ahead of myself. I was still a novice baker. The truth was, I could only reliably make one triple chocolate cake, but it was a showstopper. Well, at least to me.

Once we settled in, Elisabeth looked at Meg and me with concern and asked, "How are you two keeping?"

Mom jumped on the question. "My girls are feisty, Elisabeth. Murder and mayhem are second nature to them."

Meg gave Mom a withering glance and, turning to Elisabeth, said, "Thanks for asking. It was quite a shock, but we're doing fine."

"Well, it's no surprise that someone made small work of Deirdre Harrington," Helen Lyons, the family friend, noted while reaching for another olive and cream cheese mini-sandwich. Looking at me and Meg, she said, "That's the victim's name. Deirdre Harrington."

"She wasn't very popular; that's true," Catherine responded, looking rather distressed, "but I don't know that anyone wanted her dead."

"Last night's community meeting was a real humdinger. I know you couldn't go because you were welcoming family, Catherine, but boy, there were a lot of fireworks," Helen asserted, putting one hand on her hip.

The entire group stopped eating and looked at her expectantly.

"Helen, please enlighten us. We love a bit of village intrigue. We actually call it 'spilling the tea' at home," I said, leaning forward to not miss a word.

"All right then, I'm not one to tell tales, but here's what happened." She took a brief sip and began. "First on the agenda was the hearing about the new B&B. That young couple with the sweet baby daughter is trying to open it. What are their names? Oh, yes, Patsy and Brianna Shaughnessy. They have been in front of the town committee several times, and Deirdre Harrington always objected to their plans. She claimed that there were too many B&Bs in town. Actually, Deirdre Harrington didn't like tourists." Helen looked at us sheepishly and then concluded, "She especially didn't like American visitors."

She shrugged and continued, "Last night, she went on and on about the parking situation for the proposed B&B. Their lot is indeed small, but they have arranged with a car park a few blocks away to handle any overflow. Deirdre challenged them and brought up congestion, climate change, and everything else under the sun to try to get the committee to vote no. In the interest of time, the committee tabled the decision until the next meeting. Patsy—I think it's Patsy—well, anyway, the taller one was visibly distressed and left the meeting, slamming the door on her way out."

Elisabeth looked particularly alarmed by this news. "We all want Ballymoor to grow and thrive. Patsy and Brianna are just the type of young family we want to invest in the town and flourish here."

"Did Deirdre object to any other items on the agenda?" I asked. Meg gave me a quick, sharp kick above my ankle as I spoke. I knew she wanted me to stay out of this investigation, but I so wanted to know more. I couldn't help myself. I mean, I was the one who found the victim.

"Well, when it was time for new business, Deirdre had a list of specific dates and complaints about Delaney's Pub. She claims they stay open longer than allowed and cause too much noise. I don't know why Deirdre cared. She lives at the far end of Pinewood Road, and it would be impossible to hear any pub hubbub there. Plus, she's probably a bit hard of hearing at her age anyway."

I saw Mom, Ethel, Gaby, and Louella all sit up straighter and bristle at this remark. Helen had no idea what she was in for if she offended these women. They might be of advanced age, but they had proven themselves to be fearless warriors and did not react well to any senior discrimination.

Dolly had been refilling the sandwich trays and clearly had overheard the discussion. She was silent, but it was easy to see that she was very interested.

"Dolly, you were there, too. Didn't you think Deirdre was worse than usual?" Helen asked with an intense stare.

"Enjoy your tea, now. I don't want to interfere," she responded but didn't make any move to leave.

"My girls will need all the info they can get," Mom insisted. "Please tell us what you heard."

I held my breath. I could not look at Meg. She must be livid, knowing as well as I did that once Mom got into Magnum, P.I. mode, there would be no holding her back. She would take the lead, casting Meg and me as her faithful and infallible investigators.

Dolly pulled up a chair and joined the group. "Now, I don't want to speak ill of the dead, but Deirdre Harrington was a tortured soul. She seemed to only see the bad in situations and never gave anyone the benefit of the doubt. She came to every town committee meeting with a list of grievances. Usually, it was a long list. Last night, she also whined bitterly about Seamus Burke and his herd."

"Oh, not poor Seamus Burke again," Elisabeth said, combing her hands through her long curls.

There was silence while the visitors, one and all, waited with bated breath. It was dawning on us that this seemingly bucolic town rivaled our hometown of Langford for intrigue. Who knew?

Finishing her tea, Elisabeth placed her poppy-decorated china cup gently on its saucer and began.

"Seamus Burke worked in the tech industry for about a decade. He apparently did very well but wanted a change. Some say Seamus had a personal tragedy, but whatever. He came to Ireland, settled in Ballymoor, and became a goat farmer. His cheese is highly sought after. In fact, you had it today in Dolly's sandwiches." She smiled while looking at the serving cart, which by now was nearly empty.

"He is very highly thought of here." She paused before continuing. "Seamus Burke has been very generous to the town of Ballymoor. He provides laptops to all our students and fully underwrites the music and arts programs. He wants no recognition. He just keeps to himself."

Dolly and Helen nodded in agreement.

"But that awful hag would not let him be. Her complaints were endless. I can still hear her loud, caustic voice. 'His goats eat my flowers. His goats were blocking my car. His goats escape from his farm. You need to fine him. He should be put out of business,'" Helen said sarcastically.

"I mean goats, for goodness sake. What did they ever do to her? They are harmless. Plus, everyone was worried that if Seamus Burke was run out of Ballymoor, our children would be impacted greatly," Dolly said.

"Ballymoor schools thrive because of him." Elisabeth nodded vigorously in assent.

Helen frowned and tossed her napkin on the table. "He looked rather down in the dumps after the meeting."

The room was quiet as we all digested both food and information.

Crash! We all turned to see Sarah holding both hands to her mouth, broken china at her feet. Her face was streaked with tears.

"Sarah, what is it?" Dolly asked, jumping up.

CHAPTER TEN

———

The Euro is the currency of Ireland.

Dolly led Sarah to a seat at the table while Gaby handed her a clean napkin to dry her tears. We were all silent while she got herself under control.

"Are you feeling ill?" Dolly asked.

Sarah shook her head.

"Let me get you a cup of tea, dear," Helen Lyons suggested.

Sarah's hand shook as she lifted the delicate porcelain to her mouth. We all waited while she took a long drink. She looked at us one by one. Her eyes still brimmed with tears, but she swallowed hard and began to speak.

With a trembling voice, she said, "That awful Miss Harrington made Rory Connors' life a living hell."

Rory Connors? Who was Rory Connors? How many people had Deirdre Harrington tormented?

Dolly gently patted Sarah's back, and the girl's shoulders lowered.

"Rory Connors is one of Sarah's best friends," Dolly explained. "He works at Delaney's Pub."

"What did Deirdre Harrington do to him?" Mom asked. She was from the school of cut to the chase.

Sarah began to speak slowly, but then her words tumbled out in a rush. "Rory had a tough upbringing. His mother died young, and his father is useless. Totally useless. Rory is an only child. He was in my brother Liam's class and often ate at our house. I don't think his father ever made a meal. We became very close friends. We both loved Shakespeare and all types of poetry. Rory is a very gentle soul. Mrs. Lyons, I know that you were very kind to Rory, too. He told me."

All eyes turned to Helen, who uncharacteristically merely nodded. I noticed she was rubbing her distinctive necklace. It was silver with five small hearts, and she repeatedly touched each of them in turn.

Sarah continued, "When he finished secondary school, my mother included him in Liam's celebration. Rory's father didn't even bother to show up. By that time, Rory had started seeing Annie McIntyre."

Sarah stopped speaking and stared into her empty teacup, which Gaby quickly refilled. Then, with a frown, she began again. "When Annie became pregnant, Rory abandoned all thoughts of going to uni. His father wouldn't let him and Annie live in his house, so they rented a tiny flat above Delaney's Pub. Annie is an animal assistant at Dr. Gallagher's veterinary clinic. They don't have much money, but they love each other and are doing their best."

Sarah's eyes narrowed, and her mouth tightened. She grasped the teacup so tightly I feared the thin porcelain would shatter.

"But Miss Harrington flung horrible insults at him whenever she saw him. She said he wouldn't amount to anything and shouldn't be allowed to be the father of Annie's baby. Miss Harrington was very vocal whenever she came into Delaney's Pub. Lindsay and Cillian Delaney tried to get her to stop, but she always managed to humiliate Rory. I'm glad someone killed her. She deserved it!"

With that, she stood and ran out of the sunroom.

An unsettled hush enveloped all of us.

"She doesn't know what she's saying," Dolly finally said, getting up and smoothing her floral apron. "Sarah is a wonderful young woman, but she's obviously very distraught. I'll go to her now. Please take your time and thank you so much for visiting. I'll be back as soon as I can."

Gaby and Ethel stood and began to clear the table of plates. As she separated silverware, Gaby stopped and said, "Poor lamb. Rory is lucky to have her in his corner."

"Just place them on the buffet," Helen instructed. "Dolly has a system, and she'll be back to finish up." Helen clearly was a frequent visitor to Dolly's Tea and Pastry Shoppe.

"Well, Catherine, this village certainly has a bit of tension," Mom said.

"One person caused ninety percent of it," Helen commented while finishing the last shortbread cookie.

"It only takes one bad apple to spoil the bunch," Mom said. "But don't worry, my girls have solved tougher crimes." She looked at Meg and me proudly.

Meg's face was drawn, her mouth a thin line. "Mom, we are visitors here. The Gardaí do not need us. Maeve and I need to stay clear of their investigation."

Helen leaned back in her chair. She placed her hands flat on the table. "You know," she said, "there is another matter to attend to." She paused and looked at us. "Deirdre Harrington, even with all her faults, needs to be buried. We all often talked about the fact that we never saw any family or friends at her house. However, she was a citizen of Ballymoor and a faithful parishioner at Saint Columbkille's. We cannot allow her to go to her Maker with no one in attendance. She needs to have a proper funeral."

Catherine and Elisabeth slowly nodded their agreement.

"You're so right, Helen. We need to make arrangements," Catherine said.

"I'll talk to Sheila Whalen, the reporter, about placing an obituary in *The Ballymoor Times*," Elisabeth said.

"I'm sure the Ballymoor Garden Club will donate some flower arrangements. I'll call them," Helen stated, rising to head off.

"What can we do to help?" Gaby asked.

"Yes, we'd love to be useful," Ethel agreed as she unconsciously straightened her suit jacket and checked that her pearl circle brooch was in place. After years of serving as a Navy nurse, she was always ready to lend a hand.

Louella, garbed in citron from head to toe, didn't respond verbally but gave a thumbs-up.

That was typical of the lobby ladies. They were the definition of "All for one and one for all."

"This is your vacation. I hate to ask you to help plan a funeral," Catherine said.

"Nonsense, we are your family, Catherine. We want to help you. The four of us have had plenty of practice. In our senior housing complex, they bring out fire extinguishers when the birthday candles are lit," Mom remarked. "People die like flies there."

Mom was not going gentle into that good night.

With a smile and a chuckle, Catherine touched Mom's hand. "Thank you all. You surely are my family. Why don't you come with me to the rectory, and we'll talk to Gloria Manly. She's overseen the parish office for years. Maybe we can divide a few tasks after a conversation with her."

Mom smiled as she adjusted her sequined aquamarine cardigan. "That's a great plan."

I tried very hard to keep a solemn face. Mom read the obituaries in the local and Boston papers with a fine-tooth comb. For her, they were indeed the "Irish Sports Pages." Often, her entire day was arranged around attending wakes and funeral masses. She would then call Meg and me and, in minute detail, discuss the deceased's outfit, hair, makeup, and general appearance. Next, the relatives, friends, and nosy onlookers in attendance were all noted. We were told about any ongoing family feuds, the number and quality of flower arrangements, and most importantly, who inherited what worldly goods. Finally, beverages, food quality, and the after-party or reception and locale were ranked on an exacting scale. How one left this world was extremely important to Mom. Planning someone's final farewell in Ireland was an answer to her dreams.

After saying goodbye to Dolly and a recovered Sarah, the party set off for the church. Finn was phoned to meet us there.

The afternoon sky had turned a bit gray, and a light mist was falling. Meg and I opened our small travel umbrellas and soon realized we were the only people on the street using any protective covering.

Elisabeth waited at the gate for us to catch up.

"Come under my umbrella," Meg said.

"Ah, it's just a soft rain. I'm fine."

Soft rain.

Caring for the underdog.

Ensuring an ornery murder victim had a suitable burial.

Including everyone as extended family.

I already loved this country so much.

CHAPTER ELEVEN

———

Saint Patrick is the patron saint of Ireland.

Saint Columbkille's Church was a lovely but daunting gray edifice dating from 1890, according to the cornerstone next to the massive front oak door. It was clearly lovingly tended to by the clergy and the congregation. Elisabeth led us around to the back through a blooming flower garden with ornate stone benches. Luckily, the church office was roomy because we were now a sizeable group.

"Well, good afternoon," Gloria Manly uttered with a slight frown as she stood to welcome us. She had close-cropped black hair and wore a chestnut brown and white checked linen suit with pencil skirt and serviceable taupe pumps. Her look was reminiscent of a woman from a 1950s typing pool.

"Sorry, I didn't have time to ring. I do hope you have time for us," Catherine said.

"Of course," Gloria agreed, although her frown remained. Having a number of women appear in her office without an appointment was obviously not on her agenda today.

I could tell that Catherine was well aware of Gloria's reticence. She immediately congratulated Gloria on the captivating grounds and then introduced us. Finally, she asked Gloria about Deirdre's funeral and offered our help.

"I suspected that's why you were here," Gloria said, lightly touching a pair of blue readers that hung from her neck on a red-beaded chain.

Hmm, a little sass in her ensemble. Maybe Gloria is not as staid as she looks.

"She was a parishioner here, right?" Elisabeth inquired with a warm smile.

Gloria looked to the ceiling and then down to the floor. Her lips pursed, and she started to speak, then caught herself. She finally began with a very measured tone.

"Yes, Deirdre Harrington was a faithful parishioner. She never missed daily Mass and was very well-known to the parish staff. I just pulled her original registration from when she moved to Ballymoor. I didn't see any relatives listed."

She paused and looked around the room solemnly.

"I know it will take a while before her body is released because of the nature of her demise. But when the time comes, rest assured that Father Leahy will be happy to have input about the funeral."

"It's so nice to hear the poor soul had a home in this parish. From what we've heard, she had many disagreements in Ballymoor," Mom said, acting very demurely.

Meg gave me a sideways glance. We knew Mom was putting out the bait to lure in her catch. She was a master of subtle interrogation or, rather, manipulation. We had seen her work her magic many times in the past.

Gloria Manly looked slightly uncomfortable. I could almost see her inner debate about whether to say more.

"She must have felt so loved here," Mom said with her best impression of a saintly grandmother.

Gloria Manly cracked. "Well, I must admit that Deirdre Harrington was not always happy with the staff at Saint Columbkille's."

"My goodness, what a lovely church. I can't imagine anyone not feeling at peace here," Mom proclaimed.

I sat back to watch the master work. Miss Jane Marple could take lessons from her.

Gloria stood and paced the length of the meeting room table.

"Deirdre always found fault with something. For example, she detested the weekly flower arrangements. Although never offering to contribute to the floral fund, she criticized the choices as looking like simple field flowers. She didn't like the music the choir picked and disparaged the quality of the singing. But her biggest source of contention was that she wanted Sunday Mass to be said in Latin. She even lobbied for the altar to be turned so the priest faced away from the congregation."

Gloria stopped and put her hands on the back of a wooden chair as if to steady herself.

"Poor Father Leahy is very young and instead of just telling her no, he would listen to her rant for hours. I often had to say that he had someone waiting for him in order to get her to move along."

"It sounds like she had a lot of opinions and disliked change," Mom commented.

"Yes, she was difficult, but as we know, she still is due a proper interment. Since there's no family involved, I would appreciate your help in planning a suitable one."

"We could have a short get-together right in the church after the funeral Mass," Catherine said. "I'm sure the sodality ladies will contribute; we'll bake up some refreshments."

"That's so nice," Mom said, nodding approvingly. "I used to be in Saint Brendan's Sodality at home. It was such a nice group of women. We met once a month and did what we could to help parishioners in need."

"I wonder if she had any burial plans," Elisabeth pondered.

"Oh, I know where she'll be interred," Gloria said with complete assurance. "She had planned to be in the Ballymoor Cemetery. She had already picked out her plot and gravestone."

"That's helpful," Catherine remarked. "We'll hire a bagpiper and give her a true Ballymoor farewell."

"I'm sure it will be lovely. Again, I'm very thankful for your help," Gloria replied.

As we said our goodbyes, Catherine made plans to touch base with Gloria after the body was released. Then, as we stepped out into the courtyard, I saw that the sun had reappeared, and a rainbow was stretching along the riverbank.

Finn Walsh was ready and waiting for the ladies to get into the passenger van to take them back to the guesthouse. Surely, they needed a rest after this day.

"No, no, we can't go yet," Mom exclaimed.

We all stopped and looked at her.

"We've never stepped foot in Saint Columbkille's before and the rule is that whenever you visit a new Catholic Church, you're granted three wishes. All of us need to go in quickly and make our dreams known. You can say a prayer, too, if you feel like it."

"But I'm not Catholic. I'm a Methodist," Louella said, looking forlorn.

"It doesn't matter what religion you are," Mom said. "The wishes are available to everyone."

"Gee, I never heard about this custom in Jamaica," Gaby said, looking somewhat confused.

"My mother told me. I thought everyone was familiar with the custom. Anyway, don't look a gift horse in the mouth. Let's go." Mom raised her arm and pointed forward as if making a conquest.

My mother's view of theology was always refreshing, even when it had a dubious origin. But who was I to doubt her? I had my wishes ready. Will, Rowan, and Sloane were about to get Irish blessings. If one could have three wishes, why not four? My Fenway would be getting divine intervention, too.

CHAPTER TWELVE

———

Ireland's government is a constitutional democracy.

After that outing, I needed a quick nap; snuggling into my soft, comfy bed, I instantly fell asleep. But in the middle of dreaming of babbling brooks, rainbows, goats, and chocolate mousse, my phone startled me awake.

"Hello, honey."

"Will, it's so good to hear your voice," I said, sitting up and adjusting my pillows.

"Did I wake you? Sorry, Maeve."

"I was taking a short nap, but I need to get up. I'm so glad you called. How are you? How are Rowan and Sloane?"

"The girls are fantastic. I mean, they miss their mama, but they are being kept busy. In fact, my mother and father even took them to the park yesterday."

"What? I can barely envision your parents loading the girls into their car seats. I didn't think they knew how."

Will chuckled. "Okay, my story is not totally accurate. Kate took them to the toddler playground, and my mother and father stopped by on their way to The Country Club. Kate said they watched the girls swing for about five minutes. I know it's not a lot, but it's a start."

Lydia and William Kensington, or rather Lydia and Senior as they wanted the grandchildren to call them, were decidedly hands-off grandparents. Still, I was delighted they had made time to visit the girls, no matter how briefly.

"That sounds about right. Did they comment on the O'Reilly overseas invasion?"

"When my mother phoned, she casually mentioned she was contemplating renting a villa in Tuscany for all of us next summer. I detected a slight bit of envy that Mary O'Reilly had managed to, in her mind, upstage her."

My in-laws were very wealthy and although emotionally distant, always went in for over-the-top holiday gifts, even if they were not what the recipients wanted. Lydia and Senior had to be a bit flummoxed that my mother, living in rent-controlled senior housing, had been able to treat her family and friends like royalty. I imagined there was some late-night pillow talk about Mary O'Reilly's reversal of fortune. Who knows, maybe they started playing the lottery.

"Hey, if Tuscany is in the picture, I'm all in."

We both laughed. Then Will's voice softened, and he said, "Please, enjoy these few weeks, and don't worry about us. We miss you a lot, but we are managing."

"How is Fenway?"

"She is the most ruffled. She sits at the front window when she's not with the girls. I think she's looking for you."

"Oh, my poor girl. Fenway won't rest well until we're all home again. Now, tell me about work. How did the gala for Outlook Farm go?"

Outlook Farm was a magical place for children with cancer. They ran support groups all year, and in the summer provided a safe and nurturing environment for their campers. With livestock, trails, and a peaceful cove on Langford Bay, the farm was a well-loved oasis.

"Maeve, I'll send you the photos. It went off without a hitch, and they raised a hundred and fifty thousand dollars. Many attendees asked for A Thyme for All Season's contact info. It was a great night. I'm so proud of our team."

"Oh, Will, that's wonderful. I'm so proud of you. Look what you have built."

I stood, pulled the heavy ivory drape aside, and looked out at the garden. Will was the best. He worked so hard for me, the girls, and his staff. My voice caught a bit as I said, "You have so many added responsibilities now."

"Honey, please stop worrying. You left everything well organized, and Kate is a wonderful nanny."

He paused for a beat and then continued, "By the way, Ella and I were approached about opening a new café in Shipley. You remember Shipley, right? It's that lovely town where Tom and Mike live. Ella met with the Shipley town manager this morning, and it sounds promising."

Ella was Will's second-in-command, and she was a master of innovative solutions for the business.

"Wow, that sounds wonderful. Pretty soon, you'll have a catering empire."

"From your lips to God's ears," Will said with a laugh. "Truthfully, Maeve, I owe it all to the wonderful people working for me. I've been fortunate."

"Honey, that's because you treat everyone as family, and your food is fabulous."

Will was an accomplished chef and had followed his dream. My heart swelled with pride, listening to him talk about future plans.

"But now tell me the important news. How's everything going there? I'm anxious to hear about the woman who died."

I filled him in on what I had heard about the deceased and finally slipped in a brief mention of the murder weapon. He was shocked that I had stumbled upon another victim, but I reiterated that Meg and I were not involved in trying to solve the crime—at least not at the moment. I did not want Will to worry since he had his hands full.

Desperately trying to change the subject, I described in detail the delectable scones and mouthwatering Guinness cake we'd tasted.

"I can't wait to get there and try them."

"And see me?"

He laughed. "You are always number one. Food is a distant second."

We finished the conversation with Will promising to kiss the girls for me. We had decided not to do video calls while I was in Ireland. I knew I would cry the entire time and didn't want to upset them. I had written notes for every day I was away, and Will read them to the girls each morning. I knew Rowan and Sloane were too young to understand them, but it made me feel connected. They also had new bedtime books to look forward to in the evening.

Getting up, I took a shower and dressed for dinner. I missed my beautiful pack but also felt so lucky to accompany

Mom on this adventure. And I had to keep reminding myself that I would get to introduce my family to Ireland in a few weeks.

Tonight, Cousin Catherine was joining us at the Farrells'. It would be a low-key evening, which was just what was needed because we were all still adapting to the time change. Catherine wanted to take the opportunity to plan activities for the week. She hoped the ladies would join some local groups since they would be in Ballymoor for a while.

Although I wasn't very hungry after the exquisite afternoon tea, I had to admit that grilled orange salmon with a maple glaze, wild rice, and a crisp garden salad combined for a scrumptious meal. Molly and Owen Farrell were the best of hosts.

As we all dipped into a dessert of exquisite peach Melba accompanied by rich espresso, Catherine began to describe some of the village offerings. There was a garden club, a knitting group, a crossword club, a jigsaw puzzle club, a daily walking group, yoga and tai chi classes, and a weekly movie night at the town hall. Local craftspeople would also organize an art fair at the end of the week.

"I'd love to join the knitting group," Gaby responded.

"Me too," Ethel agreed. "I want to try learning the stitches for an Irish sweater."

"That sounds like a great fit for the two of you," Mom agreed. "You're both accomplished knitters."

"That's wonderful," Catherine acknowledged. "The group is meeting tomorrow night. I can take you to meet everyone."

"Do you knit, Catherine?" Gaby inquired.

"I do, and I have made a few Aran knit jumpers. That's the official name of the knit. It's quite an interesting story. The designs of each knit are linked to their clans."

"What's a jumper?" Gaby asked.

"That's what we Irish call your sweaters," Catherine replied.

"Please fill us in," Mom suggested.

"Let me do a 'show and tell' with help from our gracious host. That way it will be easier to understand." Smiling, Catherine began, "So, Owen Farrell is from Inis Mór. That's the biggest island of the Aran Island group. The community there is known for its fabulous knits. Now, Owen, may I borrow a jumper, please?"

"Here you go," Owen said, handing Catherine a thick ivory hand-knitted jumper from the hall closet.

Catherine gently spread the garment over the front of a dining chair so we could easily see its pattern.

"The combination of stitches on the sweaters is very deliberate. People from the islands and now knitters around the world know how to interpret them. They provide a wealth of information and reflect the lives of the knitters and their families. In the past, the stitching patterns were guarded and kept within the same clan for generations. Fishermen wore the jumpers daily, and if, unfortunately, there was an accident at sea and life was lost, often the knitwork could help identify a body. There is a register of all the historic patterns on the Aran Islands."

"These are a designer's dream. I can just imagine them on the cover of *Vogue*," Meg said, getting up for a closer look at Owen's jumper.

"I love that each sweater is unique. Can you read Owen's?" Ethel asked.

"I can tell you what I know, but remember, I'm an amateur. The knitting group members can give you more information."

Catherine traced a finger over the knit. "Let's see. The most prominent stitches are the cables. There are several different types. They represent a fisherman's rope, and it is said that wearing a jumper with that cable may bring good luck and safety to the wearer. Hopefully one would have a great day at sea. The diamond stitch represents the farmer's fields and fishing nets. That stitch is used for good luck, success, and wealth."

Catherine pointed out another area on Owen's jumper. "This is the Tree of Life stitch. It demonstrates the maker's desire for strong family ties and harmony for the wearer. This shows that the clan is of utmost importance."

Gaby bent down for a closer look at the stitchwork. "It reminds me of quilts my grandmother made back home. She embroidered various stars in bright colors to represent the branches of the family tree."

"Stitched with love, I am sure." Catherine patted the thick wool. "Ah, here is the zigzag stitch." She smiled broadly. "It is meant as a blessing and represents the twists and turns in marriage. It has become so popular that it is often used in wedding dresses."

"It's like poetry on fabric," Ethel mused.

"Well, we are a land of artists and storytellers." Catherine smiled while tenderly folding Owen's jumper.

"I am a rank beginner with yarn, but this sweater is so beautiful it makes me want to try my hand at it," I said.

"Maeve, I've seen your work. I'll buy you one," Meg said, laughing. "In fact, I think we all need one. I will be so proud to wear Irish art."

Meg wasn't wrong. I struggled with knitting. Often Fenway ended up with my attempted projects for her bedding.

Meg and I returned to the cottage when the night finally wore down. I was restless but eventually fell asleep with my Kindle beside me. At two a.m., though, I woke up suddenly, gasping. Dead fishermen washed ashore in Aran jumpers had permeated my dreams. I got up for a glass of water, but when I settled back down, I realized that one of the "fishermen" had Deirdre Harrington's face. Too bad her jumper hadn't held the name of her killer.

I shuddered. The darker side of Irish lore was somehow seeping into my pores.

CHAPTER THIRTEEN

———

*The head of the government in Ireland is called the
Taoiseach, which means chieftain or leader.*

Meg and I both slept in a bit and then hurriedly showered
and dressed to join Mom and the ladies for breakfast. We got as
far as the guesthouse foyer when Mom came rolling toward the
front door. She stopped when she saw us, just long enough to fill
us in with a quick summary of events.

"Cousin Catherine called. The Ballymoor Garda station is
releasing the body today. After an exhaustive search, they believe
Deirdre Harrington has no next of kin. A group of parishioners
from Saint Columbkille's are meeting with us to plan the
memorial service. Finn will take the four of us to meet Catherine
now. We're very interested in how the Irish bury their dead. You
never know. We might get some ideas for our own services.
Although there isn't much that we haven't seen, we all know what
one another wants." Without taking a breath, she waved goodbye
and headed out the door.

Ethel, Gaby, and Louella, all dressed in brightly colorful
ensembles, followed Mom to the van like a group of devoted
bridesmaids. Meg and I waved until they were out of sight. Then,
rolling her eyes and with a slight shake of her head, Meg went
inside. I followed, and we sat at a round table overlooking the
beautiful flower garden.

"This is the answer to Mom's dream," Meg said, placing
the beige cloth napkin on her lap. "She's in Ireland, planning a
funeral. I mean, it's almost equivalent to hitting the lottery all
over again. Who knows what she has planned for her own grand
departure when the time comes?"

What could I say? Meg was correct, as usual.

"Good morning," Molly Farrell said, pouring us coffee in thick white mugs. "I see the ladies are off already."

Although I was sure Mom had filled Molly in on the details of where the group was headed, I repeated what she had told us.

"Ah, yes. The poor woman had no next of kin." I noticed that Molly looked somewhat disturbed.

Meg and I looked at her expectantly. We had learned from our investigations that people often filled the silences, hopefully with valuable information. Molly proved to be no exception.

She filled our glasses with fresh-squeezed orange juice and said, "Deirdre Harrington made it quite clear she was leaving her house and acreage to Saint Columbkille's."

"Wow, the church must be thrilled," Meg exclaimed.

Molly was noncommittal. She asked what we wanted for our breakfast order and quickly left for the kitchen.

"Deirdre was certainly tied to Saint Columbkille's. Funny how Gloria never mentioned anything about her property," Meg said. "I'm sure Catherine and Elisabeth know about the will, but they were too polite to mention it."

"Maybe Gloria isn't allowed to talk about it," I speculated. "Deirdre Harrington had no family. She probably felt very welcome at Saint Columbkille's and wanted to repay them."

"I wonder what the parish will do with the property. You know, there were probably some investments, too."

Molly returned with our eggs, sausage, bacon, baked beans, grilled tomatoes, potato hash, and, of course, toasted brown bread. Irish breakfast! What a treat!

"Does Father Leahy have plans for the property?" Meg asked as our plates were put in front of us.

Molly's brow furrowed. "I just know what I hear around town." She paused before continuing, "Young Father Leahy doesn't have much say. He can't be held accountable for what happens. Everyone knows it's ultimately up to the diocese. There's been a lot of discussion in Ballymoor, as you can imagine." Molly looked uncomfortable and swayed from side to side as if her feet suddenly ached.

"I bet the citizens of Ballymoor have some ideas about what would benefit the town," Meg pondered.

Molly sat down beside me. "We're all worried that if the rumors are true, Saint Columbkille's will sell the land to a big developer, and a flock of holiday houses will spring up. They can make an enormous amount of money that way."

Meg poured tea from a large white ceramic teapot decorated with a lily-of-the-valley motif and placed a cup in front of Molly.

"What would most of the townspeople like to see done with the property?" I asked.

Molly took a sip and gave a weak smile. "It would be lovely if year-round homes could be built for young families and our seniors. The town needs that so much."

"Do the townspeople sometimes feel overrun with tourists?" I asked.

Meg's eyes bored into me. Perhaps I should have rephrased that.

Molly frowned deeply. Her cup trembled a bit in her hand. "Tourists are how Owen and I make a living. Ballymoor would not be as prosperous without them."

Ouch, I did not want to alienate her.

"Molly, our town at home is very similar. We get an influx of tourists in the summer, which helps our businesses greatly, but as the weather gets colder it's nice to feel less crowded."

"We get most visitors from May through August. The town is bustling then but in a nice way. All the merchants agree that's how we make ends meet. The rest of the year Owen and I are booked by people going to conferences or by family or schools for reunions."

"I can see why the town would prefer hotels and B&Bs and not a development of vacation homes," I said. "They would not have a connection to Ballymoor and would take up space where families could live."

"Exactly. I grew up here. It's where Owen and I decided to make our home, and we care deeply about the town."

"Will the church ask for input?" Meg asked.

Molly shrugged. "It's going to be theirs, free and clear. I know that Catherine and members of the parish council have discreetly discussed their concerns in the past with Father Leahy, but the official decision will be made at a much higher level."

"Did anyone ever talk to Deirdre Harrington about her plans?" Meg asked.

"I know Martin Ryan tried a few times. The poor man, I think she laid him out in lavender."

"Who is he?" Meg queried.

"Martin is a wonderful man, a retired banker. He's helped so many in Ballymoor over the years with mortgages, loans, and all manner of financial matters. He told me he visited Deirdre a few times but that she would not listen to him. No one wanted to cheat her. It's just that we wanted our village to thrive. We don't want to see people displaced because they can't afford lodging."

My phone pealed, and I saw it was Catherine's niece, Aisling Doyle.

"Excuse me, I need to take this call. I'll be right back."

Walking to the sitting room, I answered. "Hello, Aisling."

"Good morning, Maeve. I wanted to see if you were free to visit me."

"Of course, I'd love to come and see your midwifery practice. I am at your beck and call. When would you like me there?"

"How about this afternoon? I can give you a tour of the labor unit, and then you can stay for as long as you like for my antenatal session."

"That sounds wonderful. I'll be there."

"Grand. Meet me at the Ballymoor Health Center. It's on Mill Street, next to the main hospital building. You can easily walk from your inn. You'll see a sign on the right side of the Center that says *Ballymoor Maternity and Infant Care Unit*. Go in the red door and ask for me at the desk."

I was so excited. I was going to meet with midwives from another country! Would our protocols be similar? How was the Irish obstetrical system set up? Were our struggles alike? I had so many questions.

As I was returning to the dining area, Owen Farrell stopped and gave me a small sticky note.

"Sheila Whalen, a reporter for the *The Ballymoor Times*, called to ask if she could interview you and Meg today. I wrote down her contact information. I told her you were having breakfast now and you'd probably call her afterward. I hope that's all right."

"That's fine, Owen. Thank you." As I turned to rejoin Meg, I added, "I don't know how much we can add to what she already knows, but we'll be happy to talk to her."

At our corner table, I saw Meg eating yet another slice of buttered and toasted brown bread and finishing another cup of tea.

She smiled like the Cheshire cat and said, "This bread might be my new favorite food. I mean, I love chocolate, especially here, but this brown bread is the best thing I've ever tasted."

"It is delicious," I agreed.

I'd have to insist that Will put Irish brown bread on his menu, or Meg would have a nasty withdrawal when we got home.

I sat down to take a last nibble and handed Meg the sticky note.

"A reporter from the *The Ballymoor Times* wants to interview us. We need to call her." I paused as I drank iced water. "Also, I'm visiting Aisling at her midwifery practice this afternoon at one p.m."

"That's fine. I want to check out the shops today to see what gifts I want to buy for the family," Meg responded.

Meg proceeded to call Sheila Whalen and set up a meeting for eleven a.m. in her office.

After hanging up, Meg gave me a wry smile. "Maybe we can find out some inside information from the reporter."

I shrugged. "I'm sure she's only going to ask us for the details of what we witnessed."

"Come on now, Maeve. You know how we operate. We are the M&M's, after all. We may not be in the thick of this, but we'll still want to follow along, right? And what if we can find out who killed Deirdre Harrington?"

I shook my head slowly. What had gotten into my sister? "I thought you were the one who didn't want to get involved, Meg?"

"Well, maybe I caught the bug a little," she admitted. "We've solved four murder cases already, haven't we?"

Solved might be a stretch. A few times we were lucky to escape with our lives.

Meg held up her phone to show me the notes section. She had already begun making a list of suspects. I noticed it was titled, *M&M, Case #5.*

There was no question that Meg was all in.

I realized now that our Irish holiday would involve a bit of sleuthing. Oh no, I had told Will we were not investigating. Well, how much could we really do? Meg and I didn't even know how the Ballymoor crime unit operated.

Well, I supposed we could poke around a bit. A few questions still bothered me, though. If we got involved and had our usual roller-coaster ride of sleuthing, would Ballymoor ever be the same? Did the United States embassy in Dublin offer free legal help? Could one be banned from their homeland?

CHAPTER FOURTEEN

As of 2023, the population of the Republic of Ireland was about five million.

After finishing breakfast, Meg and I walked Ballymoor's main street so she could begin her initial survey of the shops. As we made our way along the cobblestones, the sidewalk was crowded with shoppers, workers, and more than a few tourists. Hearing a variety of accents, I remembered that Molly said most visitors were from Germany, the UK, France, and of course, the States. What a bustling town. The shops were a mix of local services and ones clearly aimed at the tourist trade. We passed a grocery, Donovan's Alehouse, Blooms by Rose, and a few art galleries before stopping in front of an adorable children's shop called Little Treasures, which had beautiful hand-knit Aran sweaters in the window. I decided I would have to return to this shop later to scope it out.

Looking back, I saw that Delaney's Pub was at the far end of the block. It was just as Helen Lyons had described. There were no residential properties anywhere near it. So, how could Deirdre Harrington possibly have been bothered by any noise emanating from the site? Did she have a grudge against the owners? How far away did she live?

"Hey, Maeve, let's take a peek in here," Meg said, bringing me back to the present. While I was musing about the deceased, we came upon Eire Gold, a small jewelry shop with a captivating window display of pearl necklaces and gold chains.

I followed Meg inside, where we were warmly greeted by a twenty-something woman with strawberry-blonde hair and a glowing alabaster complexion. She told us to take our time and to call her if we had any questions.

I gravitated toward the pearls while Meg headed to the ring cabinet.

"Maeve, look at these," she said, calling me over after a few minutes.

There were trays of exquisite Claddagh rings of every description. The Claddagh was a traditional Irish style showcasing two hands, a heart and a crown. Some were gold, some silver, and some held emeralds, rubies, or diamonds.

"Meg, they are lovely. Are you thinking of buying one?"

"Maybe—I've always admired Mom's wedding band."

Dad had given Mom a rose gold Claddagh ring when they married. Mom had always cherished it. Now that arthritis had made it impossible for her to wear it on her finger, it took pride of place on her necklace.

We were the only customers in the shop, and seeing us hover over the rings, the saleswoman came back.

"May I show you anything?"

"I'd like to see the gold one on the top right with the emerald, please," Meg said.

I looked where she was pointing. It was a gorgeous piece.

"Would you like to see one, too?" the saleswoman asked me as she handed the ring to Meg.

"No thanks," I said with a smile. "But they are lovely."

Meg slipped the ring onto her finger, turning her hand from side to side to admire it.

"It looks very nice, Meg."

"Are you familiar with the meaning of the Claddagh?" the shopkeeper asked.

"I know they denote love and are often used for weddings or engagements," I said.

The sales clerk picked up a silver ring and looked at it wistfully. She turned it to us as she spoke, "The heart represents love, the crown loyalty, and the hands are a sign of friendship. They are often used for marriage, but nowadays, mothers give them to daughters, and many women gift them to friends. Traditionally, if one is engaged, you wear it on your left hand with the heart facing out. Once married, you'd wear it with the heart facing in. But today, as I said, both men and women wear them. This one with the emerald is charming, but there are all types of Claddagh rings—one to fit every budget. We also have

Claddagh brooches, necklaces, and earrings. It's a wonderful symbol of loyalty, friendship, and love."

Meg put the ring down on the black velvet pad on the glass countertop, and we thanked the woman for her help. We left, promising to stop back.

As we walked past one of the flower shops, Meg started giggling.

"What, Meg?"

"If we tell Mom that Claddagh rings are often given to friends now, she'll want to buy one for all the Ladies of the Lobby. Of course, they'll have to have them fitted with jewels in their favorite colors."

"You know Mom. She loves to give to her people, and with her newfound fortune, she is being the philanthropist she was meant to be. It has made her so happy."

"She was always happy, but I do agree that money put a pep in her step." Meg smiled.

My mother always looked on the bright side. Losing her husband, being left with four children to raise, and now needing a wheelchair to get around may have slowed but never stopped her. She had an immense love of life, no matter what it threw at her.

"I can only imagine what she will buy the family when they arrive."

We continued along the brick walk, getting a better sense of the town. A white van pulled up across the street. It had *BURKE'S GOAT CHEESE* lettered in red on the side.

A tall, slim man with a chocolate brown scally cap and worn jeans exited the driver's seat. I nudged Meg to take notice of him. We were very familiar with his attire. Scally caps—with their unpretentious style consisting of rounded tops and small, stiff brims—were often seen in Boston. Opening the van's back door, the man unloaded two boxes and headed into the grocery store with them. I noticed he had a scruffy beard and some long red scratches on the right side of his face.

"That must be Seamus Burke," I whispered to Meg.

"Looks like he was in a bit of a tussle," Meg said.

"It certainly does. I wonder if the Gardaí has questioned him? Let's add that scuffed face after his name on his suspect page," I said.

"I'm so glad you are committing to this investigation. I just hope he's not the killer because his cheese was delicious when we had it in sandwiches the other day," Meg said wryly, as she typed into her phone.

"Perhaps we should rank suspects according to their contribution to our lives," I mused.

"Hilarious, Maeve."

Since it was close to eleven, we wound our way onto Elmwood Street, which was directly behind the main thoroughfare. The address we searched for belonged to a very stately, clearly historic red brick building set far back from the road. *The Ballymoor Times* was displayed in large black letters on a white sign out front.

As we entered, it was evident that this paper was far more modern than its facade suggested. Striking white walls and large glass windows made the room light and bright. By the door, a receptionist sat at a rectangular white acrylic desk that supported a large computer workstation. Three offices with glass partitions ran side by side on the right side of the room. A large wall-mounted TV and a long oak desk with printers took up the left side.

"Good morning, may I help you?" asked an older woman with a distinctive Dominican accent. She was dressed in cobalt blue and had bright orange octagonal glasses. Her spiky brown hair framed her face becomingly.

"Good morning. We're here to see Sheila Whalen. We're Maeve and Meg O'Reilly. She called and asked us to come in for an interview at eleven," I said.

"Ah, you are the Americans who found the victim."

Yup, we were known here, all right. What a way to make an entrance to Ballymoor. I guess news traveled here at the speed of sound, just as it would in Langford. Then again, it wasn't every day that two foreign women found a body on arrival.

"Well, welcome. I'm Evie. Come right in and have a seat. May I get you a cup of tea or a glass of water?"

We both shook our heads. "No, thank you. We're fine," Meg said.

"Okay then, I'll tell Sheila you're here."

Meg reached into the large glass container of mini-wrapped chocolates on the low waiting room table. She took two and handed me one.

As the chocolate melted in my mouth, I knew Meg was correct, as usual. Irish candy was unlike anything I had tasted in the States. These treats were in a whole new ballpark.

We watched Evie walk to the farthest office and knock on the door. A few minutes later, she came back, accompanied by a tall, thin, copper-haired woman dressed in chic, black tailored pants and a soft white silk blouse.

I was still amazed by the large number of gingers here. The myriad of shades of red hair was fascinating and so beautiful.

"Hello, Meg and Maeve. Thank you so much for coming. I know it's your holiday, and I appreciate you making time for an interview."

Sheila led us back to her office and invited us to sit in two high-backed black leather chairs. Gorgeous prints of Kylemore Abbey, the Rock of Cashel, and Killarney National Park adorned the walls.

As we settled in, Sheila turned her full attention to us. "Well, what a visit you've had so far. I don't imagine that finding a corpse as soon as you got here was on your to-do list. That must have been a little disconcerting."

I held my tongue as I did not want Sheila to know that I had a propensity for finding dead bodies.

"It was shocking. We suffered no ill effects but feel bad for the poor victim," Meg replied.

Sheila was silent momentarily, then said, "I hear your family hails from County Galway."

Meg nodded. "Our mother's parents emigrated from Ballinasloe, and she was born in Boston. Our father was from Cork but came to the States when he was nineteen. They met at a parish dance."

"So lovely. And such a common story of people of a certain age. I've been to New York but not to Boston yet. I do hope to visit sometime. I interned in Manhattan after uni and had a grand time there. I absolutely miss the pizza," Sheila said with a laugh.

"Nothing like a New York slice—it's the best!" Meg agreed.

"So, I'd like to hear your story and ask a few questions. Unfortunately, I don't know much about Deirdre Harrington." She paused for a few seconds. "I know she was very vocal at town council meetings since I cover those. I can't find anything about her past, and I've been searching. For tomorrow's edition, I wanted to report how she was found. So, in your own words, could you please tell me what happened?"

Meg nodded at me to begin. I told Sheila how we had decided to take an early morning stroll to get scones and tea and decided to sit on Ballymoor Green to eat. She listened intently as I told how Meg spotted something that looked like trash in the weeds but turned out to be a body. After the part where we called 9-9-9, she knew the rest of the story.

"Did you see anyone suspicious on your way to the Green?"

"No, we were early birds," Meg replied.

Sheila shrugged her shoulders. "I appreciate you repeating your story to me. It's such a mystery. I tried to write her obituary, but Deirdre is a blank slate. It's almost like her past life was a secret. I know she moved here from Dublin four years ago, but I don't know why she picked Ballymoor. She bought an older non-working farm with a lot of land."

"That's interesting," Meg said. "It seems like an odd choice for a senior citizen."

Sheila leaned back in her chair with a look of chagrin.

"Deirdre Harrington was a woman of means. She outbid a local contractor for the property, and then she had the farmhouse updated but left the accompanying fields unplanted. The contractor had envisioned a multigenerational neighborhood. He planned smaller homes for elders and larger homes for growing families."

"What did the people of Ballymoor think of that?" Meg asked.

Sheila's eyebrows raised, and she gave a slight shrug. "No one was pleased. The town could use the housing, but you know, money talks."

"We heard that Deirdre Harrington had some issues with a few citizens," I said.

Sheila was briefly silent as if contemplating how much to say. "Well, you've likely heard that she was very outspoken and liked the status quo. She adamantly opposed any new business in town and was a stickler for rules."

"We heard there was a problem with stray animals on her property," Meg said.

A bright red streak appeared from Sheila's chin to her forehead. "You've obviously heard about her run-ins with Seamus Burke. Yes, sometimes a goat or two of his got loose and headed for her property. They were never near the farmhouse but always in the back fields." Sheila looked a bit exasperated. "I know he mended his fence, but Deirdre still asked the town council to fine him."

This topic was clearly near and dear to Sheila's heart. She took a large drink of water, which seemed to help her get her bearings.

"I know the people from Saint Columbkille's are planning Deirdre Harrington's final goodbye. I'll publish the service details when they're available."

Sheila looked at her watch and closed her laptop. "I should let you two be off now. A million thanks for stopping by. Would it be all right if our photographer took your photo for the paper?"

"Sure," Meg responded. She was always ready for a cover shot.

Oh brother, here for a few days and already in the newspaper. What would Cousin Catherine and the family think?

I rapidly put on lipstick and fluffed my hair. As the photo was snapped, Sheila said, "It will only be used to add interest to the piece."

Standing outside *The Ballymoor Times*, Meg asked, "Are Sheila and Seamus an item? She seemed very distressed by Deirdre's interest in his goats. Does he have an alibi for the time of the murder? And how did he get scratched? I hope Deirdre Harrington's fingernails were checked for a DNA sample."

I was trailing slightly behind, astonished that my big sister had turned into Hercule Poirot. It seemed we were becoming global spies. I might need a classier wardrobe.

"Come on, Maeve, keep up."

Well, I guess the game *was* afoot.

CHAPTER FIFTEEN

———

As of 2023, the population of Northern Ireland was approximately 1.9 million.

Looking down the busy street, Meg gestured towards Delaney's Pub. "Hey, Maeve, how about a cup of lamb stew before your appointment with Aisling?"

"Sounds great," I said.

The heavy wooden and glass door opened into a very large, handsomely decorated dining room with a mahogany host stand directly to the right of the entrance. As soon as we stepped through the doorway, a medium-height, thin, black-haired man in his late thirties greeted us.

"Hello there. Welcome to Delaney's. I'm Cillian Delaney."

"Thank you. What a beautiful pub you have," Meg remarked, taking in the décor.

Cillian beamed at Meg. "Thank you. We feel so lucky to be the proprietors. We've put a lot of work into it, but the result was well worth the effort."

Looking around, I noticed that the stucco walls were painted a creamy linen white, drawing your eyes to the majestic arched ceiling and showcasing the polished dark hardwood beams. At one end of the main room was a massive limestone fireplace next to an extended bar area. The rest of the space held about thirty round tables. The white tiled modern kitchen was an open concept, and two chefs were preparing meals. It all effortlessly added to the charm.

"Two for lunch?" Cillian inquired with a wide grin.

Meg nodded, and he guided us across the dining area to a set of French doors that faced a lush, colorful flower garden.

"I thought you might enjoy looking out at our fountain and plantings."

"The grounds are breathtaking. Someone has a green thumb," I observed.

"Yes, it's all my wife, Lindsay's, doing. It's her pride and joy. Well, after the children, of course," he said with a laugh. "But truthfully, everything she touches just blossoms, even with our Irish weather."

We took our seats, and Cillian handed us menus. He poured water from an etched glass pitcher and said, "Gracie, our daughter, will be over to take your order in a few minutes."

"Gee, Meg, what a gorgeous pub. Every little touch is thought-out and special." I inspected the small rectangular cobalt blue vase, which held a lacy white hydrangea blossom. In keeping with the table décor, there were small, blue and green swirled handblown glass salt and pepper shakers. The very comfortable captain's chairs had dark green leather seats. Together, the furnishings gave off an upscale yet peaceful air.

Meg was eyeing the majestic fireplace. "I bet they have traditional Irish music here at night. We'll want to take that in as much as possible while we're here."

After perusing the menu, I decided that lamb stew would indeed be a tasty lunch.

"Good afternoon," said a brown-skinned girl with chin-length braids and large brown eyes with lush lashes. She appeared to be about sixteen. "I'm Gracie, and I'll be your server today. May I get you a cup of tea or coffee?"

"Do you have lemonade?" Meg asked.

"Yes. Would you both like a glass?"

"I'm fine with the ice water, thank you," I said.

"We'd both like a bowl of lamb stew, please," Meg said. "Does it come with brown bread?"

Gracie smiled as she took a pencil from her ear. "Of course. All of our soups and stews come with a platter of brown bread."

"Wonderful," Meg said.

"Lamb stew sounds fitting on a day like today," I said.

"I agree," Gracie said, smiling. "Even though it's still technically summer, there's a bit of a nip in the air." She collected our menus and commented, "I can tell you're visiting from abroad."

"Yes, we're from a town about an hour south of Boston. We're visiting relatives in Ballymoor," Meg answered.

"Oh, isn't that wonderful? It's always so good to see family. Well, let me go and put this order in for you. If you need anything, just flag me down, and I'll be back in a jiffy."

The dining room began to fill up with the lunchtime crowd of mostly locals. By their numbers, I'd say that Delaney's Pub was a very popular spot, and Meg and I soon felt fortunate that Cillian had put us at a table set off from the rest of the diners. We needed privacy to review the meeting with Sheila Whalen.

After Gracie dropped off our beverages, Meg leaned back in her chair and folded her hands on the table. "Well, that was certainly an interesting session with Sheila. It strikes me as odd that she could find absolutely no information on Deirdre Harrington, although that might go along with the fact that she had no close friends and no family." She took a sip of lemonade and then took a long look at the icy glass. "That's delicious lemonade," she said with a degree of contemplation. Then, looking at me, she said, "You know, it makes me wonder what our victim did for work in Dublin."

"I find it impossible to believe no one knows," I said.

"Sheila is an experienced reporter, but there has to be information hiding somewhere." Meg's forehead wrinkled as she pondered that thought. "And why move to Ballymoor? I mean, it's a beautiful town, but Deirdre was older, and without family or friends nearby, it certainly seems like a strange choice, especially purchasing a farmhouse and acres of land."

As we were speaking, Gracie returned with a tray holding two steaming bowls of lamb stew and the promised platter of brown bread—with Kerrygold butter, of course. As she placed our entrées in front of us she said, "I don't mean to intrude, but I just realized that you are the women from Boston who found Miss Harrington's body."

I handled the explanation. "Yes, unfortunately, we made that grim discovery on our first morning here."

Gracie shuddered a bit and then somewhat cryptically said, "Well, it's sad that she was killed in such a gruesome manner, but she certainly caused a lot of misery in this town."

At that instant Cillian Delaney appeared and put his arm on Gracie's shoulder. "Hello, there. Is everything all right?"

"Everything is great," I answered.

"Excellent. Gracie, why don't you help the new girl? That party of eight just arrived and she might need assistance."

Gracie glanced quickly at her father and then gave Meg and me a shrug. "Fine, Dad. I'll get right on it." She hurried off, and Cillian quickly departed.

When we were alone again, Meg tilted her head and stared at me with her discerning baby blues.

"Hmm, is it me, or does it seem that when Cillian overheard Gracie mention Deirdre Harrington's name to us, he made sure to shut down the conversation?"

"It wasn't just you, and it is very interesting. Or else maybe he didn't want her to disturb our meal."

"Perhaps he didn't want Gracie to tell us about the deceased's vendetta against Delaney's Pub."

"Meg, can we just enjoy this tasty lamb stew and try not to add any more suspects to the list?"

"Oh, come on, Maeve. We're wasting too much time already. Remember we are only in Ballymoor for a few short weeks. Once the family arrives, we won't have time for crime-solving. Plus, we need to visit Dad's family in Cork. I want this murder solved soon. We can't go back to the States with our reputation damaged."

I shut my eyes for a few seconds and opened them slowly. My sister, adamantly opposed to sleuthing at first, was now channeling Jessica Fletcher of *Murder, She Wrote* fame. My head was spinning.

"Meg, have another piece of brown bread. Maybe it's the time difference, but I am overloaded today."

As she dipped her knife in the tasty Irish butter and began fixing a slice, she said, "Well, I am already taking copious notes. Seamus Burke is right up at the top of the list. Apparently, Deirdre Harrington upset his well-ordered life. Also, the scratches on his face? What were those from? Then there's Rory, that young guy she taunted. Had he finally had enough?"

She stopped for a spoonful of stew and a bite of bread. A rapt look crossed across her face, and then she continued, "Now add to that her complaints about Delaney's Pub. She clearly was not a fan, a fact that Cillian confirmed by conveniently pulling Gracie away from us."

I was silent. Meg was making many valid points. Who else should we be looking at?

Oh, brother, I could just feel the ground shifting under my feet, sucking me back into detective mode.

"Next up, we need to dig into Deirdre's background. Her past cannot be a total secret. Why was she in Ballymoor? And why leave everything to Saint Columbkille's? While you're visiting Aisling, I'll be very busy with Ms. Google."

Finally, Meg's hunger made her concentrate on the stew. I had to admit that it was positively delicious, with tiny potatoes, carrots, peas, and very tender bites of lamb. Will was absolutely going to have to duplicate this in Langford.

After we finished, Cillian returned with the bill and bid us a good day. Although he was very cordial, he obviously did not want to engage in further conversation. I noticed there was no sign of Gracie in the dining room. What was he so worried that we might hear? Had we ruffled some feathers?

All in all, it had been a very interesting, or rather intriguing meal.

CHAPTER SIXTEEN

———

As of 2023, there were approximately 4,200 midwives practicing in Ireland.

I left Meg in the heart of Ballymoor, knowing she would be busy browsing shops and then spending the afternoon with her laptop. I headed off to my appointment with Aisling Doyle.

The Ballymoor Health Center, which was adjacent to Ballymoor Hospital, the main medical facility, had a bright white façade fronted by a glass revolving door. Standing in front of the main entrance, I immediately saw the sign for the maternity unit pointing to the right. I walked to the side of the building and opened the red lacquered door. When it closed behind me, all street noise stopped.

The waiting room was painted in muted tones of peach and cream. There was a slight hint of eucalyptus in the air. What a mellow waiting room. It was decorated tastefully with pale gray synthetic leather couches and side chairs. One corner of the room had been converted into a play area with a primary-colored rug, toys, and books for young children. It was apparent that much planning had gone into this warm setting, and the result could not have been more welcoming.

I went to the beige quartz reception desk and asked for Aisling Doyle.

"Ah, you must be the midwife from Boston," said the petite woman with a charming Irish brogue. She wore her light brown hair in an intricate chignon. "We're so happy that you're visiting us. All the midwives are very excited to meet you." With that, she stood and escorted me to the staff room, where Aisling sat with four other women.

"Hello, Maeve! Welcome!" Aisling said as she shook my hand warmly. Then, she turned and addressed the group. "This is

Maeve O'Reilly, visiting us from the States. She lives south of Boston and is an experienced midwife. Today, I'm going to give her a tour, and then she'll accompany me to my afternoon clinical session. But first, I thought we would all sit, say hello, and give her a little glimpse of how we practice."

"That sounds great. I'm so happy to meet you. I must say, even though I'm having a delightful holiday, I'm missing my midwifery colleagues."

What a welcome. I couldn't help smiling as I slid into one of the chairs at the table. I immediately felt at home looking at each midwife in turn. I couldn't wait to hear their stories.

"Everyone, please introduce yourselves. Maeve, may I get you a cup of tea?" Aisling asked.

"I'd love one. Thank you."

Tea clearly was the most beloved national drink. I noticed there wasn't even a coffeepot in the room.

"Hello, Maeve. I'm Amara," said a dark-skinned, slim fortyish woman. "I've been a midwife for sixteen years. I was born in Nigeria, studied in London, and then took a position here."

She started to laugh. "And, of course, I fell in love with a charming Irish lad, and four babies later, here I am."

"And we are so thankful to Cathal Driscoll for having the good sense to fall in love with you," Aisling said as the group spontaneously applauded.

Next, an older woman with black curls streaked with white piped up, "Well, I guess I'm the unofficial elder of the group. I'm Cara. I've been here for my entire career. Welcome, Maeve. I can't wait to ask about midwifery in the US."

The third woman, who appeared to be in her late twenties, said, "Hi, Maeve. I'm Orla, the newest midwife. I'm a Ballymoor native. I've wanted to be a midwife since I was a young girl. I have a lot of questions about American midwifery educational programs."

Without missing a beat, we began an animated discussion of all aspects of midwifery. The five of us talked about the highs and lows, as well as the support and the nonsupport from hospital administration. We reviewed the similarities and differences in our respective practices. It was so invigorating to hear new perspectives. I was surprised and happy to hear that currently there was a high demand for midwives in Ireland.

After a much too short twenty minutes, Aisling stood. "This has been so much fun, but we must hurry now. I want to give Maeve a tour of the birth unit, and then we need to get to my clinic session."

I stood and addressed the group. "It was so wonderful to meet fellow midwives. You've made me feel right at home. It's as if I'm back with my group. Thank you so much for sharing with me."

"Well, we are fellow midwives," Amara said, toasting me with her teacup.

I received hearty handshakes as I was leaving and made promises to return. Aisling took me on a tour of Ballymoor Hospital. The birth suite was painted a soft pale blue, and sheer white curtains framed the large windows. Immediately upon entering, a feeling of calm enveloped me. It was a very peaceful place, but I knew that, inside the cabinets, emergency equipment was readily available, if needed.

"Aisling, it's such a charming place to give birth."

"We're so happy with the way it turned out. It was just remodeled last year, and the midwives had a great amount of input."

As we ambled down the corridor, she continued, "Our group is in a very good place right now. Five midwives are on staff, and we have a full caseload of patients. Also, our consultant obstetricians are very supportive."

I nodded. I knew intimately how important staffing and support were to midwives. My own practice had gone through some dark months when a totally unsupportive chief was temporarily in command.

Aisling continued, "I hope one day to make the trip to meet your group and visit your birthing unit."

"I would love that, Aisling. And I know everyone in my practice would be happy to show you around."

Aisling opened the stairway door. "Off to clinic now. I have a light afternoon because this was an add-on session."

Aisling reviewed the health center's electronic medical records system with me. It was quite similar to what I had back home. I quickly scanned the charts of the patients we would see today.

The first two patients were newly pregnant, and I watched Aisling take a complete history and conduct a thorough physical exam of each one. She expertly incorporated patient teaching into the visit. It was a unique experience to watch how another midwife, especially one from a different country, practiced, and I appreciated seeing how things could be said in an alternate manner.

The afternoon flew by. In what seemed like minutes, Aisling was greeting her last patient of the day. The young woman was thirty-eight weeks pregnant. I was half following the conversation when, about five minutes into the encounter, I realized she was Annie McIntyre, the girlfriend of Rory Connors, the young man Deirdre Harrington had bullied. She suddenly had my full attention.

"So, Annie, I see you've been keeping well. All your vital signs are great, and your baby sounds fine. Are you and Rory all set for the birth?" Aisling asked.

"I think so," Annie smiled a bit tentatively. "I've read the book you gave me on labor and newborn care. I am a little worried about how I will cope, but I know the midwives will be there with me."

"We absolutely will. Remember, take every contraction step by step. The nursing staff is excellent. If you need anything for discomfort, it will be available. Now, I don't want you to listen to any scary birth tales. Sometimes, well-meaning people exaggerate their stories and cause pregnant women to worry. Did you and Rory get to the birthing class?"

"I took the class that Amara taught. She was terrific. I learned so much. Rory couldn't come because of his work schedule, but I told him everything she discussed. My friend Joan went with me."

"That's wonderful, Annie. Do you have supplies for when the baby comes home?"

"I think we're all set, at least for the first few months. One of the women at the vet office had a baby last year, so she gave me blankets and a lot of newborn clothing. The staff at Delaney's gave Rory a gift card, so we stocked up on diapers. Mrs. Lyons, a friend of Rory's, gave us a bassinet." Annie smiled broadly, and I finally saw her green eyes sparkle. "It's small, but it will do for the first few months, and it's all we can fit into our flat right now. Hopefully, we'll get a bigger living space soon." She paused and started twirling a piece of her long hair around her index finger. "Well, if Ballymoor gets some decent housing."

"That's so true," Aisling commiserated. "Well, it sounds as if you're well prepared. You and Rory are doing a good job. Now, I'll see you in a week, but remember, if you experience any signs of labor, call us."

"I know that I should call if I break my water or if the contractions are every five minutes," Annie said.

"Exactly. Remember to also ring us if there is any bleeding or if the baby is not moving as usual," Aisling said.

"Thank you so much, Aisling. And it was nice to meet you, too, Maeve."

"Thank you, Annie. Best of luck now."

Suddenly, it hit me. Everyone in Ireland knew how to say my name. No more Mraeve, Mavis, or Maida. No more of my helpful suggestions:

Like *Dave* with an *M*.
Like *cave* with an *M*.
Like *save* with an *M*.

It was yet another reason to love Ireland.

As Aisling finished charting, she said, "Well, that was a nice session for you to see. We had a variety of ages and stages of pregnancy."

"It was the best, Aisling. You put women at ease, and you're so caring. I enjoyed being a spectator. I feel I got a bird's eye view of midwifery in Ireland. Thank you so much."

Aisling smiled and said, "You know, Maeve, I hesitate to bring this up, but if you want to attend a birth here, let me know, and I'll try to arrange it. It would have to be during my call time, and the patient and her partner would have to consent, but it is possible."

"I would love that. Being present at a birth with a fellow midwife is always special. And to have that midwife be a cousin in my ancestral homeland makes it even more exciting. In my practice, we rarely get to observe each other."

"Be careful what you wish for," she said with a laugh. "I do a lot of night call. I might be calling you in the wee hours. But you can always say no. This is your holiday."

"Please call me anytime, Aisling. I would be thrilled. As you know, all midwives are aware that sleep is overrated."

Aisling laughed again. "If you say so. Maybe the stars will align."

As we packed up, I decided to gather some information. I guess I *was* in detective mode.

"Annie McIntyre looked well. I recently heard about Deirdre Harrington's treatment of Rory Connors. That must have upset Annie."

Gee, couldn't I sound a little vaguer? Was I losing my edge?

"Everyone in Ballymoor knew how Deirdre treated Rory Connors. Often, she embarrassed him at Delaney's Pub." She looked up from the workstation with a frown. "Annie never said anything about it to me. Those two kids are trying so hard to provide for their baby. They need support, not someone dragging them down."

We were both silent.

"Anyway, I guess that's no longer an issue," Aisling shrugged.

She was right. Dead is dead.

I thanked Aisling again and started the walk back to the guesthouse. I was still feeling the glow from having connected with the midwifery group. Although an ocean apart, we all strived to care for women the best we could. The walk back seemed short as I replayed the visit in my mind.

Smiling and ready to chat, I walked into the sunroom. Meg was sitting in a tufted ivory armchair with her laptop open. "Hi, Meg. Did you have a nice afternoon?"

Meg's face looked grim. "Why don't you get a cup of tea, Maeve? You're going to need it."

"What's up?" I asked. My thoughts immediately went to Mom and her crew. Had there been an accident?

Meg could, as always, read my mind.

"Everyone is fine. Well, everyone except for Deirdre Harrington. There was a press conference about fifteen minutes ago."

"What?" I asked.

"The knife that was used to kill her came from Delaney's Pub."

CHAPTER SEVENTEEN

———

A brogue refers to the distinctive Irish accent.

Meg was right. I needed a cup of tea—a strong cup. Although I usually drank it black, I added cream and two lumps of sugar. Then, I sank into the beige striped upholstered glider and studied a row of majestic hosta plants.

"Sounds like Deirdre Harrington was killed by someone from this town."

"I would say so," Meg replied.

"Did the Gardaí say that they were questioning anyone?"

"They are holding their cards close to their vests. I am sure the Delaney family and Rory Connors are at the top of their lists, though."

I had come in basking in the glow of my delightful afternoon, but now I suddenly felt wholly deflated.

"Meg, I was so hoping she wasn't killed by a local. Now it looks like she probably was." I tasted my tea, appreciating its sweetness just now. "Everyone in this town seems so lovely. It's so tranquil here. Couldn't it just be a random killing?"

"There you go again, Maeve. As I've told you so many times before, there is evil in the world. Look at Langford. It's so scenic and seems idyllic, but it's certainly had its share of murders. Come on now, this is Ireland, not Shangri-La. Get a grip."

"I know, I know. So, what's next?"

"Well, I assume Delaney's Pub is temporarily closed while the staff are questioned."

"They must be fingerprinting everyone. But the knife probably was kept in a wooden block in the kitchen. With such an open cooking area, it seems anyone could have taken it."

We were both silent as we let that thought sink in.

"We did hear that she made Lindsay and Cillian Delaney's life miserable," Meg said, setting her laptop on a side table.

"Miserable enough to kill her?"

"Well, if she impacted their business, who knows?"

Even if the situation sounded dire, Meg had a valid point.

Our conversation went back and forth, and we discussed various motives and suspects. Finally, Meg sat forward, balancing her laptop on her knees. "I spent a few hours researching Deirdre Harrington, and sad to say, it's exactly as Sheila Whalen described. She is a near-total mystery. The best I can find is that she ran some type of business in Dublin. But I did find an old address for her, so we'll want to check that out."

I didn't answer right away, but I knew Meg was right. She was clearly taking the lead in this investigation.

Trying to recapture some of my mellowness of the day, I asked, "Did Mom and the ladies have an enjoyable day?"

Meg gave me a broad grin. "They had a wonderful time. Ethel, Gaby, and Louella joined various groups, from knitting to gardening. And Mom and Catherine have planned the funeral to the last detail, bagpipes and all."

Stretching my arms, I laughed. "Mom must be on top of the world."

"She is very pleased with herself."

"Meg, I know that this trip was a lot to coordinate, and we were reluctant at first, but Mom is so happy. It was all worth it, even with a murder thrown in."

I wanted that to be true. I wanted nothing to mar this trip. Our last few escapades had almost resulted in bodily harm. Hopefully, this one would not.

"They're all taking a rest now and then are off to Catherine's. I said you and I would be on our own tonight. I hope that's fine with you."

"That sounds good. Where were you thinking of dining?"

"Delaney's Pub is out, but I saw a cute place called the Hungry Fox. We could eat, formulate a suspect list, and listen to traditional Irish music. After that, it can be an early night."

"Just what I need."

I took a brief nap, followed by a long, warm shower. Then, dressed in my favorite boyfriend jeans and navy fleece, I headed out with Meg. There was a slight chill in the air and the wind was brisk.

"So much for summer," Meg said, turning up her fleece collar as we made our way to the Hungry Fox.

Stepping into the warm, lively pub, we were seated at a booth near the fireplace. Although we looked at the menu, I had already decided, and Meg readily agreed. We ordered fish and chips baskets with pints of Guinness.

Meg raised her glass to me. "*Sláinte.*"

"*Sláinte.*"

The entrees were done to perfection. We could judge because, as New Englanders, Meg and I knew how fish should be cooked. It was served with malt vinegar, and even though I liked to try new condiments, I stuck with my traditional coleslaw and tartar sauce.

As we finished our meal, the band started setting up. It was fascinating to watch. I saw that the musicians carried flutes, fiddles, tin whistles, mandolins, and a drum I recognized as a bodhrán. I had read that it was made from goatskin stretched over a wooden frame and was played with a double-headed stick. There was also some type of bagpipe, which I had never seen before.

Although I was rather full, Meg ordered bread pudding with whiskey-caramel sauce for two and another Guinness each. She loved dessert and intended to try every Irish one she came across.

I smiled and shook my head.

"What? Look, we're on vacation, and it's only pudding. Well, and two pints apiece. We're walking home. Just think, it will help us sleep."

What could I say but *Sláinte*?

After the waitress placed our desserts on the table and left, Meg pulled out two large Cadbury bars.

"These are just in case we want them," she said.

My sister did love her sweets. I broke off a piece of one. It was truly delicious. What could go better with a Guinness?

"Well, hello, are the two of you alone tonight?" Helen Lyons stood in front of our booth dressed in a burgundy and white plaid jumper and beige slacks. Her heart necklace was at her collar. It was clearly a favorite piece.

Before we could answer, Helen leaned into the booth and, in a loud whisper, said, "Your Mom brags about your detective skills. Well, Ballymoor needs you now."

CHAPTER EIGHTEEN

———

Ireland is comparable to the state of Maine in size.

Meg looked at Helen Lyons with surprise but quickly recovered.

"Hello, Helen. It's nice to see you. Yes, Maeve and I decided to have a quiet night. Catherine, Mom, and the rest of the group have been planning the requiem. They wanted to review all the arrangements tonight."

"Yes, I heard the funeral Mass will be tomorrow at ten a.m. at Saint Columbkille's. Even though Deirdre Harrington wasn't well-loved, I bet there will be a noteworthy turnout. Ballymoor people will pay their respects."

Or, like Mom, maybe many of the citizens just liked the pageantry, the gossip, and the free food.

"We're very interested in hearing the music tonight. But there's one instrument I don't recognize," I said. I gave Meg "the look." Every sister knows it. I was trying to distract Helen from asking us questions about the murder. We didn't need to share what little information we had.

Helen slid in next to me and looked at the band with admiration. "They are the Mulcahy Project. They're deadly *craic*. What instrument were you wondering about, Maeve?"

Although the term sounded ominous, I knew that deadly *craic* meant the band would be great.

Meg nodded slightly at me. She realized I had diverted Helen's attention.

"The one that resembles bagpipes," I answered.

"Those are Uilleann pipes and are often called Irish pipes. Unlike Scottish bagpipes, these are not played by mouth. The pipes are inflated by a set of bellows, which are placed under the musician's elbow, and they are played while sitting. Wait until you hear them. I think they have a sweet and soft sound. They are the national bagpipe of Ireland."

Despite her long explanation, I could sense that Helen was getting ready to launch back into a discussion of the murder. Giving her a broad smile, I said, "Helen, your necklace is lovely. Tell me about it."

Helen's face went ashen. Her hand reached up and grabbed her necklace tightly. "Jack…Jack," she sputtered.

Then she swallowed hard and seemed to regain her composure. "My Jack bought it for me ten years ago for my birthday. He was my husband. He passed on three years ago," she said, still rubbing the hearts.

The gift clearly had a deep significance for her. My fingers lightly touched the locket Will had given me one Christmas. How tough to lose her husband. I decided to ask about her necklace later.

Meg had ordered a pint for Helen, and she took a sip. I thought she would be silent until the music started, but Helen was clearly on a mission.

Her hazel eyes went from Meg to me. This time, there was no way to deflect her. "I know that you have solved crimes in the States. Do you have a list of suspects for Deirdre Harrington's murder?"

Helen had indeed recovered fast.

I hesitated before answering. We didn't know much about Helen Lyons. I mean, she was Cousin Catherine's friend, but were we going to discuss our thoughts with her?

"What are you thinking, Helen? Ballymoor is your home, and you know all the players. Do you have any ideas?" Meg asked, smiling brightly.

It was a flawless response. Meg was a master at lobbing the ball back into her opponent's court.

Helen's face clouded over, and she scowled. "I'm worried that poor Rory Connors will be blamed. He's an easy target who's never had a fair shake. Rory's mother died when he was five, and his father was never there for him. Rory's very intelligent, you know. He could have attended uni. The lad doesn't have a mean bone in his body."

I noticed that the hand fingering her necklace was shaking. Why was she so attached to Rory?

Helen's eyes narrowed. "And he stepped right up when Annie became pregnant. He could have taken off, but he didn't. He's a good man and will be a wonderful father."

She spread her hands on the wooden table as if to gather strength. "Deirdre was relentless. She was the original wicked witch. She was always disparaging Rory Connors, and her comments were absolutely vicious. She delighted in taunting him while he worked at Delaney's Pub. Cillian and Lindsay were appalled and spoke to her about it often. She ate there frequently, even though she lodged complaints against them. That woman has been pure trouble since she moved to Ballymoor."

So, a knife from Delaney's Pub was the murder weapon. Maybe this case was that easy. Perhaps the trail from Ballymoor Green stopped there.

Before more conversation started, one of the flute players tapped the mic to get people's attention.

"Welcome, everyone. I hope you're all having a grand night. Tonight, we have Matthew on tin whistle, Riley on pipes, Andrew on the bodhrán, Brianna on fiddle, and I'm Brian on the flute. Now we're going to start with 'Morning Lark' and then go right on to 'Shoemaker's Jig.' If you have any requests, please let us know."

They began to play. I leaned back in the leather booth, closed my eyes, and let the music invade my soul. It was hauntingly beautiful. My mind drifted to Will, my girls, and eventually to my entire family. I thought of how lucky I was to be of Irish descent and visit this country as I became lost in the music. Maybe Mom was right. She had urged all the siblings to apply for dual citizenship. Maybe I would. I began to imagine enjoying holidays here. Then, a knife and a body began to infiltrate my thoughts.

Who had Deirdre Harrington pushed over the edge?

Who had lost control?

When there was a lull in the music, Helen leaned closer to Meg and me. In a low voice, she said, "Brianna, the dark-haired woman on the fiddle, and her wife are the couple trying to open the new B&B. Hopefully, with that pesky Deirdre out of the way, they won't have a problem now." Helen straightened, stood, and gathered her purse. "Well, I'm off now. I'll see you tomorrow at the burial."

We said goodbye, but the music was so wonderful I didn't want to leave. After a quick tête-à-tête, Meg and I agreed on another half an hour.

As "The Wind that Shakes the Barley" began, a wide-eyed Helen abruptly rushed back to our booth.

"Rory Connors was just taken in for questioning. You must help him. He didn't kill Deirdre Harrington."

CHAPTER NINETEEN

———

Ireland has over seven million tourists a year.
Most are from the UK, the United States, Germany, and France.

Light, or rather soft rain, was falling the next day as Meg and I walked to Saint Columbkille's for Deirdre Harrington's rites. The dreary day seemed only fitting for seeing her off. Finn Walsh was picking up Mom and the ladies in his trusty van, and we were to meet them at the church steps.

As we approached the church, we saw that true to form, Finn had parked directly in front of Saint Columbkille's. Meg and I went to the passenger door and helped the quartet disembark. Their outfits looked, quite honestly, like they could raise the dead. Mom was in an emerald green pantsuit with sequined sleeves. Gaby wore vibrant purple slacks under a hot pink slicker. Ethel was a bit tamer with a pleated teal skirt and magenta tights. Louella, as usual, was in sunshine yellow from head to toe. All were adorned with long black lace mantillas, clearly resurrected from the 1950s and obviously gifts from Mom. A band of rogue nuns or the Golden Girls on holiday? Whatever, they were fearless and the best.

"Meg and Maeve, don't worry, I have head coverings for you, too," Mom sang out when she saw us.

We filed in and sat in a side pew in the middle of the church. It had a cutout where Mom's wheelchair could fit in without obstructing any of the guests.

"Do you think the mantillas were in Mom's deep storage, or do you think she raided a convent?" Meg whispered to me.

"Oh please, like the royals, she's always packed for a funeral."

"Don't you want to wear the veils? You'll look lovely," Mom suggested, waving a pile of black lace at us.

Meg gave Mom a dagger of a stare. Depositing the mantillas in her large purse, Mom shook her head and put her hands up in mock surrender. She knew she had crossed the line.

I sat back in the ornately carved pew and looked around at the stunning gold-painted sanctuary. They certainly didn't make churches like this anymore. As I surveyed the surroundings, it was apparent that Saint Columbkille's had gone all out for the memorial service. The altar was decorated in an abundance of white. Roses, calla lilies, tulips, baby's breath, and hydrangeas covered every surface. It was stunning. The décor was not being overlooked today. Well, Saint Columbkille's *was* Deirdre Harrington's sole beneficiary, and she'd had a lot of benefits to bestow.

Cynical, Maeve, very cynical.

The church was becoming quite full, as Helen Lyons had predicted. Deirdre might not have had any close friends or family, but the town of Ballymoor, with the help of our beloved mother, was going to make sure her departure to the great beyond was memorable.

As the service began, a tall priest in his thirties and with wiry chestnut hair blessed the casket and then stood silently off to the right. A much older, heavyset man dressed in deep purple and gold vestments led the way onto the altar. This must be the archbishop.

"The big brass," Meg whispered to me.

As the Mass began, I surveyed the crowd. I saw Catherine, Helen, Lindsay and Cillian Delaney, and Brianna and Patsy Shaughnessy in the pews ahead of us. Seamus Burke and Rory Connors appeared to be among the missing. Well, at least some of our suspects were present.

The solemn rite proceeded in typical fashion. After the reading of the gospel passage, the congregation stilled as Father Leahy began to give the homily. What would he say about a woman with whom so many of his parishioners had issues? Would he address her untimely death? Father Leahy chose to talk about life after death in general terms. He stated that Deirdre Harrington was now on the way home. He was noticeably not very specific about *her* life. After a rather brief ten minutes, Father Leahy summed up by thanking everyone who had come together to pick out the readings, arrange for the flowers, and put together the social afterward. He said that the funeral demonstrated the compassion and kindness of the people of Ballymoor. Although not personal about the deceased, the homily was heartfelt and seemed to provide temporary closure to this tough chapter in the town's history. When he finished, there was a long moment of silence.

When the Mass concluded, the organist pumped out the opening bars of "Be Not Afraid" as the choir director strongly encouraged the congregation to sing. That signaled six burly men in dark suits to lift the casket in unison and start down the long aisle. The funeral home must have hired them.

"Men in black," Meg murmured.

The pews emptied in an orderly fashion, and when we went out the front door of Saint Columbkille's, a bagpiper with Scottish pipes led the casket and the mourners—well, perhaps not mourners but participants—down the street to Ballymoor Cemetery. We all gathered on the grass as the archbishop and Father Leahy said some final prayers. When they were finished, a deep hush overtook the crowd. Then, one by one, people began to leave and head back into the basement of Saint Columbkille's to have a bite to eat and socialize. I knew this was one of Mom's favorite parts of a funeral. No matter what the reason, Mom loved a "time." She would relish meeting the townspeople and rehashing the entire service.

As I pushed Mom towards the reception, we passed a few elderly women sitting on a stone bench. They must have decided to sit there during the burial service. I smiled as we passed, and then heard a distinctive hiss, "Don't forsake the babies." My head snapped to the right. The small woman at the end of the bench, bundled in a black raincoat and hat, was pointing a slightly shaky blue-gloved finger at me. "The babies…don't forget the babies."

Nan! It was Nan, the Irish Zeena from Blooms by Rose.

"What did she say?" Mom asked.

Picking up speed to distance us, my thoughts frantically scrambled for a credible response. "I think she said, 'Keep up with the ladies.' You know, Mom, she was just putting her two cents in. People love to give directions."

Mom turned her head to look up at me. "Maeve, I was born at night, but not last night."

Thankfully an older gentleman was holding the door for us, and we were swiftly enveloped into the crowded hall.

There was no way I was introducing Mom to the Irish Zeena. Who knew what Pandora's box that could open? But why did Nan keep admonishing me about babies?

Meg, the ladies, Catherine, Helen, and Elisabeth all sat at a table near the front of the large banquet hall in the parish center and had saved places for Mom and me.

"Well, that was lovely," Meg said. "You women planned a beautiful funeral. You should be very proud."

"Thank you, Meg," Catherine said, looking pleased. "The entire community worked together to put this on. We wanted it to be as elegant as possible and hopefully what Deirdre Harrington would have wanted." She hesitated a bit before continuing. "The poor woman had a harsh death, and none of us know exactly what her life was like. Who knows why she was so against change? Who knows why she had a bit of a mean streak? No matter, at least she was laid to rest peacefully."

"A bit of a mean streak?" Helen almost shrieked, her face florid and her bottom lip quivering. "She tormented Rory Connors, prevented Brianna and Patsy Shaughnessy from making a living, tried to put Lindsay and Cillian's pub out of business, and ensured Seamus Burke was heavily fined. I would say that's a bit more than a mean streak."

Helen was going down our suspect list, one by one.

Catherine sipped her tea and took a bite of a ham sandwich, but she didn't respond. She was from the school of 'don't speak ill of the dead.'

"The only thing I would have changed is the closed casket," Mom opined. "I prefer an open casket unless there's been a terrible accident or something. We could have picked out some nice clothing, maybe a pale pink chiffon blouse to offset her white hair. And perhaps a gold chain, maybe with a cross since Deirdre Harrington was very religious. Other than that, though, I thought the whole service was lovely."

Mom was one of a kind.

My siblings and I had attended wakes from an early age. Did seeing corpses harm young children? Was that even a consideration? In my family, attendance was expected. Death was part of the cycle of life. The oppressive scent of gladiolas in a heated room always brought me back to the thought of people I hardly knew lying in pastel silk-upholstered caskets clutching rosary beads. I always worried whether someone had remembered to put their shoes on because their legs were hidden. Often mementos ranging from photos and medals to letters and sports memorabilia were placed with the deceased. King Tut had nothing on my relatives.

A famous O'Reilly story, never repeated outside our home, was eight-year-old Aidan showing us the extremely valuable Boston Red Sox rookie card of Hall of Famer Carl Yastrzemski, which he planned to bring to show-and-tell at school. It turned out our distant cousin, Mr. Cormac Linehan, went into the great beyond without his prized possession. Aidan had clearly thought door prizes were included with the viewing.

Taking a chicken salad sandwich, Mom looked at Meg and me and asked, "Where are we now in the investigation?"

Meg rubbed her temples as if in pain, but merely said, "Mom, as I said before, Maeve and I are not part of this official inquiry."

Mom sat up as straight as she could and shook her shoulders. "Don't give me that. You two can solve this case with your hands tied behind your backs. You've been down this road before."

Gaby put her white cafeteria-style mug down and looked at Meg and me with her deep brown eyes. "You two have an incredible record of catching murderers. You are intrepid."

Ethel, who was beside Gaby, nodded and said, "I know we're on foreign soil, but American citizens always follow the call of duty." That was spoken like a true veteran.

All eyes were on Meg and me.

"Don't waste time. It's precious. Ballymoor needs you," Louella said in a rarely used raspy voice.

Meg looked at me. We were outnumbered.

"You do need to get involved," Helen agreed. She leaned forward conspiratorially and said in a whisper, "Poor Rory Connors doesn't have a strong alibi. Like I told you last night, you must help him."

CHAPTER TWENTY

———

Gaelic football is one of the most popular sports in Ireland.

Everyone's attention was intently focused on Helen Lyons.

"So, here's the story," she said. "I talked to Annie McIntyre, his girlfriend, and she said that Rory was distraught after the town council meeting. When it broke up, Deirdre said some very mean things to him about Annie's pregnancy. She caught Rory at the back of town hall and berated him for not being married, not having a good job, and getting Annie pregnant. He was so out of sorts that when he came home, he decided to go for a run. Unfortunately, it was around the same time that the murder took place."

Meg lightly tapped me on the elbow. Sister ESP at work again. Things were not looking good for poor Rory Connors.

"What about Seamus Burke?" I asked. "I noticed that he had some scratches on his face. I wonder what he was doing at the time Deirdre Harrington was killed?"

"See, there you go," Mom declared.. "I knew you would have started a suspect list and begun writing down clues."

Meg looked at me with an exasperated expression. Her eyes were like daggers. Oh, if looks could kill. Why did I open my big mouth?

"Let's not forget there's an open kitchen at Delaney's Pub," Elisabeth said, meeting everyone's eyes one by one. Clearly, she was used to making sure her students understood her lessons. "Anyone could have stolen that kitchen knife and used it to kill."

"That's true," Catherine said. "And I'm sure that after the town council meeting, almost everyone stopped in for a quick pint or bite at Delaney's."

As they spoke, I pictured Delaney's Pub in my mind. Elisabeth had a valid point. To get to the restrooms, you passed by the open kitchen on your way down a long hallway. Indeed, anyone could have taken that weapon without being seen.

"So, let's see," Mom said. "We have questions about Rory Connors, we have questions about Seamus Burke, and I suppose we have questions about anyone who was at Delaney's Pub that night. Well, that ought to keep the two of you busy."

I closed my eyes. Meg and I were losing control of this narrative.

"What about the staff at Saint Columbkille's?" Helen asked. "The church is not exactly overrun with parishioners. They must be in the red, and Deirdre conveniently left everything to them. Maybe they helped her along the path to the great beyond."

"Helen, do you really think Father Leahy murdered Deirdre Harrington? Come on now, he's a man of God," Catherine said, clenching her napkin tightly in her hands.

"Men of God have been known to do a lot of evil things, Catherine," Helen said, her eyes narrowed into slits.

"So, I heard we're going to see a football game," I piped up, desperately trying to change the subject. "I can't wait. I've tried to study up on Gaelic football. I read that the field size, the balls, and the rules are all different from American football. I think it will be so much fun to watch."

Meg said back in her chair and watched me without saying a word. Gee, did she think I was trying too hard? I guess I was, but I didn't see my fearless sister jumping in to stop this from becoming a brawl. We would talk later.

"Yes, I got tickets for all of us," Catherine said, with a noticeable sigh of relief. At least someone was happy that I had changed the subject. "I thought you'd like to see a true Irish sport while you're here. It's at Pearse Stadium, which is a great venue. It'll be a grand outing."

"Finn's all set to drive us, and we got him a ticket to the game. We're going to have stadium snacks there. I can't wait," Mom said bubbling with enthusiasm.

"Me too," Gaby chimed in. "We'll all wear our green sequined scarves."

Of course, they would.

Mom noticed that the crowd in the parish hall had thinned out and decided it was time to leave. "Ethel and Gaby, why don't you get us some treats to take back to the guesthouse?" she asked. "And please make sure you get some of that apple cake. I just love it."

Putting their bags into the back compartment of Finn's van, Meg and I watched while Mom and her group were safely tucked in for the ride home. They had, unsurprisingly, filled two large bags with leftover treats. Mom and the ladies were experts at scoring food at any gathering, especially funerals.

As we stood outside Saint Columbkille's Church, looking at the gardens, I noticed a man walking swiftly down the side street. He looked so familiar that I wondered if he could be someone from home. I racked my brain trying to place him. But he was out of sight before I could get a better look.

"Come on," Meg said. "Let's take the long way home. I want to stop and get a few things at the corner store."

Meg's sweets supply must have been dwindling.

We wound our way through the garden and the Ballymoor Cemetery. Deirdre Harrington's grave was now covered with fresh soil. Flowers from the church service had been laid on top. As I walked on and studied the other gravestones, I realized Meg wasn't keeping up with me.

I turned around to see her waving me back. As I approached, she said, "Maeve, look at her grave."

"I already looked at it. There's no headstone yet, so not much to see."

"Look again."

I walked over and studied the fresh earth.

"Come over to this side," Meg commanded.

Looking down, I saw the heads of the calla lilies and tulips had been chopped off. The stems had been arranged to spell the word EVIL.

A chill ran up my spine. Were we caught in a Stephen King novel?

Someone was still very angry with Deirdre Harrington.

"Talk about saying it with flowers," Meg commented.

I took Meg's arm and steered her out of the cemetery and toward the corner grocery. My sister needed her chocolate fix.

While Meg resupplied and I looked through the newspaper stand, a thought suddenly popped into my head. The man I saw walking down the street outside the church was the guy from the plane.

Rob Larson!

Why was he in Ballymoor?

And what had he been doing at Deirdre Harrington's funeral?

CHAPTER TWENTY-ONE

———

Ireland has the largest number of red-haired people in the world.

After an early dinner of roasted chicken, carrots, and colcannon that evening, we all headed off to the Galway versus Donegal football match. Finn collected Mom, Gaby, Ethel, Louella, and Catherine in his passenger van. They were decked out in every shade of green imaginable and ready to encourage Galway on to victory. The Dallas Cowboy Cheerleaders could take a lesson from them. Meg, Elisabeth, and I followed closely behind in our rental.

An atmosphere of anticipation started in the parking lot. The crowd was extensive but orderly, and the stadium was packed by the time we entered. Catherine had picked great seats. We were smack in the center and could see the entire length of the field. Excitement, laced with a bit of apprehension, was palpable. A disproportionate number of Galway fans were in attendance, and they desperately wanted their team to win. Even though the atmosphere was a bit tense, it was still very festive.

Just before the game started, the fans rose en masse and faced the Irish flag. All headgear was removed while "*Amhrán na bhFiann*," or "The Soldier's Song," the Irish national anthem, played.

Tears sprung to my eyes while I listened to the stirring piece. How lucky we were to have this experience. I hoped we could attend another match when the rest of the family arrived so they could feel this pride, too.

The game started too loud and sustained cheering. I quickly saw that while the players did not wear body pads or helmets, Gaelic football was highly physical. There were fifteen players on each team, and there would be two halves, each thirty minutes long. The players could kick, punch, throw, or pass the ball to get it over the goal line.

Back and forth the score went, and cheers and groans rang out from the stands. As the clock ticked down in the second half, Galway desperately needed to score.

Suddenly, the Galway fans stood as one and began to sing. Meg and I stood with them but had no idea what was going on. Elisabeth quickly passed us the program and pointed to the back cover. Quickly scanning it, I saw that the lyrics to the piece, "The Fields of Athenry," were printed in full.

The song was extremely sad but also very powerful. As I read the words, I saw it documented the Irish famine. It told the tale of a man named Michael who was exiled to Australia for stealing food for his starving family.

"It's such a beautiful but heartbreaking song," Elisabeth mouthed in my ear. "It demonstrates the resolve of the Irish. It's become the unofficial national anthem of Irish everywhere."

It described an act of rebellion for one of the most basic human needs. I could see how it lifted everyone's spirits and united the spectators. Well, hopefully, that would be just the Galway fans tonight.

The clock was winding down. With less than a minute left, the score was tied. Suddenly, Tim Flanagan, one of Galway's veteran forwards, caught a pass, gave a mighty kick, and sent the ball flying through the goalpost! Galway wins! The fans went wild. There was clapping and hugging all around.

When the final buzzer sounded, all the athletes were soundly cheered. For a few minutes, no one made for the exits. It was as if everyone just wanted to bask in the victory.

Eventually, though, the crowd made its way out of the stadium. Many were still singing the chorus of the "Fields of Athenry."

"I need to make a quick pit stop at the ladies' room. I'll meet you at the car," I said to Meg when we reached the ground level.

"Take your time," she replied. "The parking lot will take a while to empty."

As was typical, the line to the ladies' room was about a mile long. Just as in the States, there were never enough stalls built for women. The world needed more women architects.

Standing in the long line, I began surveying the crowd. Seamus Burke! He was walking with an older man. In a few seconds, he was so close I could almost reach out and touch him. As I turned slightly to the right to get a better look at his face, the crowd stalled momentarily.

While Seamus and his companion waited patiently for people to move forward, I could hear their conversation.

"Well, I won't have to worry about her anymore," Seamus said gleefully.

"That's right. Peace and quiet can finally be restored to our village," the other man chimed in.

"She will not be missed," Seamus said, giving his friend a high five.

They slapped each other on the back, and the line started to move. I lost the rest of their words to the crowd noise.

Deirdre! They had to be speaking about Deirdre Harrington's demise. He was overjoyed that she was dead.

Seamus Burke just went to the head of the class. Seamus Burke was now suspect number one in my book.

When I finally finished up and returned to the car, my thoughts were swirling. I held my tongue, though. I did not want to discuss what I had heard in front of Elisabeth Devlin. I needed to get Meg alone.

While the two of them rehashed the game, I was noticeably not contributing to the conversation.

After we dropped Elisabeth off, Meg turned to me and said, "Were you a trifle preoccupied, Maeve? I mean, you could have acted slightly interested."

I ignored the dig. "Meg, as I was waiting in line, I overheard Seamus Burke and a friend talking. He said he didn't have to worry anymore now that 'she' was gone. He was gleeful. He had to be speaking about Deirdre. Who else could it be?"

Meg pulled out a Dairy Milk Oreo Cadbury bar and broke off a large chunk. She did have an endless supply. Would there be any left in Ireland when we departed?

"It could be a lot of things. Maybe he was going on about a former girlfriend. I mean, they didn't mention Deirdre Harrington by name, did they?"

"No, but I'm pretty convinced it was about her. The other guy referred to the fact that the village could now return to normal."

"You're probably right, but what will we do with that information?" Meg asked, pulling up to the guesthouse. We parked behind Finn's van and went into the main inn to say good night to Mom and company. As we entered the foyer, Owen and Molly Farrell were standing there to welcome us. Although she was usually upbeat, Molly looked very troubled.

As we were about to greet them, Mom, in her typical no-holds-barred fashion, wheeled over to us and went straight to the heart of the matter. "Molly, did something happen? You look upset."

Molly's face crumbled a bit, and her brow furrowed. "Oh, Mary. Everyone in the village is on edge. Rory Connors has been brought in for more questioning." Owen put his arm around her shoulders. Taking a shaky breath she continued, "Rory Connors has no alibi for the night of the murder."

CHAPTER TWENTY-TWO

———

There were approximately 54,000 births in Ireland in 2023.

Mom turned to us. "Girls, the M&M detective agency needs to investigate this case immediately. Hurry up and put your thinking caps on. You need to get out of holiday mode and find the murderer. We don't want a young man accused of killing her if he did nothing wrong." With that, she spun around and rolled off into her bedroom.

Well, the queen had spoken. There was nothing left for Meg and me to do except to say goodnight to Molly and Owen and head back to Briar Cottage. After our showers, Meg called me into her room, where we sat on her queen-sized sleigh bed together.

"It's time to get serious," she said. I could tell she meant it because she was holding a red leather notebook and Montblanc pen instead of her phone. She fixed me with a no nonsense look and began. "First, it's time we updated the list of suspects."

I couldn't help myself. "That's a very fancy ledger and quill," I said, smirking.

"Just supporting the local economy, Maeve."

I let it go at that. Nothing good could come from challenging Meg at this time of night.

"Seamus Burke is still at the top of the heap for me," I said.

"I agree. Then Lindsay and Cillian Delaney come next," she said.

I nodded my head in agreement.

"How about Brianna and Patsy Shaughnessy?"

"Definitely add them."

"And, of course, there's Rory Connors." Meg grimaced slightly as she added his name to her notes.

"Who knows how many more people she antagonized?" I sighed.

At that moment, my phone chirped. It was Aisling Doyle.

"I need to take this, Meg." I swiped the phone. "Hello."

"Hello, dear Maeve. It's Aisling. I realize it's very late, and you've probably had a hectic day. If you want to hop into your bed and sleep, please do. However, I thought I'd tell you that Annie McIntyre is in labor."

"Really?" I said.

"Yes, and I'm on call tonight. I've already talked to Annie, and she is fine with you accompanying me. It was so nice that you met the other day, but Maeve, please don't feel obligated. This is your holiday."

I didn't even need to think about the offer for a second. "I'll be right there, Aisling. Thanks so much for thinking of me."

When I hung up, Meg looked at me with an air of resignation. "Midwifery is calling you, even in Ireland."

"Meg, I can't believe I'm so fortunate to be with Aisling tonight."

HIPAA was so ingrained in me that I didn't say who the patient in labor was. I mean, I wasn't bound by any laws here in Ireland, but I felt it was not my news to share. What a coincidence to be with Rory Connors' girlfriend in labor. Maybe I could get some information on what the Gardaí were thinking.

Meg gave me the once-over. "Go get dressed. I'll drop you off at the Ballymoor Hospital. Call me when you're ready to come back here. I don't want you walking home in the dark."

I nodded but didn't want to tell Meg that since this was Annie's first baby, I expected to be welcoming the dawn.

When I returned to the sunroom, Meg was applying her signature, deep crimson Chanel "Gabrielle" lipstick. When she was done, she said, "Just think, now we can add international midwife to your resume."

Meg dropped me off at the hospital entrance, muttering under her breath about crazy midwife hours. I checked in at the front desk and followed the signs to the labor unit. I rang the bell at the birth unit door, and Aisling came to let me in. She greeted me warmly and placed a temporary badge around my neck.

"Welcome, Maeve. I'm thrilled you decided to join me."

"Aisling, thank you for inviting me. This is a dream. I get to see you in action and hopefully see a birth in Ireland. I can't believe my luck."

"Come on, we'll go to the midwifery call room, and you can change into scrubs and store your belongings."

Aisling led me down a back corridor that contained bright lights and institutional green paint. Seeing the familiar color here made me wonder if they sold this paint to every hospital and prison in the world. And how, even in Ireland, could a shade of green be that depressing? Thank goodness the birth unit had been redecorated.

At the end of the hall, we came to a brown steel door with a small white sign labeled *MIDWIVES*. As I stepped inside the drab portal, I entered a beautiful oasis. Soft lighting bathed the room in a gentle yellow glow. Against the far wall was a long maroon chenille couch with a gorgeous watercolor of Galway Bay above it. A lovely dark brown braided circular rug, two small, upholstered armchairs in ivory, and a low table with a small pot of pink cyclamen completed the tableau. I immediately felt at home. The space was so inviting. Wasn't it interesting that the Creighton Memorial and Ballymoor midwifery sanctums were so similar? We might be from different countries, but midwives have similar cocoons.

Aisling handed me a pair of bright blue scrubs, gave me a key to the call room, and told me to meet her at the labor desk when I was ready.

I changed into the familiar-looking outfit, and fastened my long hair into a French twist. After checking my appearance in the mirror, I quickly brushed my teeth and applied some light rose lipstick. Putting my phone on silent, I slid it into the pocket of my scrubs. I'd covered my sneakers with booties when I arrived on the unit. I was ready!

A slight shiver of excitement ran through me. Every birth was special and always energized me.

As I walked out to the central labor desk area, I saw Aisling talking to several people.

"Hello, Maeve. Let me introduce you to our wonderful staff." She proceeded to go down the line one by one. I met the consultant obstetrician, three nurses, and Orla, the midwife I had met the other day, who was just about to sign off.

I immediately felt as if I fit in. Maybe it was our shared life experiences, but it was uncanny that hospital staff always made me feel at home wherever I was. Although our terminology or practices may be somewhat different, so much was familiar and comforting.

Aisling pulled up Annie's chart on the computer workstation. "So, Annie has already been admitted. She broke her water a few hours ago and is about four centimeters dilated. As you probably remember from the other day, it's her first baby."

"She was lovely and seemed well prepared."

Aisling smiled and nodded. "I don't know if you heard, but her partner, Rory Connors, was brought in for questioning again. I've called the Ballymoor Garda station to tell them that Annie is in labor. My husband, Thomas, is an inspector on the force, and I pleaded with the shift captain to allow Rory to finish with them later. Hopefully, they'll let him come soon."

"I hope so, Aisling. Missing the birth of one's child is tough. At home, we have used video calls if a partner could not be present. Is that an option?"

"Let's see what unfolds. We may have to resort to that." Aisling frowned and continued, "Rory Connors seems like a kind, gentle young man. I can't imagine he committed that terrible deed, but who knows?"

I did not comment. I wanted to hear her perceptions and see what I could learn about Rory.

Aisling folded her hands on the counter and looked pensive. "I worry how Rory's absence will affect Annie."

We both knew that many factors influenced a woman's labor.

"Is anyone with her now?" I asked.

"No, she's alone." She gave me a small smile. "That's why I'm so glad you're here. You can be her support person until Rory arrives." She stopped and sighed deeply. "That is *if* he arrives."

"It will be my pleasure," I said.

Being in labor with your partner under investigation for a local murder had to be one of the most stressful scenarios ever. I would need to gain Annie's trust quickly to help her on her way to motherhood.

Well, *midwife* means *with woman*, and I intended to give Annie my best.

CHAPTER TWENTY-THREE

————

As of 2023, less than 1 percent of births in Ireland were home births.
However, the demand is growing.

Aisling opened the door to room four, and I followed her inside. Annie was on her side, breathing well through a contraction. A tall nurse with deep brown skin and short black curls was rubbing her back. When the contraction ended, Aisling smiled and said hello.

"You are doing wonderfully, Annie." Then Aisling gestured at me and said, "I know you remember Maeve from the other afternoon."

"Annie, thank you for allowing me to be here," I said.

She gave me a quick smile, but I saw her attention return quickly to the door. I knew she was hoping that Rory would appear soon.

"Maeve, this is Lucinda. She's a very experienced nurse, and I am happy to say will begin studying midwifery in a few months."

Lucinda beamed. She looked happy and ready to start her transition.

"And Lucinda, this is Maeve. She's a midwife from near Boston. She's here to observe."

Looking closely at Annie, I noticed her freckles were more pronounced than ever on her pale skin. Her light brown hair was pulled into a thick braid. Her face and eyes betrayed that she had recently been crying.

Annie's eyes locked onto Aisling's.

"Did you hear anything about my Rory?" she asked, gripping her hands together.

"Nothing yet," Aisling said, taking her hand.

Annie closed her eyes. "I just wish he was here."

"I know, Annie, I know. Hopefully soon. But I want you to concentrate on your daughter. Try to focus on her birth. Everything else is out of our control right now."

Another contraction started, and I relieved Lucinda, who had stepped out to check on another patient. Rubbing Annie's back, I could feel the tension. She needed to know that Rory was on his way.

As Annie's breathing slowed, she opened her eyes and spoke rapidly.

"That old woman tormented my Rory even though she had no reason to. She never let him be. After the council meeting, she caught us in the foyer as we were leaving. Deirdre said our infant should be taken away at birth. Rory was furious. I started crying and couldn't stop."

Annie took a breath while a fresh torrent of tears spilled down her cheeks. She finally stopped and then began speaking again. "Once we got home and I calmed down, Rory couldn't settle, he felt that a run would help him clear his mind."

"That must have been so upsetting. I can see why Rory needed to calm down. Many people find running therapeutic to reduce stress," I commented.

"He said exercise might help him sleep. I must have dozed off while he was gone, and when I woke, he was beside me."

She was quiet for a bit and then gasped. "Oh no, a contraction is starting."

Annie had a difficult time riding out that strong wave. Her concerns about Rory were preventing her from concentrating on herself.

When she caught her breath again, she continued, "I know Rory. He's a wonderful, honorable man. As nasty as Miss Harrington was, he would never retaliate." She suddenly made a face. "Oh…another one."

I rubbed her back firmly and again tried to help her deal with the discomfort.

Aisling and I exchanged glances. We would need all our midwifery tricks to put Annie's sadness out of her mind and help her get through this labor.

The long night wore on, and Annie did the best she could. Even under these difficult circumstances, she handled her labor superbly. At six a.m., she felt the urge to push. Aisling checked her cervix and found that Annie was fully dilated. We began to prepare for the birth. Aisling left the room quickly, and I figured she was probably making a furious call to the Ballymoor Garda office.

Lucinda and I helped Annie into a comfortable position, and I gently bathed her face with a warm washcloth. Her labor room had a beautiful view of trees and the morning sky beyond, and I encouraged her to look at it. Annie pushed for about an hour, and I could see that she was getting tired.

"Your daughter's going to be born today," I whispered in her ear.

She smiled at me and then began to gather her inner strength as the next contraction started. Just as she began to push, the door opened, and Aisling entered, followed by a tall, gangly young man. Rory Connors! Just then, though, Annie was intent on her pushing. She didn't even look up. I motioned Rory to take my place at Annie's side. When the contraction ended, Annie realized he was finally present.

"Oh, Rory," she cried out.

"Sorry I was so long, beautiful."

"You're here now," Annie said. Rory kissed her gently on her forehead.

Lucinda checked the fetal heart rate, which was nice and steady.

Aisling spoke up from the foot of the bed. "Annie, I can see your baby's hair. She'll be born with the next few pushes."

"Now remember, we want her to come into this world nice and slow. When I tell you, blow out like we discussed."

Annie's head dropped back, and her eyes shut. She held Rory's hand tightly and gave a long, steady push.

"Perfect," Aisling said. "Now blow out, Annie."

Slowly, a cap of dark hair appeared and began to emerge.

"Oh, my goodness," Rory exclaimed.

Aisling expertly guided the head and then the shoulders from the birth canal. The baby's body followed quickly, accompanied by a large splash of amniotic fluid.

"Let's settle your daughter on your chest," Lucinda said. She took the newborn from Aisling and put her on Annie to cuddle as she covered both of them with a warm blanket.

"She's as beautiful as her mother," Rory said, choking back tears.

Annie smiled and kissed him.

"You will be a great Dad," she said.

"Does this beautiful girl have a name?" Aisling asked.

"This is Emily Andrea," Rory said, beaming at the newborn.

"What a lovely name," I said.

"Andrea is after Rory's mother," Annie said, kissing Rory's hand.

Tears glistened in Rory's eyes as he lovingly looked at Annie and Emily.

After tidying the room and ensuring Annie was fine, Aisling and I exited. As we did, I saw a tall, lean Garda at the desk.

"What's going on?" I asked Aisling.

Aisling walked up to the uniformed woman. "Hello, Sergeant Mullaney, are you here about Rory?"

"Yes, ma'am. As a favor, we let him come to see his baby be born, but I'm taking him back into custody now. He's being charged with the murder of Deirdre Harrington."

Aisling's hand flew to her mouth, but she said nothing. My breath caught. I felt as if the wind had been knocked out of me.

Turning to me, Aisling said, "Maeve, go ahead home. I'll stay with Annie when Rory leaves."

With a heavy heart, I went into the midwifery room to change. This might be Rory Connor's best and worst day.

CHAPTER TWENTY-FOUR

———

Saint Raymond Nonnatus is the patron saint of midwives.

Meg insisted on picking me up at Ballymoor Hospital. As we made our way back to the cottage, I was soon made aware that many people, including my older sister, knew that Annie and Rory's baby had been born. Nothing went unnoticed and unannounced in a small town.

"You never told me you were attending Annie's labor. Talk about keeping information close to the vest. Please, fill me in on the birth. You know I'm the sister of a midwife and can handle talk of any complication."

Smiling, I said, "There were no complications. Annie McIntyre was amazing, and Aisling Doyle is a wonderful midwife. The staff at the maternity unit is outstanding, too. Really, Meg, I was fortunate to be invited to see a birth in Ireland."

"And how was Rory Connors? Did he come straight from questioning?"

"He made it for the birth but just barely. It was very moving to see him and Annie together." I paused for a moment, remembering the Garda's words. "The problem came when he was taken back to the station after Emily Andrea was born."

"Emily Andrea. What a beautiful name."

"She's a gorgeous little girl."

We were stopped in traffic, and Meg turned and gave me an appraising look. "What's wrong, Maeve? I'm sure they just had some follow-up questions."

I tapped the dashboard lightly. "Oh, Meg, Rory's going to be charged with Deirdre Harrington's murder."

"What? Are you kidding me? What timing. I can't believe it. I don't think he's guilty," she said.

"I know. I don't either but the Ballymoor officers must believe they have a strong case." Unfastening my hair and shaking it out, I said, "I hope they are wrong."

"Well, Maeve, as much as we hate to admit it, facts are facts." Meg sighed deeply. "The murder weapon is covered with Rory Connor's fingerprints, he had access to the knife, and Deirdre belittled him horribly and constantly."

"Everything is stacked against him, I know. But we also know things are not always what they seem," I said as I yawned.

"Spoken like a true detective. I knew I'd get my partner back. Maeve, what a night you've had. Why don't you take a rest and a shower, and I'll get some light snacks for when you wake up?"

"How about a late lunch?" I asked.

"No can do. We're going to Catherine's for an early dinner."

"Fine. But Meg, can you do me one small favor?"

"What?"

"Please don't just get candy. I love it, but I'm about to overdose."

"Silly woman. One can never have too much chocolate," she replied as I shut the car door.

Back at the Briar Cottage, I snuggled into my four-poster bed with my earplugs in and pulled out my Kindle. I started *Small Things Like These* by Claire Keegan but was asleep in minutes.

When I awoke, I took a delightful warm shower and dressed simply in comfy jeans and a sapphire tunic.

As I walked into the sunroom, I saw Meg typing on her laptop.

"I'll make us tea. Did you get any snacks?" I asked.

"Sit, please," was all she said.

Meg pulled out a tray with shortbread biscuits, Dubliner and goat cheese, a few varieties of Tayto crisps, a loaf of brown bread, and, last but not least, a pile of Cadbury Starbars and Butlers Milk Chocolate Truffle bars. She then made a pot of tea.

I dug in. The cheeses were creamy and so flavorful. The Taytos were delicious, but then I never met a crisp I didn't like. I was famished after the all-nighter in the hospital, and I could have made a meal of the cheese and crisps alone. However, I knew I better pace myself if I wanted to have room for dinner.

As I sat back and looked out at Molly Farrell's flower garden, I said, "That's so nice of Cousin Catherine to invite us again."

"She's the best," Meg agreed.

As Meg combined her helpings of cheese and onion crisps with chunks of Dairy Milk Cadbury added in, she said, "Catherine called me today. That retired banker, Martin Ryan, has talked the archdiocese into separating Deirdre's farmhouse from the rest of her property. Elisabeth and her husband, James, are considering making an offer. Even though I'm an American real estate agent, they would like me to walk through the house with them before they decide."

"Look at you. Now it's your turn to practice your profession in Ireland."

"Truthfully, home sales are very different here, but I can still look at the rooms and the comps and help them come up with a reasonable value. They can also bid on some of the furniture. To get ready, I've spent all day researching Irish land issues."

"Can they buy any additional acreage and farm it?"

"That's a thorny question. We'll know more tonight when we speak to Catherine's friend."

"Well, Meg, they couldn't ask for a better person to help them than you."

"Thanks, Maeve, but my expertise is in the New England area. I'm a bit out of my league in Ballymoor."

We were both silent for a while, lost in our thoughts. I had a second cup of tea and leafed through *The Ballymoor Times*. I was still tired from the night before.

"Have you spoken to Will recently?" Meg asked, breaking the silence.

"I had a long email from him today telling me the girls were great, and he texted photos of Rowan, Sloane, and Fenway. Will said Kate has been a godsend. And he says they feel pampered by all the calls and treats that have been dropped off. I'll call him tomorrow to check in. What about you? Have you heard from Henry?"

Meg's face lit up. How she loved that boy.

"I spoke to him today, and he's doing great. He and Artie drove down the Pacific Coast Highway, and they saw seals, toured Hearst Castle, and even managed to get in a round of golf at Pebble Beach. Artie is pulling out all the stops. Henry's having a wonderful time."

"I'm so happy to hear that. Meg, can you just imagine when the whole family is here? Mom is planning a goodbye dinner in Ballymoor for everyone before we leave to tour the rest of Ireland. You know I love Ballymoor but I'm ready to explore. Will and Henry want to go to Skellig Michael. They'll have to hope for good weather."

Skellig Michael is an uninhabited island, eight miles off the southwest coast of Ireland. It contained a monastery until the thirteenth century and has an extremely steep, uneven, rocky landscape. Because of the rough seas, it can only be visited in summer and autumn. The location was famously used in the *Star Wars* films.

"It will be great," she answered but seemed distracted.

I could tell that she had an agenda. I knew my sister. She stood and looked out at the garden. After a few minutes, she turned and faced me. "Maeve, I think we should keep investigating. It just seems too pat that Rory was the killer. What was his motive? Revenge? Would he really commit murder on the eve of becoming a new father?"

That pulled me back to reality. "I agree, Meg. Something just doesn't feel right. We better work speedily though. Our time here is limited."

"That's true. We certainly don't want Patrick to arrive and discover that the Gardaí are our new best friends. There would be hell to pay." Meg checked her watch. "Hey, Maeve, we have to leave in about ten minutes."

"Okay," I agreed.

"I told Catherine we'd bring dessert. Give me a second to grab it from the kitchen."

"What did you get?"

"I found this lovely shop in town that has every flavor of cupcake you can imagine, so I got an assortment. I bought a box of chocolates too, just in case anyone doesn't want a cupcake."

"Covered all the bases, as usual."

As we headed to the car, Molly and Owen Farrell were in the courtyard. Molly had a basket overflowing with fresh-cut dahlias.

She was smiling but I could tell she had something to tell us.

"We just heard that Deirdre Harrington's home was broken into," Molly said.

"Really?" Meg said. "Did they catch whoever did it?"

"No, we heard someone driving by, saw a broken window and the front door ajar, and called emergency services. Who knows if anything was taken?" She paused and thoughtfully said, "It will be good to have that house filled with new people. Ballymoor needs to heal."

We said our goodbyes, and as we headed off, Meg said, "Was it a random break-in or was it tied to the murder?"

Somehow, this must all fit together, but right now I felt like I was looking at an unsolvable jigsaw puzzle.

CHAPTER TWENTY-FIVE

―――――

Newborns can recognize their mother's voice after birth.

As we walked into Catherine's home, delicious aromas filled the air. I didn't know what was being served, but I could smell onion, carrots, and homemade bread. Whatever the menu, I knew it would be delicious. I guess the snacks hadn't quite filled me up.

Catherine greeted us warmly as we entered the sitting room.

"Something smells amazing," Meg said.

"I hope you like the selection. I made bangers and mash and a large pot of Irish beef stew. Everyone can take their pick." Looking at Meg, she added, "And of course, there is some brown bread. Don't you worry."

"Sounds great to me, Catherine," Meg responded.

We had all gathered to have a pre-dinner cocktail when there was a heavy knock on the front door.

Catherine left to answer it and returned with a tall, distinguished-looking gentleman. He was dressed very formally in a navy pinstriped suit and pale blue tie.

Catherine was smiling broadly as she introduced him. It was clear that this was the revered guest of honor.

"I'd like to present Mr. Martin Ryan. He was a banker at Ballymoor Savings and Trust for many years. He's retired now but still aids many families in purchasing homes."

Catherine then went around and introduced us individually. Martin shook every hand. His demeanor and shy smile were very welcoming. Catherine continued to sing his praises.

"He has helped so many Ballymoor citizens get mortgages and loans. He's always looking out for young families and seniors. Martin is well loved in Ballymoor."

"My goodness, Catherine," Martin demurred. "You'll have me canonized soon. I was merely doing my job."

"We know how much you've accomplished," Catherine said with a laugh. A flush appeared in Martin's cheeks as he sipped his Negroni.

At that, we all moved to the large dining room. The table was set with vintage Royal Tara shamrock bone china. Catherine and Elisabeth served the meal. I could see that the candles, the entrees, and, most notably, the company would make this a memorable feast.

"Martin, could you please say grace tonight?" Catherine asked.

After making the sign of the cross, Martin began, "Bless us, Oh Lord." He was strictly sticking to a traditional prayer. When he was done, Catherine stood and lifted her Waterford Powerscourt crystal goblet and said, "To family and friends. May we have many more nights like this."

Everyone raised their glasses, and toasts of "*Sláinte*" reverberated around the table. As we all dug into the meal, we complimented Catherine effusively. After that, the conversation was light and breezy. The weather forecast and highlights of Galway's football win dominated the talk. Martin questioned Mom and the ladies about Hanville Grove, their senior residence back in Langford. He was very interested in how residents were selected and the sliding scale for monthly rent.

After a bit of a lull, Elisabeth looked around and said, "We all know that Rory Connors was arrested for Deirdre Harrington's murder. I know you were with him at his daughter's birth, Maeve. How did he seem?"

Martin looked at me quizzically. I'm sure he was wondering why I was at the birth.

"I'm a midwife back home, Martin. Aisling Doyle, Catherine's niece, is a midwife at Ballymoor Hospital. She invited me to be on call with her, and Annie McIntyre, her patient, happened to be in labor and agreed to have me there. It was wonderful to see midwifery in action in Ireland. That's how I met Rory at his daughter's birth." Addressing Elisabeth, I added,

"Rory and Annie seemed thrilled with their daughter. They're a lovely couple."

Martin's face clouded over. "That poor young man. I heard that Rory had a very rough early life. Being arrested is a tough way to start out as a new father. I truly hope it turns out he didn't resort to violence."

"What are you talking about? There is no way that Rory Connors killed Deirdre Harrington. That young man wouldn't harm a fly," Helen said with deep conviction. "I have a feeling that he is being railroaded. Rory's convenient and has no one to speak for him. The officials want to put this murder behind them."

Everyone was still for a few minutes, studying their plates.

"Not to worry, Helen," Mom announced. "My daughters Meg and Maeve are here, and this case will be child's play for them. In fact, I know that they are already studying the situation and have a list of suspects."

Meg and I were stone-faced. Mom was impossible to stop, and I feared someone would ask about our suspect list.

Martin looked at Meg and me as if sizing us up. "I did not realize that we had amazing detectives in our midst. Are the Gardaí aware of your qualifications? Have they asked for your help?"

"We're just amateur sleuths," Meg responded. "We got lucky and uncovered some clues in a few police cases at home."

"That's not how I see it," Mom said.

"And you know how mothers are," Meg said with a laugh. "They think their children are magnificent." As she said this, Meg shot Mom a look. She wanted Mom to hold her tongue.

"What are your thoughts, Martin?" Helen asked. "We all know that you met with Deirdre to discuss leaving her property to the town for development."

Martin looked down at his hands.

"Deirdre Harrington was a complex woman. She was very attached to the Catholic Church, especially Saint Columbkille's. She wanted to provide for them. I tried to get her to see that Ballymoor would benefit from more housing, but she wouldn't listen. I couldn't get her to change her mind. So, with her untimely demise, all her property now belongs to Saint Columbkille's parish."

Martin poured himself more wine.

"I heard that her home was broken into," Meg said.

"What?" Helen exclaimed. "I bet it was the killer! Maybe they were looking for money. See, it couldn't be Rory Connors."

Everyone looked down at their plates. No one knew what to say.

"I happened to see the town manager on my way here. I met him at the petrol station. According to the detectives, a window was broken but the house looks otherwise untouched. They believe that the intruders were scared off and left by the front door. The best guess is that some teenagers did it," Martin commented.

It seemed to me that the young people of Ballymoor were taking the blame for all manner of crimes.

"Saint Columbkille's was notified, and the home has been secured. The area will be patrolled more frequently," Martin said.

"Has Archbishop Flaherty decided how the land will be divided?" Catherine asked.

"I had a conference with him this week. He is willing to sell the farmhouse on its own but is still deliberating about the rest of the property."

I gently tapped Meg's foot. I could feel the tension rising in the room.

"He'll sell to the highest bidder. The Church will always go for the money. They need it to pay off a multitude of lawsuits." Helen said, raising a hand to her neck. No, I corrected myself. She was grasping her heart necklace.

I found myself asking the same questions I'd had about Helen from the start. Why was Helen Lyons so angry? What was the story behind her necklace? And most importantly, why did she defend Rory Connors so fiercely?

CHAPTER TWENTY-SIX

––––––

Newborns can detect their mother's scent.

Martin Ryan grimaced. He looked forlorn and weary. From what he said, he was trying his best to intervene for the people of Ballymoor.

"Helen, I'll see Father Leahy again in a few days. As you know, he's a young priest and quite dedicated, and he agrees with the town's vision."

"But he has no say, Martin. The little people have no say," Helen responded.

"Well, I still have many connections with the Ballymoor Savings and Trust and the town council members. I will advocate for year-round housing for the town rather than holiday homes. I offered my time to assist with the financial aspects to lighten the burden," Martin replied.

Elisabeth leaned forward as she traced the pattern of the tablecloth with her fingers.

"James and I are very interested in purchasing the farmhouse, Martin. We're going to walk through it with Meg. She's a very experienced estate agent in the States. We know that Ireland has different rules, but she's looked at so many homes, I believe she'll be a great asset to us."

"That's wonderful," Martin agreed. "I believe it will be priced fairly. The home was kept in very good repair. I know the archbishop would like it sold to a family with Ballymoor roots."

"Well, we're trying not to let our hopes get too high. We are keeping our fingers crossed, though."

"A prayer to Saint Joseph might help, too," Martin replied with a wink.

"He's the saint for selling a house, not buying one. Here's what you do. First, get a Saint Joseph statue. They even sell them on Amazon. Then you bury his statue upside down and facing your house. There's even a special prayer you say and your house will be under agreement in a flash," Mom commented knowingly. "I think it would be better to pray to Saint Anthony for help buying a house. It just makes sense. He's the patron saint of lost items and miracles. So, if you need a house, he's your man," Mom concluded with a pleased look.

"I love that Catholics have saints for every life event," Louella said. "It's so handy."

No one spoke for a minute. No one would dare tread on Mary Margaret Callahan O'Reilly's knowledge of novenas and saints.

"Is there a special saint for finding the murderer of a crime?" Helen asked.

There was another silence as no one wanted to touch that remark. Except, of course, for Mom.

"You know, Helen, I think Saint Jude is the best person for that. He would be ideal because Saint Jude is the patron saint of hopeless cases. I'm not saying that Rory Connors is hopeless, but I think he needs all the help he can get."

Tell it like it is, Mom.

Helen sat up as tall as she could in the high-backed dining chair.

"Come on, it was in an open kitchen. Anybody visiting the restroom or just walking to the back of the pub could have reached in and taken that knife. Meg and Maeve, please don't let Rory be the scapegoat."

Helen, Meg, and I were thinking alike.

Catherine rose from her seat at the head of the table. "How about some dessert? Meg brought us a selection of mouthwatering cupcakes and chocolates. I'm going to put on water for tea. There's also Baileys Irish Cream liqueur for those wanting a stronger beverage. Let's all move to the sitting room to be comfortable."

Catherine was valiantly trying to change the subject.

As chairs moved back and people stood, Martin looked at Elisabeth and Meg and said, "Let's plot your strategy for getting the farmhouse. I want you to offer a fair price that doesn't overstretch your budget."

The three of them retreated into the far corner of the room.

"I'm going to take dessert to go, Catherine," Helen said while helping to clear the table.

She seemed a million miles away as she grabbed her sweater and a red velvet cupcake. "Thanks for a wonderful evening." And with that, she departed abruptly.

After getting Mom and the ladies settled with tea, sweets, and Baileys, I helped Catherine clear the table and stack the dishwasher.

I loved her homey kitchen. Copper tile lined the fireplace. A lineup of tiny multicolored vases, all holding purple statice, lined the windowsill. The room exuded warmth and a feeling of well-being.

"Thank you, Catherine," I said to her. "This has been a great night. You are so good to us."

"Maeve, you are my family, and I am thrilled you are visiting. Mary and I have been planning this for a long time."

As I wiped the caramel-veined granite countertop, my thoughts returned to the night's conversation.

"Helen Lyons has a soft spot for Rory Connors, doesn't she?"

"That she does," Catherine answered. "He is like one of her own. It pains her deeply to think that he could have any involvement in this mess."

Catherine paused as she put the white cotton napkins in the laundry bin.

"Helen is one of my dearest friends." With a very soft voice, she continued, "You know she has four boys. She originally had five, but she lost one. I think she looks out for Rory Connors as if he is her fifth son."

"Catherine, please leave those dishes and come in here with us," Mom called from the other room.

We took off our aprons, picked up mugs of Barry's Gold tea, and went to join the others.

How had Helen's son died? And did that explain why she was so protective of Rory? Was Rory an innocent or a killer?

Somehow it always came back to children. Was the Irish Zeena onto something?

CHAPTER TWENTY-SEVEN

———

Legend has it that bakers make a cross on the top of Irish soda bread to let the fairies out while it's baking.

My sleep schedule was off due to the all-night midwifery session, so the next day, I was up at the crack of dawn. Since Meg was still asleep, I decided to take a stroll and get scones and tea to bring back to the house. As I was waiting in line at Maggie's bakery shop, I hungrily eyed the selection. Besides many varieties of scones, there were rows of apple and rhubarb tarts, tea cakes, éclairs, soda bread, shortbread, and lace biscuits. I was going to miss these treats when we returned to Langford unless I could convince Will to expand his offerings to include a taste of Ireland. As I was gazing, I felt a tap on my shoulder.

"Hey, Maeve, how are you keeping?" Sheila Whalen asked. "You're certainly up early."

"Good morning, Sheila. I'm great. I couldn't sleep, so I decided to get out and take a little jaunt before breakfast. Well, and get a little snack," I said, laughing.

"I'm so happy I ran into you. I'd like to talk for a minute." As she said that, she looked at the line and realized many ears could overhear our conversation. "Let's meet outside once we get our orders."

"Sure thing," I responded.

I ordered two large teas to go and four scones. I'd entered the shop meaning to get just two pastries, but the display looked so tempting that I couldn't help myself and came away with two raisin and two cinnamon apple scones. This was only meant to be a pre-breakfast snack, so we could always save some for later.

As I picked up my brown paper bag, I knew that although I would miss Ireland for many reasons, a major one would be the fabulous scones.

Sheila emerged from the shop with a medium-sized cup and a small bag. She motioned me to a bench across the road where we could have some privacy from the early morning dog walkers and Dublin commuters. Other shops were starting to open and soon Ballymoor would fully come to life.

We both took long sips of tea, and I reached in and broke off a sizable piece of a raisin scone.

"So, Maeve, I'm happy I ran into you. I was going to call you and Meg later today. I've been a reporter for a long time and thought nothing could surprise me anymore. But I must tell you that the Deirdre Harrington case has me scratching my head. At the beginning, I was writing her obituary, and now I find myself investigating a murder. Currently, it's a tangled web because so many things just don't add up."

"Deirdre has certainly turned out to be a mystery, and in more ways than one," I said.

"That's so true, but I did find out a few things I thought you and Meg would be interested in knowing." She took a long swallow before she continued.

"As far as I can tell, she ran an export business. I don't know what she was exporting, but it was definitely from an office in Dublin."

I knew Meg had some information about Deirdre's address in Ireland's capital, but I didn't want to share that with Sheila Whalen just yet. I wanted to see what else the reporter knew and was also curious about her relationship with Seamus Burke. He was, after all, still high on our suspect list.

Sheila reached into her pastry bag and took out a frosted blueberry scone. She took a bite before continuing. These scones were incredibly addictive.

Sheila pulled out a pad and began reciting the facts she'd gathered. "Now, I think we went over some of this before. Deirdre Harrington left home when she was eighteen. Her family was from Limerick, and as far as I can tell, she never returned home. I'm guessing that, for some reason, she was estranged from her parents. She was an only child. I find it odd that she would have no acquaintances if she ran an export business. I mean, what about work contacts? Some people must have known her through her agency."

Looking down, I realized I had finished one scone and was halfway through another. So much for mindful eating. Deirdre's story was fascinating and troubling.

"We know she was very connected to Saint Columbkille's, and at times, I've wondered if she was an ex-nun. However, I can't find anything to support that theory. I've called some of my contacts in Dublin, but they've run into a complete dead end. I didn't know if you and your sister were interested in looking further into this since you are on holiday. I don't want to burden you."

Sheila looked at me a little sheepishly. "I heard some people say that you and Meg have been involved in solving crimes in the past. I even checked the stories about you in *The Langford Times*. Do you run a detective agency?"

"Detective agency? Oh, my goodness, no. We just happened to get involved in a few local crimes."

She handed me the slip of paper with Deirdre's last known address in Dublin. I saw it matched the information that Meg had found. Even as she stood to go, Sheila seemed hesitant to leave. She grasped my elbow and said, "Maeve, I don't know who killed Deirdre Harrington, but I do know that Seamus Burke is a wonderful man. He had absolutely nothing to do with any of this. He's only ever done good things for the town of Ballymoor." And with that pronouncement, she was off.

Aha, so she and Seamus were an item. Well, now we had two women protecting two men. How novel was that? Regardless of their wishes, though, the cold fact was that someone had murdered Deirdre Harrington.

I got up and brushed scone crumbs off my lap. Closing the paper bag, I was happy for the extras I'd gotten on impulse. With two scones left for Meg, I returned to Briar Cottage.

Meg was up and dressed in impeccably fitted dark wash jeans with a crisp white shirt. She looked flawless as usual. I reheated her cup of tea in our microwave and handed her the brown bag. Thank goodness I had stopped after eating two scones. As Meg got comfortable, I filled her in on what Sheila had relayed and the reporter's perception of our investigative skills.

"Sounds like Mom's been talking to many people," Meg commented. "Nothing unusual there."

She leaned back and took a large bite of a cinnamon apple scone. "How can we ever go back to Langford?" she moaned. "Malia must duplicate these beauties."

Malia was the magnificent French-trained pastry chef at A Thyme for All Seasons.

Meg and I had the same tastes and often thoughts. No DNA test necessary. We were definitely sisters.

As she finished her tea, Maeve said, "I've talked to Artie and got a little background on our friend, Seamus Burke. It just so happened that Artie was meeting an old friend from business school in Montecito for coffee, and she had the scoop on our buddy, Seamus. Word is that he was an amazing entrepreneur with his own company in Silicon Valley. However, he was very high-strung with a pure type-A personality and apparently a tad aggressive to boot. Hmm, how can I say this nicely? Okay, I can't. He left corporate life after an arrest for hitting one of his partners. After that, his board of directors urged him to go for extensive anger management counseling. Instead, he sold the company and left the US for greener pastures, so to speak."

What? Was farmer Seamus Burke a wolf in sheep's or, rather, goat's clothing?

CHAPTER TWENTY-EIGHT

Ireland produces highly sought-after cheeses.
Cashel Blue, made in Tipperary, is the most popular.

Meg said Artie was not exactly sure where Seamus had gone, but he was not surprised to hear that he had started goat farming in Ireland. He reported, per his friend, Seamus had always marched to the beat of a different drummer. After his arrest for fighting, Seamus attended some new age retreat center and yearned to change his life.

"That's very interesting. He had an arrest for fighting in his past, an anger management issue, and now has scratches on his face after a woman he had problems with was found dead."

"Do you have a plan, Sherlock?" Meg asked, popping the last of her scone in her mouth.

"How about we visit him at his goat farm? We could tell him that Will is a chef, he's coming to Ireland in a few weeks and would like to sample his products."

"He sold his business for millions, Maeve. I doubt he's interested in exporting goat cheese to the States."

"Come on, Meg. You're the one who taught me what big egos some business tycoons have. We can say that Will is here to do a tour of local Irish produce for inclusion in a Boston foodie magazine. You know he'll want to be included in that promotion."

Meg looked up and shrugged. "That's not a bad way to approach him—appeal to his inner diva or rather divo?"

"There you go. Score one for the younger sister."

We made our way over to join Mom and the ladies. I'd just had two scones, but who could resist Molly and Owen's delicious offerings? This was vacation, after all, and I needed to sample all the Irish food I could.

Although the morning sky was a bit hazy with clouds, I almost needed sunglasses as I surveyed Mom's table. Luella did not disappoint in her dandelion yellow boiled wool jacket and slacks. Gaby wore a burnt mandarin blouse with a high ruffled collar and a mid-calf length teal checked skirt. Ethel, consistently a bit more conservative, was in a peach cardigan and tangerine and coral striped pants. And Mom, who never felt a day was complete without sequins, was seated in the middle of the group and sported a Kelly green raglan sleeve top covered in glittering sequins and dark green slacks. Mom would wear her green proudly for the entire holiday.

"Good morning, girls. Did you sleep well?" Mom asked.

"Heavenly," Meg said. "My bed is a dream."

There were nods of agreement all around.

Molly bustled over to us. "Here, let me pour you some tea."

"Thanks so much, Molly. I was a major coffee consumer back home, but now I will have to take a few cartons of Barry's Gold tea back with me," I said, laughing.

"Today, there's a buffet of scrambled eggs, sausage, ham, beans, fruit, and, of course, brown bread for Meg. You can toast it if you'd like."

"Thanks so much. This all looks wonderful," Meg replied.

Once we were all settled and happily munching away, I asked, "What are your plans for today?"

Ethel jumped on the question. "Gaby and I are off to the knitting group. They call themselves, 'Keep Calm and Carry Yarn.' Isn't that just the cutest? Gaby and I are learning to make Aran knit scarves. It's so much fun," Ethel said with a big smile.

"Louella, Catherine, and I will help coordinate a jumble sale," Mom said. "I love that name. At home we call them rummage sales. People donate all types of used items for charity.The proceeds will go to the Ballymoor Village Childcare Center. We can't wait. I'm sure there are some great treasures to be found. Louella and I will oversee setting up the white elephant table."

Meg put her head down and twisted her neck slightly. Did she have a headache?

She looked up slowly. "Mom, just remember that we'll have to take a plane to go home. If you buy anything, it must be small."

"Meg, don't be such a worrywart. We can always buy more suitcases if we need them. I know that we each get two checked bags. Besides, I'm sure our family, when they come, will have room for a few of my things."

Meg picked up some brown bread, buttered it, took a bite, and was silent. She knew this was a battle she would not win.

"Then tonight we're all going to meet at Delaney's Pub at six to eat and then listen to more wonderful music. Catherine, Helen, and Elisabeth will join us. It will be great *craic*."

I had to smile, as did Meg. Mom was enjoying herself thoroughly and even picking up the native lingo. I was thrilled this trip had come together.

"What about you two? What are *your* plans for the day?" Mom asked.

I quickly bit off a piece of toast so I could remain silent. I was going to let Meg take one for the team.

"We still have some shops to visit, and then we'll probably drive around the surrounding area. We'll keep the day open and see where things take us," Meg continued, breezily.

"That's a great idea," Gaby said. "Just be free to roam and see what pops into your head."

Mom looked at us with a long, penetrating gaze. Did she have X-ray vision? She probably did with us. There was no fooling her. She was our mother, after all.

"Yes, what a wonderful idea, girls. Go with the wind, and who knows what you might uncover?" she asked with a slight hint of sarcasm. Mom did not like being out of the loop, especially when she knew we were in full investigative mode.

After ensuring Mom and her crew were safely off in Finn's van, Meg and I headed out to Seamus Burke's farm. First, however, we decided to take in more sights around Ballymoor. The rolling hills and beautiful rock walls were enchanting, and as we rounded one high bend, we saw the ocean sparkling in the distance. A mild breeze accompanied the bright morning sun. It was shaping up to be a beautiful day.

"Do you think it's strange to just drop in on Seamus's farm?" I asked Meg.

"Were we supposed to call first? I don't know what proper farm etiquette is, Maeve. But really, what else were we going to do?"

As we followed the GPS and began to get closer to Seamus Burke's farm, the roads became increasingly narrow. I had warned Meg about getting a big car, but she, as always, knew best.

Then she turned right onto Blue Ridge Way, and about sixty bleating sheep suddenly surrounded the SUV. They let their displeasure be known in no uncertain terms. How dare a car take up their road? At the far end of the flock, we could see a woman and a black-and-white sheepdog. They were moving the sheep to another field.

"Well, this is a different type of traffic jam," Meg said.

We could only wait and watch until the last ewe went by. Then the woman gave us a nod, the dog barked, and we could finally move forward. I didn't say a word about driving a massive SUV on country roads in Ireland. I knew better.

About a mile down the road, we saw a small black-and-white sign hanging from a wooden fence at the beginning of a long dirt driveway. It read, *Burke's Goat Farm. Goat Cheese for Sale.*

"Wonderful, he has a store on the property. We can be shoppers," I commented.

"Here goes nothing," Meg said as she steered the car toward the house.

CHAPTER TWENTY-NINE

———

There are about 17,000 family-owned dairy farms in Ireland.

Now, this was a farmhouse fit for Martha Stewart's glossy magazine! Seamus Burke must have spent some of his millions to update and expand the property. The main house spread out around a lush flower garden, and it looked like at least three new wings were built off it. To the immediate right was a massive red barn that also looked like a recent addition. *Burke's Goat Farm* was painted in large white letters on the side. To the left was a white building with dark red shutters. A large sign hung out front that read, *Burke's Farm Store.*

"Quite an operation. This renovation certainly cost a pretty penny," Meg said. "You called that right about his ego, Maeve. He obviously left nothing to chance when he refurbished this place and wasn't shy about getting his name all over it. This may go easier than I thought."

Perhaps because it was a weekday morning, we were the only customers. Meg parked over to the far-left side of the courtyard. Once we were out of the car, I spotted Seamus's white van parked on the other side of the barn. Across the acres of pasture, dozens upon dozens of goats roamed the hills, secured behind wire fencing.

As we made our way to the farm store, a man with dark, curly hair tied back in a ponytail stopped and watched us approach. Dressed in weathered jeans, boots, denim work shirt, and requisite scally cap, he looked every bit like an Irish goat farmer. Had Seamus Burke googled what to wear in the role?

Oh, stop, Maeve. This was his life.

He squinted at us in the morning light, and when he did, I saw his face still held four long scratch marks. They were healing but still apparent. This was Seamus Burke, all right.

We better have a convincing story.

"Good morning," I called out, maybe a little too gaily. "We're here to see your shop and sample your products. We had some of your exquisite cheese at Dolly's Tea and Pastry Shoppe. It was so yummy."

Yummy? Seriously, Maeve?

Seamus did not reply but simply nodded, walked over to the shop, and held the door open. Upon entering, we saw a massive wall-to-wall refrigerator case filled with various sizes and varieties of goat cheese. On the walls, ribbons and citations attested to the quality of this artisanal cheese. A large oak table held note cards with watercolors of various scenes of Galway and Ballymoor, in particular. A wire rack held an assortment of knitted goods. There were hats, mittens, and scarves in primary colors for children.

"Good morning," said a young woman with a sleek black bob with a deep purple streak on one side. "Welcome to Burke's. Would you like to try some cheese?"

Meg and I nodded.

"Come and sit, and I'll get you some samples and cream crackers."

As Meg and I settled at the round white table, I noticed Seamus Burke was still at the front of the shop, where he appeared to be redoing a bulletin board. Or was it just an easy way to eavesdrop on our conversation? Maybe he was interested because we were from the States, or perhaps he had seen our photo in *The Ballymoor Times* and knew we were the duo who had found the body.

"Here you go," said the attractive young woman. "My name is Penny. I brought you a few samples that I'll tell you about. But first, let me explain that our cheese is made in tiny batches. The original blend has a subtle peppery taste. It's quite popular here in Ireland."

Meg and I spread some of the original on a cracker and tasted it. This was the cheese we had had at Dolly's and was as good as I remembered.

"I can see why it's so sought after," Meg said. "It's very creamy but has a slight kick."

"I've tasted a lot of goat cheese, and this is unique," I said. "My husband has a catering business near Boston. He's coming over in a few weeks, and I know he'd love to sample some. While he's here, he will explore Irish foods and list them in a promo book in Boston."

I gave all my attention to Penny, but I knew that Seamus Burke was watching and listening the entire time I spoke.

"That's wonderful. I so look forward to meeting him. Let me get you some of our aged cheese. Seamus even makes a goat brie. It's delicious."

As I took another bite, I heard a gravelly voice ask, "What type of catering does your husband do?"

I turned and gave him my broadest smile and said, "His name is Will Kensington. His company is called A Thyme for All Seasons. Will caters many events in Boston and the surrounding area. He is usually fully booked for weddings a year in advance and also has a café where he offers breakfast, lunch, and dinner as well as takeout. He's currently in the process of opening a second one. After college, he went to Johnson and Wales because he realized that cooking and hospitality were his passions. His pastry chef is Cordon Bleu–trained, and most of his employees have been with him since the start."

Seamus gave a slow, pensive nod.

Penny wasn't nearly so reticent. She animatedly said, "It's wonderful how food brings people together. Seamus doesn't like me to talk about him, but he has done remarkable things for Ballymoor. People clamor for his goat cheese, and Seamus provides it to most pubs and restaurants in the area and beyond. I told him that he needed to think about exporting his products. It's not my call, but I think it would be a grand time to meet up with your husband." Turning, Penny gave Seamus a shy smile.

"Do you work here full-time, Penny?" I asked.

"Just for the summer season. I'm in my third year at uni. I study food science and nutrition. I'm very interested in the current food landscape in Ireland. When I graduate, I want to help let the world know about our fantastic products."

Suddenly, Seamus smiled and looked at Penny. "She's been a godsend this summer. Penny keeps the schedule in check, knows when all the deliveries need to take place, and writes ad copy for the products. She's probably right about exporting our goat cheese."

"How long have you been a goat farmer?" I asked.

A cloud came over Seamus's face. Had I stepped too far? But this was my only time to get information.

"Oh, just a few years now." He was purposely being very vague.

"Did you relocate from the United States? I can't quite place your accent, but I'd guess you're originally from the Midwest."

Seamus turned as if to leave but then turned back and replied. "I was born in Cincinnati. I spent some time in corporate life but got very tired of it. I obtained Irish citizenship through my mother and decided to move here. I've been very happy being a goat farmer. It suits me well. Of course, at times, it can be a little physical," he chuckled.

"Yes, I see that you have scratches on your face. What happened? Did you get in a tussle with a goat?"

Seamus's hand immediately reached up and covered the abrasions. He gave me a stern look with his dark eyes. "These are just from some thorny bushes. I was very careless. And now I'll be off. Enjoy your cheese. Penny, don't forget to lock up when you leave tonight. I'll be out on deliveries." Without another word, Seamus was off.

Meg and I finished our samples. We bought an assortment of cheeses for Catherine, said our goodbyes, and headed home.

Oh, Seamus, what are you hiding?

CHAPTER THIRTY

———

Opened in 1745, the Rotunda Hospital in Dublin is the
oldest maternity hospital in the world.

"You're unusually quiet, Meg. What did you think of Seamus?"

"Honestly, Maeve, I don't know what to think. He's hiding something. He must have been in an altercation of some sort."

"Maybe with Deirdre Harrington?"

"Could be. But meanwhile, Rory Connors is under arrest. I mean, he is a likely suspect. But once the Gardaí examined Delaney's Pub, they had to realize that many people had access to that knife. Of course, Rory had reason to detest Deirdre, and it was his special knife. The authorities are being cautious and methodical. He's the lead suspect right now."

"I'm sure they've questioned Seamus or will soon. I wonder what he told them about his scratches."

"You know, it surely makes a difference not having Patrick around to give us a little information. We're functioning in a vacuum here," Meg said.

"Which reminds me," I said. "We still need to investigate Deirdre's life. Perhaps that will give us some answers or a direction to go in. We need something soon because Mom will never forgive us if we don't solve the case."

"You're right. Plus, we'll hear about it forever."

With that, she pulled out two caramel bars and handed me one.

"Lunch," was all she said.

Later that night, there was a very festive atmosphere at Delaney's Pub as our group came through the door. By now, we all felt we were part of Ballymoor village because we had slipped right into daily life with the citizens. Catherine had the waitstaff join two tables so that our large group could sit together. We were positioned so that we had prime seats to watch the musicians after our meal. Everyone was pleased.

"Catherine, everyone in Ballymoor is making us feel so welcome," Mom said, looking up from her menu.

"Yes, they are. Ethel and I are coming along learning Aran knitting. We even traded some yarn. They're a great bunch," Gaby said.

Louella as usual was silent but looked very happy.

"Mary, you and Louella have a distinct sense of style. I think with your help it will be a very successful jumble sale," Catherine beamed.

Meg lightly touched my elbow. I could not look at her or I would burst out laughing.

Since Mom wore sequins daily and Louella solely donned shades of yellow, I could only imagine the display they had created.

Mom and the Ladies of the Lobby were thoroughly enjoying themselves.

Lindsay came and took our orders. As usual, she was very upbeat. Most of us decided on fish and chips with a cup of chowder, but Meg ordered Irish lamb stew with, of course, extra brown bread.

"So, Meg, tomorrow we're all going to Dublin," Mom said, leaning in close to be heard over the other voices. "I told Finn we want to visit the woolen mills. I think I have everyone's size. I want to get them all Aran knit sweaters before they come. I'm going to need you to go over the list with me later." Mom took a sip of her Manhattan.

"No problem, Mom," Meg said, saluting her with a pint of Guinness.

"We're going to see *Pygmalion* at the Abbey Theatre. I've never seen it on stage, but I loved *My Fair Lady*, the film adaptation with Audrey Hepburn," Gaby gushed.

"Be sure to get there early to check out the venue. The Abbey is the national theatre of Ireland and a source of pride for all Irish," Catherine said before sipping merlot.

Lindsay came and delivered our meals with Gracie. I noticed that Lindsay nodded to Gracie to help at another table after the plates were put down. It seemed that neither Cillian nor Lindsay wanted Gracie to have the chance for any small talk with Meg or me.

"Yes, Finn has the trip all arranged," Mom said. "Catherine graciously helped us get tickets for the play, and before that, we'll stop by Trinity College because I desperately want the ladies to see the grounds and the Book of Kells."

The Book of Kells is an intricately illuminated manuscript containing the gospels. It was created in a monastery in Scotland or Ireland around 800 AD. Its pages contain colorful illustrations of humans, animals, mythical beasts, and Celtic knots. It takes its name from the Abbey of Kells, which had been its home for centuries. The Book of Kells is now on display in the Trinity College Library. Only two pages are visible at a time, and they are changed every twelve weeks.

"Finn knows a great spot for lunch. We'll see the play in the late afternoon and then be back here at night. It should be a wonderful day."

Meg took another swallow. I could see her mind working overtime. "You know, Mom, it sounds fabulous. Maeve and I are thrilled that we're joining you. I thought we might even stay over an extra night because I'd like to visit some museums, and I bet Maeve would love to see the Rotunda Hospital. That's the famous maternity hospital in Dublin."

"That would be magnificent," I said. "I'll call Aisling and see if she has any contacts there. Perhaps I could have a tour."

Mom continued to sip her cocktail but leaned back in her wheelchair and gave us a long, stern look. I briefly felt like I was at an inquisition.

"That sounds just ducky, girls."

Ducky? Oh boy, Mom was not happy. There was no hiding anything from her. She knew we had other plans. We would hear about this later.

As we finished eating, I could see that there was a celebratory gathering on the opposite side of the pub. I recognized Brianna Shaughnessy drinking champagne and hugging people at a round table.

"I wonder what's going on?"

"Brianna and Patsy Shaughnessy received wonderful news. They got permission from the town council to open their inn. They're just thrilled," Catherine said.

"That's great," Meg responded. "Apparently, Deirdre really was holding up their business venture."

"Well, now it's all set to open. They can start accepting guests this week," Helen said.

Before the music started, I ordered dessert and then visited the restroom. As I walked past the open kitchen, I thought again how easy it would be for anyone to take the knife and hide it. I also observed that all the cutlery was now stored somewhere else.

On my left, I noticed a door was slightly ajar. I couldn't resist peeking inside. It suddenly opened, and I found myself face-to-face with Gracie Delaney.

She quickly scanned the corridor and, in hushed tones, whispered, "Maeve, come in, please," as she pulled me by my left arm.

The next thing I knew, Gracie and I were in a large supply closet. Boxes of napkins, utensils, and cups were stacked high on shelves.

Gracie looked up at me with her wide brown eyes. She bit her bottom lip and seemed unsure of what to say. She had something to tell me. I smiled at her and perched on one of the knee-high cartons. She was very petite, and I knew my height could sometimes intimidate shorter people.

Gracie clenched her hands and then seemed to find her voice.

"Maeve, I know you and your sister solve crimes. I know something about the murder, but my parents want me to stay out of it."

Why would Lindsay and Cillian prevent Gracie from telling what she knew?

She wiggled from side to side as if debating what to say before giving a slight nod. "The night that Miss Harrington was murdered, Rory Connors left early. He had worked very late the night before. But that night, because there was a town council meeting and Rory wanted to attend it, my father let him go home right after the dinner service."

She twisted the strap on her apron as she went on. "My mum was in charge of shutting down the kitchen that night. She said she didn't mind because she stayed up late to do the payroll. Mum liked the peace and quiet."

She looked at me with eyes as wide as saucers. "I left soon after Rory, but I saw it. I saw the knife. It was right where Rory left it."

Gracie stood up taller now, having found her courage. "Rory's knife was in the kitchen. Someone else took that knife and killed Miss Harrington."

CHAPTER THIRTY-ONE

———

There are approximately 9,000 births a year at the Rotunda Hospital.

"Gracie, I need you to clear table twelve," we heard Lindsay call as she knocked sharply on the door.

Gracie's eyes widened with fear. "Be right there, Mum. I was just grabbing some cocktail napkins for the bar."

Gracie looked at me pleadingly. "I'm trusting you. My parents can't know that I told you." Before I could respond she continued, "Stay here, Maeve. Please, stay here. You can let yourself out a few minutes after I leave." She was gone in a flash without looking back at me, and the door closed behind her.

Out of habit, she had shut the light off as she left, and now I was in the storage closet entirely in the dark. Well, it gave me more time to think. Did Gracie realize the implications of what she had said? Her mother was alone at Delaney's Pub the night of the murder. What happened at Delaney's after the dinner rush? Did the pub have late-night customers? Why would Cillian and Lindsay not let Gracie tell what she knew? It would definitely help Rory's case. Did Lindsay have something to do with the murder? There were so many questions and so many loose ends. Without betraying Gracie, I had to get this information to the proper authorities.

Groping my way to the door, I put my ear on the cold metal. I didn't hear anything, but I had to be sure. As quietly as I could, I opened it a crack. The hall was silent. I looked both ways. The coast was clear. I made my way to the restroom and took the farthest stall. It was around the corner from the main bathroom area and looked like it had been added on willy-nilly. Or maybe it was part of the original design and had never been remodeled. I wondered if anyone had ever had too much to drink, fallen asleep, and was forgotten in this tiny cubicle for a few hours.

Sitting there, I heard a few people enter, laughing and talking. It sounded like two women, but I suppose it could have been three.

"Can you believe it, honey? Our dream is going to come true."

"Oh, Brianna, it's just so wonderful. After all this time and red tape, we'll have our B&B."

Brianna and Patsy Shaughnessy! It had to be them. I held perfectly still to listen to their conversation.

"Thank God that witch is finally dead. I dreamed about her demise for so long, and now she is gone."

"Maybe you could add the song from the *Wizard of Oz* to your set tonight. The one about the witch."

"Ding, dong, it is."

That led to lots of laughing and giggling.

"I feel some guilt, but not much."

Just then, another group of women entered, and their conversation abruptly stopped.

Guilt about what?

I stayed in the stall, listening to lively banter before all the women finally left. I was alone. As I looked in the lavatory mirror, I thought that perhaps Meg was right. We might genuinely be out of our league. This crime was shaping up to be the Orient Express on steroids. Were Brianna and Patsy Shaughnessy guilty of murder, or were they just among the many people who were happy that Deirdre Harrington had left this earth? Had Rory Connors slipped back into Delaney's and taken the murder weapon? What about Lindsay Delaney and Seamus Burke?

I knew that there was nothing much I could do tonight. When I got back to our table, I saw a cream puff with chocolate sauce at my place, just waiting to be eaten. Well, I might as well enjoy dessert.

Helen was to my right, and as I took my first bite, I asked her what was happening with Rory Connors. I knew the question might upset her, but I felt connected to Rory since the birth of his child. I needed to hear the latest.

Helen rubbed her right temple as if she had a fierce headache. Then she took a sip of ice water and said, "I'm so upset that Rory has been charged with murder. A group of us from the neighborhood have collected some money to get him a good attorney. He insists he's innocent, and I believe him. I've known that boy for years. He certainly had enough reasons to hate Deirdre, but I know he would never have the heart to get rid of her."

My cream puff suddenly lost its taste. I was brought right back to the supply closet. How could I possibly get Gracie's information to the detectives? I needed to debrief with Meg as soon as possible.

"Have you seen Annie McIntyre and the baby at all? It must be a pretty tough time for them."

"We're all looking after her. In fact, I had them move in with me. I have the room and can help her with the baby until she can get back on her feet."

"Helen, that's so kind of you."

"Postpartum is a special time, as you know, Maeve. Mothers and babies need to be cared for carefully. Annie will need all the strength she can garner to overcome this ordeal. We all have to take care of her so she can care for the baby."

What a wise woman, I thought. That's precisely what it was all about. Helen knew all the tenets of postnatal care.

The music started, and our conversation stopped. I watched Brianna playing the fiddle for all she was worth with a massive smile. She had the face of an angel. Was it also the face of a murderer? Would it really be worth it to her to have committed murder? Well, I guess her livelihood depended on stopping Deirdre Harrington's objections to the B&B. Or maybe Patsy, her wife, was the murderer.

All I knew for sure was that as soon as we got back to the cottage, I needed to go over the suspect list again with Meg and tell her what I had heard from Gracie tonight. Then, a thought struck me. I remembered that Aisling Doyle's husband, Thomas, was a Garda Inspector. I wondered if he could be as discreet as my brother, Patrick. If so, maybe I could relay the information that Gracie had given me without betraying her confidence. But even if I had to name a source and it made Gracie uncomfortable and, in turn, meant that Meg and I would be unwelcome at Delaney's Pub, the truth had to prevail. Gracie wanted Meg and me to know the information. She knew it could shake her world, but she also knew what was right.

I sat back in my chair and let the Irish music transport me yet again. The town of Ballymoor and this trip was a dream come true. The scenery was gorgeous, and the people were welcoming and gracious. Unfortunately, evil was also lurking about.

CHAPTER THIRTY-TWO

---

*The Wild Atlantic Way, in the west of Ireland, is the
largest coastal driving route in the world.*

Meg and I talked late into the night. We reviewed our
suspect list.

"It's so frustrating having so many," Meg said, tossing her
elegant red leather journal onto the coffee table.

"And they all had reasons to dislike the deceased," I said.

"More than dislike, Maeve. You don't kill people you
merely dislike. We need more information."

She wasn't wrong.

"Well, there is one small thing I learned tonight, although
it may affect only one person," I offered.

Meg said nothing, merely raising a lone eyebrow, and
waited for me to speak.

I relayed what Gracie Delaney had offered up in the
supply closet. Meg was stunned to hear the news. Putting our
heads together, we devised a plan to get her information to the
officials without betraying our source. Neither one of us knew
what to think about Brianna and Patsy Shaughnessy. When Meg
and I were alone, we, too, could make scathing remarks about
people who had wronged us. It didn't mean we thought about
murdering them.

I had texted Aisling Doyle before leaving the pub, and
luckily, she was on call and awake. She called my phone and told
me she had some friends at the Rotunda Hospital and would
touch base with them in the morning to see if I could have a tour
as a visiting midwife. Then I briefly explained to her that I had
some information I thought her husband might want to know
about the murder case. I told her it would need to be handled

discreetly. I had found Aisling Doyle warm and welcoming when I spent the night on call with her. I hoped Thomas was the same.

She said that she would be off duty at seven a.m. and suggested I meet her. She could introduce me to Thomas then since he was due at the Ballymoor station by eight. It would give us ample time to talk.

Meg and I decided to go together. Luckily, we weren't meeting Mom and the ladies until nine to drive to Dublin.

After the meeting was scheduled, I had a very restless night. Dreams of knives, rivers, fiddles, cocktail napkins, and goats kept waking me from sleeping. Or maybe they were nightmares.

I woke up early to shower and dress for my day. Meg and I had already packed overnight cases the evening before. When we were ready, we took off from Farrell's Garden Estates, walking rapidly toward Ballymoor Hospital. Hopefully, Mom, Gaby, Ethel, and Louella would not even be aware of our early morning rendezvous.

Aisling met us on the first floor. The hospital was mostly quiet at this time of the morning. The day staff had already arrived, and most of the people passing through were hospital personnel on various rounds. Aisling led us to a small conference room off the main corridor. As we entered, I saw a broad-shouldered man in his late thirties with wavy jet-black hair dressed neatly in a navy and yellow uniform. This must be Thomas Doyle, Aisling's husband.

"Maeve and Meg, this is my husband, Thomas. I told him you wanted to talk about the Deirdre Harrington case. I will leave you now to give you all some privacy."

As she turned to leave, she said, "Oh, Maeve, I've made a call to the Rotunda Hospital, and Sadie Ahearn, a midwife there and a dear friend of mine, can give you a tour later this afternoon. I'll text you all her information."

"Amazing! Thank you so much, Aisling. I'm so looking forward to it."

"Anything for a fellow midwife. I'll see you later. Love you, Thomas."

Where to begin? First of all, could we trust that Thomas would be discreet? The truth was, we would just have to lean on my relationship with Aisling and trust him. As they say, in for a penny, in for a pound.

Thomas began, "It's nice to meet you, Meg and Maeve. Aisling tells me that you've solved several cases in the States. I also heard that your brother—Patrick, is it?—is in law enforcement."

We filled Thomas in on our background and emphasized that we did not want to interfere, but we had come across some information that we believed was valuable.

The three of us sat in silence at the conference table. Meg and Thomas both looked at me. It was time to tell what I knew, whatever the consequences. It would be devastating if Gracie's parents were involved in the murder in any way.

"Thomas, what I'm about to tell you was told to me in confidence. I trust you can find a way to say you got the information yourself without saying you heard it from me or Gracie Delaney."

"Maeve, I promise I will do everything possible to keep both of your names out of it."

I told him what Gracie had told me, and I stressed that her parents had forbidden her from sharing her observation about the knife. Thomas meticulously wrote everything down and nodded thoughtfully. I didn't tell him about overhearing Brianna and Patsy Shaughnessy's conversation because I hadn't heard anything definitive. Also, I couldn't prove it was them since I hadn't seen anything. I wanted to find a killer, not damage reputations.

"Is there anything else that you want me to know?" he asked when I had finished.

"That's everything," I said. "When I heard it, I was shocked, of course. But I don't know why the information wasn't shared. That might put a different light on Rory's situation."

Thomas thanked me. I could tell he was anxious to get to the station, share the information, and probably reinterview Lindsay and Cillian Delaney. I was trusting that he'd keep his promise and not mention my name.

We all left the hospital together, and then Meg and I slowly made our way back to the guesthouse.

"Well, Maeve, that was the best we could do. Thomas seems as methodical and cautious as Patrick. I believe he'll do all he can with that information."

"I agree, Meg. And I do feel better now, having told him."

"As long as we're not banned from Delaney's Pub forever, which we might be if they found out you're the source. That's not going to make me happy. I love their lamb stew," Meg said, nudging me. "I'm going to stop in Maggie's and get a few scones. Do you want a cup of tea as well?"

"That would be great. Can you get me a raisin scone?"

"Will do."

I opted to stay outside. I had a slight headache from not sleeping well and thought the morning air might help. As I waited, I surveyed a few shop windows to pass the time. The sidewalk was empty except in front of Murphy's Property Office. There, I saw a gentleman looking at photos of Ballymoor homes for sale that were posted for passersby to browse. It was early, and the agency was closed. Why was he there so early? Perhaps, like me, he just liked looking at the inventory.

When I stopped to get a good look, I saw about ten homes posted in the window, and I noticed that one of them was Deirdre Harrington's farmhouse. It appeared Archbishop Flaherty wanted it sold as soon as possible, which led me to wonder if Elisabeth and James would have any chance to buy it.

As I got closer, I did a double take at the guy looking in the window.

Rob Larson! It was Rob Larson studying Deirdre Harrington's house listing.

"Hello," I said. "I remember you from the plane. How's your conference going?"

"Yes, yes…uh, you are here with your family, correct?"

"I am. We're visiting relatives in Ballymoor." I gestured at the property listings. "What are you up to? Have you decided to move here?"

"No, no. I was just passing the time. Gosh, I need to get back to my conference. So nice to see you. Have a great day."

Turning in mid-sentence, he rushed off down the other end of the street.

Rob Larson, I mused. What was going on with him, and what was he hiding? Our suspect list might need adjusting, and my headache required medication.

Where were Cagney & Lacey when we needed them?

CHAPTER THIRTY-THREE

The cesarean section rate in Ireland was about 36 percent in 2023.

After another great breakfast, we set off for Dublin. By the time I got back home, I was going to have a hard time settling for a bagel on the run.

A slight breeze was in the air, and the sky was a bit overcast. I began to realize that this was quite common for August. The day would probably warm up, but autumn was on the horizon.

As we followed Finn Walsh's white van, I reflected on what an accomplished young man he was. He cared for Mom and her friends as if they were his family. He was an expert driver, kept up a running commentary on the wonders of Ireland, and was always cheerful. Finn loved his work. Of course, by now Mom and the ladies knew where he lived, how many siblings he had, and all about the young woman he was dating. Finn had no chance versus the Hanville brigade.

There was a moderate amount of traffic on the road to Dublin. We had budgeted two hours for the trip, and I knew that was what it would take us, at least. Finally, my headache was gone, and I was simply enjoying the journey.

On the outskirts of Dublin, Finn turned on his blinker and maneuvered off the highway. This was the first stop on a day-long journey.

At the end of the ramp, we saw signs for McCarthy's Woolen Mills. Then, about a mile down the road, there was a turnoff into a large industrial complex. The factory store was inside a vast brick building.

Meg maneuvered Mom's wheelchair across the lot and through the large glass doors. We all stopped momentarily and took in the sales floor as we entered. Everywhere the eye could see was stocked with a wide array of beautiful Irish knit items. It was stunning, not to mention a bit overwhelming, even for seasoned shoppers like Mom and Meg.

The main floor was about the size of an American football field and had everything from children and adult clothing to pet clothes. Mom pulled out three pages of notebook paper with a hot pink floral border. It was a very long list. She had a laundry list of people for whom she intended to shop. We decided to start in the children's area. Meg wheeled Mom over, and we took on the role of saleswomen ready to serve. Mom read off the sizes, and we held up each item for her inspection.

"Let me see the front of that one again, Maeve." Mom looked at every stitch of the Aran knit jumper. "I like it, but I want them all to match. Now, I'm thinking of cardigans for the girls."

This was going to be a very long, very involved shopping trip.

"Wouldn't it be great if we had a family photo when everyone comes?" Mom pointed out. "We could all wear our brand-new sweaters."

"I can arrange for that, Mom," Meg said. "It sounds like a fantastic idea."

As Mom read off sizes, sweaters began to pile up without rhyme or reason. I could tell that even Meg, the queen of organization, was feeling overwhelmed.

Meg was genuinely being a saint. How long could she keep this up? I needed to step up my game.

"Read me the list, Mom. Start again at the top," I said.

Mom started with the youngest, who were my two, and then proceeded to name all her granddaughters and their sizes. One by one, Meg and I held up items, folded cardigans, refolded rejects, and packed the winners into the shopping cart.

"I think that does it for the children," Mom commented.

"What about my Henry?" Meg asked.

"I put Henry in with the adults," Mom said. "He's my only grandson, and I want him to match his uncles."

"Henry will love that," Meg agreed.

"Let's move on to the adult section," I said. Time was moving, and we needed to wind up this shopping expedition.

After a bit of back and forth, Mom settled on identical pullovers for all the guys. She was very particular about the type of stitches she wanted featured. Meg and I modeled a few cardigans, and Mom decided all the women should have ones featuring shawl collars and patch pockets. I rubbed my hand over the wool. The sweaters were beautiful. I had to smile thinking of new outfits that Olivia would put together with this sweater as the showpiece.

Mom's haul was beginning to overwhelm even the largest shopping cart. Finally, an official saleswoman offered to take the sweaters to the counter.

"Gaby, Evelyn, and Louella, what have you decided on?" Mom asked.

"Mary, we can buy our own sweaters. After all, you paid for our entire trip," Gaby said.

"Nonsense, I'm going to buy them. I won that lottery money, but I intend for all of us to share in it. Now, let's look at the styles. I think the four of us should get matching ones. We'll be the envy of everyone at Hanville Grove."

With that command, the ladies perused several cardigans and pullovers. Finally, the four of them decided on soft green cardigans with carved wooden buttons. I could just see them at home. They would grace the Hanville Grove lobby with their finery.

At the cash register, I counted twice to ensure we had a sweater for everyone. It would be a disaster if one person were left out.

Two saleswomen rang up the sweaters. They both had broad smiles. This was a banner day for McCarthy Woolen Mills. Mary Margaret Callahan O'Reilly looked equally pleased. She had certainly outfitted her family and friends in style.

I piloted the shopping carts out the door and gave everything to Finn, who neatly stored it in the cargo section.

With that task accomplished, we set off for Trinity College. Now, it was my turn to be excited as we set foot on the grounds.

Trinity College was founded in 1592 and is counted among the leading universities in the world. As we entered the gates, I marveled at the stunning architecture and the sight of students in academic dress leading campus tours. Seeing students and professors crossing the courtyard in long black robes felt otherworldly.

After checking out the vast courtyard, we headed to the Trinity Library to see the Book of Kells. We waited in a thankfully small line, and one by one stepped up to view the book. Today it was opened to two pages in the Gospel of Matthew. It was awe-inspiring to see the intricate details and rich colors of this ancient manuscript in this famed library.

After all this excitement, Finn took us to his favorite restaurant. He told us it was where all the locals dined, and the food was indeed excellent.

After lunch, the group wound its way down O'Connell Street, which was bustling with shoppers, business people, and students. I don't think I will ever forget the look of joy on Mom's face. I also noticed that Meg stopped at a small food mart, undoubtedly, to restock her candy stash.

Finn kept us on schedule and had us to the theater for the matinee. Sitting in the Abbey Theater gave me a great sense of history, and *Pygmalion*, by George Bernard Shaw, the famous Irish playwright, was terrific. Mom loved Broadway musicals and plays, so I knew she would talk about this performance for a long time.

Afterward, Meg and I waved goodbye as Finn and the ladies set off for the return drive to Ballymoor. Meg dropped me at Parnell Square, in the heart of Dublin, where I met Sadie Ahearn and had a private tour of the historic rounded reception rooms and then the Rotunda Hospital itself. What a thrill. If these walls could talk. I could only imagine the history they had witnessed. Finally, I came to the famous chapel. As advertised, it was lavishly adorned with Baroque stucco saints and cherubs.

Finishing up, I made my way to the storied Shelbourne Hotel where Meg had booked us. Walking into the foyer, I felt as if I was dreaming. A few years ago, I watched a PBS special about this fine establishment and had always wanted to visit. It did not disappoint. The lobby had an incredible flower display stretching from ceiling to floor. Today, it went from the palest of pinks all the way to vivid red. There were roses, peonies, carnations, hydrangeas, and tulips. The staff was magnificent and took care of one's every need. After a light room service meal, we settled in for the night, and I felt like royalty.

Stretching out on her bed, Meg said, "The day couldn't have gone any better. It was a wonderful time, and I don't think Mom will ever forget this. We were so right to take her on this trip, Maeve."

"I agree. It has just been magical."

We were both silent, lost in our thoughts.

"Now, if we didn't have a murder to solve, it would be even better," Meg pointed out.

"What's on the agenda for tomorrow?" I asked.

"I thought we'd start with Deirdre's last known address and see what we can find out. Hopefully, someone there remembers her."

"This case is so up in the air. I feel like an inept juggler."

"Hit it. Let's hear the list." Meg was poised with her newly acquired pen and notebook to check off suspects as I named them. The journal was clearly a beloved purchase.

"Rory Connors, Seamus Burke, Lindsay and Cillian Delaney, Brianna and Patsy Shaughnessy, Rob Larson."

"Rob Larson? The guy from the plane? I think you're stretching there, Maeve."

"I may be, but let's leave him on for now. Something is going on with him. For some reason, he's very attracted to Ballymoor and maybe to Deirdre Harrington. We need to find out why."

"Will do," Meg said, carefully writing in her trusty new notebook.

Maybe I should get her one in every color. Who knows? This could be a low-tech side of her that I had yet to discover.

CHAPTER THIRTY-FOUR

———

In 2023, the cesarean rate in the United States was about 32 percent.

I had a peaceful night and felt refreshed and ready for the day. I heard Meg in the shower as I opened my laptop.

Pulling up *The Ballymoor Times*, I saw an article from Sheila Whalen noting that Lindsay and Cillian Delaney were being questioned about the Deirdre Harrington murder. A photo of the two of them going into the Ballymoor Garda Station was on the front page. Was Thomas able to keep Gracie and me out of the official record?

Actually, I was more curious about why Sheila would put this on the newspaper's front page. I'm sure a lot of people were being questioned. Was it to direct attention away from Seamus Burke?

Pulling open the shades, I saw that the sun was shining again. We were having a string of lovely days. But truthfully, no matter the weather, every day here was beautiful to me. Well, maybe not the day we found a dead body, but I could manage to overlook that.

A few minutes later, Meg came out of the bathroom looking like the runway model she could have been. Her makeup and hair were flawless, and she wore tailored navy slacks and a navy wrap blazer over a rose silk tank. Somehow, her outfit was unwrinkled despite having come directly from her suitcase. "Did you see *The Ballymoor Times*?" she asked.

I nodded, grimacing.

"It looks like Sheila Whalen is desperate to showcase anyone but Seamus Burke."

I shrugged. "The lady doth protest too much, methinks."

"My thoughts exactly. Maeve, as soon as you're ready, let's grab breakfast and search Deirdre's past life. This may be our only chance to check out her Dublin connections."

Meg was right. Our holiday time was marching by quickly. We needed some solid information in this case, and this was probably our best shot at getting it.

I could have lingered over the delicious Shelbourne Hotel breakfast for at least an hour, but time was of the essence. After a quick cup of tea, a hard-boiled egg, fruit, yogurt, and toast with some delicious orange marmalade, I signaled to Meg that I was ready to start the day. Trying to look as professional as my big sister, I had put my blonde hair in a high ponytail and dressed in black slacks and a pale blue embroidered Johnny Was jacket.

After successfully navigating Dublin traffic, Meg parked down the block from Deirdre Harrington's former address. The neighborhood was in the Liberties section of Dublin, which looked like a covetable combination of older and new housing. Properties in Dublin were very pricey, and this building with its pristine red brick façade, ornate black gate and railings, and immaculately tended front garden had to be on the high end of offerings. Deirdre clearly had enjoyed a comfortable lifestyle here. At the top of the front stairs, the directory listed six apartments. Of course, Deirdre's name did not appear on any of the mail slots.

"What now?" I asked Meg.

"I guess we could try ringing a bell. But look at the name tags. Do you notice that these five look like they were recently put in, but the one on the top left looks like it's been there for a long time? The paper has turned brown, and it's written in cursive. Let's try that one."

"You bet, Captain Benson."

Meg bowed slightly and rang the bell. There was no answer, but then a young woman came flying out the front door. She stopped just long enough to hold it open for us and then was on her way again.

"And that, my friend, is how crimes are committed," I commented as we walked into the lobby.

"You are so right, but the luck of the Irish is with us today. We don't look like thieves or murderers, at least in her book. Maybe no one ever told her not to let random strangers into an apartment building."

We walked up the three flights and knocked on the door corresponding to the older nameplate. We heard movement inside. It took a minute, but finally, a short, slightly stooped older woman opened the door a tiny crack. I could see that the safety chain was still on. I hoped we hadn't frightened her.

"Yes, may I help you?"

"Good morning. Thank you so much for answering your door. We're Meg and Maeve O'Reilly, visiting from the United States." Meg spoke in a soft, calm voice, with a wide smile. "I know this sounds strange, but we're looking for a woman we believe used to live in this building. Her name is Deirdre Harrington, and we were wondering if you knew anything about her or if you could give us the address where she moved to."

Meg was a master in these situations. She was doing her best to make this woman feel at ease.

The older woman looked us up and down, or rather as much as she could look us up and down from behind the barely opened door.

Apparently, she decided that we were trustworthy enough to provide information to. In a soft lilt, she said, "Deirdre Harrington moved away from here about four years ago. I wasn't friends with her, and I don't know where she went. I do know she left no forwarding address."

Pay dirt—finally, someone who knew Deirdre Harrington.

The door closed while she undid the chain. "Come in now, and we can chat for a minute."

She was barely five feet tall and very slight. She wore her white hair braided around her head. A green paisley dress reached to her ankles. Under that, sturdy black shoes peeked out. Nun shoes—or at least that's what Meg and I always called them.

Stepping into her apartment was like stepping out of a time machine into the past. The sepia wallpaper had a vintage flower basket motif. There were crocheted doilies under all the lamps, and the apartment was furnished with old-fashioned wooden rockers and a velvet sofa. A glass cabinet displayed Hummels, Royal Doulton figurines, and porcelain characters from the *Peter Rabbit* books. A large white cat sat on the back of the far sofa. Uh-oh. Meg was not fond of animal hair on her clothes. She sent her black Lab, Brady, to the groomer's weekly.

"My name is Geraldine Shea. I've lived here for about forty years. Deirdre Harrington used to live next door." She looked up at the two of us as we towered above her.

"Come and sit now, please. I'll get you a cup of tea, and we can chat."

"Thank you so much," I said, "but we don't want to put you out."

"I already have the kettle on. It will be no trouble."

Geraldine returned to the kitchen as Meg gave me a thumbs-up. Hopefully, Geraldine could provide a few answers about the mysterious Deirdre Harrington.

CHAPTER THIRTY-FIVE

————

May 5th is the International Day of the Midwife.

Geraldine returned to the parlor carrying a silver tray with delicate Belleek china teacups and teapot under a pale yellow cozy. After she had poured our tea and offered us custard cream biscuits, she turned and, in her low voice, asked, "So tell me. Are you any relation to Deirdre Harrington?"

I looked at Meg. I would let her take the lead on this.

"No, we are not related to her. We're here with our mother, visiting a town in Galway called Ballymoor. We have family there."

Meg paused slightly before breaking the news to Geraldine.

"You may not have read about it because it probably wasn't covered in the Dublin papers, but Deirdre Harrington was murdered recently."

"Murdered? Oh, my goodness." Geraldine's hand flew over her heart.

"Yes, it's awful," Meg commiserated. "She moved to a farm there about four years ago. From what you said, it sounds like she left Dublin and moved directly to Ballymoor. My sister and I are trying to find some information on her previous life."

At that moment, the large cat, who I noticed had yellow eyes, jumped up and plopped on Meg's lap.

"That's Snowy," Geraldine said, smiling at Meg. "Are you working with the local authorities?"

I decided to step in to give Meg a bit of a break. I could see she had her hands full.

"We are police deputies back in our hometown in the States. We found Deirdre's body. We know how busy the Gardaí are and what a great job they do, but we thought we could lend a hand since we're on holiday."

All right, Meg and I had been auxiliary deputies in the Langford police force for a hot minute, but desperate times called for creative stretching of the truth.

Geraldine gave me her full attention. I just hoped she didn't ask to see my badge.

I continued, "We took our mother to see a play in Dublin yesterday. She's back in Ballymoor now, but we thought that perhaps we could uncover some information that would aid the officials in their investigation."

Geraldine was quiet for a few minutes. She put one finger to her lips and tapped it as if trying to decide how much she would say. Eventually, she paused and looked at us. For the first time, I noticed she had pale blue eyes accentuated by her frosty white hair.

"I'll tell you what I know. Maybe it will help. Like I said, I was not a close friend of Deirdre Harrington. She wasn't friendly with any of the neighbors in the building, and now most of them have moved on to other living situations. Well, except for me."

Geraldine looked at her front door as if remembering the past.

"Deirdre Harrington was very, very secretive. She told any neighbors who asked that she was in the export business. One time, I got a letter of hers in my mailbox by error. It was addressed to Deirdre Harrington, Social Worker, so I knew that that was her profession. I never asked her about it. I just slipped the letter under her front door."

She gently moved her head from side to side, wondering if she should continue.

Please, Geraldine. Tell us what you know.

I smiled encouragingly, hopefully spurring her to continue. I was afraid to interrupt her train of thought. I certainly did not want her to stop speaking.

Snowy stretched and nuzzled Meg's neck. Although Meg was decidedly a dog person and had always been leery around cats, she smiled lovingly at Snowy. My sister may earn her Garda badge today.

"You are so sweet, Snowy," Meg said, petting the purring feline as white fur slowly drifted to the carpet.

Geraldine beamed, her expression softened, and she began again. "I wasn't nosy, but I saw couples come to her apartment on a regular basis. She would spend an hour or so with them. And I know Deirdre Harrington traveled around Ireland. She was often gone for a few days at a time."

Geraldine took another sip of tea and continued, "She must have made a good salary. She never seemed to lack for money. She dressed very well and always drove a late-model car."

Geraldine stopped and looked out the lace-curtained front window. She seemed to be debating what else to contribute to the conversation. Meg and I held our tongues. We did not want to appear too eager.

Geraldine gave a slight shake of her head as if to convince herself to continue. It was as if she silently decided to say all that she knew. "I believe that Deirdre Harrington had something to do with adoptions."

Adoptions? I certainly didn't see that coming.

Geraldine's voice became deeper and took on a commanding tone. "Deirdre Harrington was very religious. She was always at the Holy Rosary Church on the corner, and she was buddy-buddy with the priests. I don't know for certain, but I've always suspected she had something to do with arranging the adoptions of Catholic children."

Again, Geraldine went silent, and her eyes were downcast.

Meg and I quickly glanced at each other. What else was Geraldine going to tell us? I noticed that Meg was absentmindedly stroking Snowy, who was purring contentedly. I guess sleuthing took precedence over cat hair.

Geraldine leaned back in her rocker. She placed the teacup in the saucer on the side table and gripped the sides of the chair. Her demeanor mimicked a reluctant patient about to have dental work.

"Now, I don't want to sully her reputation, but you know there has been a lot of trouble about adoptions in Ireland."

My brain quickly ran through what I knew about Irish history. Could this have anything to do with the infamous laundries that the Catholic Church ran? I knew that nuns were involved and that many young unmarried pregnant women were sent by their families to the laundries. They had to work in abysmal conditions and then were forced to surrender their babies. Could Deirdre Harrington have had anything to do with that?

Geraldine Shea spoke in a clear voice that belied her age. "I've thought about this for a long time. I do believe that Deirdre Harrington was involved in placing babies from the laundries with families in America."

I gasped, and Meg gave me a warning look. But I couldn't help it. I had read some accounts of what had happened to those poor young women. I knew that the government of Ireland had formally apologized and had arranged for compensation. Still, the facts remained that the Catholic Church had mistreated the women and most of the mothers had no idea where their children had gone.

"Oh, I've read about those. Why did you think the babies were from the laundries?" Meg asked.

"I'm not sure that I'm correct," said Geraldine. "But the couples who came to her door were always from the States. Deirdre Harrington traveled around Ireland for days at a time and was very friendly with the priests. She was a social worker, and she must have been familiar with the court system. That could have worked in her favor. She always seemed to have plenty of money, much more than an average social worker would make. I believe it all fits. And then she retired very suddenly. As far as I know, she had no friends or family. I think she didn't want anyone to ask any questions."

Snowy jumped from Meg to Geraldine's lap, perhaps sensing the new tension in the room.

"And now to hear of her murder. It's all so sad." She paused and looked at us. "I believe she had many sins to atone for, and I suspect many people were very unhappy with her. So, girls, I'm sorry to say this, but I'm not surprised to hear about her death."

CHAPTER THIRTY-SIX

―――――

In Ireland, the Magdalene Laundries for "fallen women" or unmarried pregnant women were run by Roman Catholic orders from the late eighteenth century until 1996.

I barely remembered leaving Geraldine's apartment. I was in a total fog. Meg made sure that Geraldine had our contact information in case she thought of anything else she wanted to tell us. But really, what else could she say that would have more of an impact?

Meg and I were silent at the beginning of the ride out of Dublin, each lost in our own thoughts. Finally, I let out a desperate sigh. I felt like I had been holding my breath for hours.

"I feel so sad, Meg. Those young women were treated so poorly for so many years. It was a national tragedy for Ireland."

"If Deirdre was truly involved in this, imagine how many people could be angry at her," Meg said solemnly.

"We need to think about where we go from here," I pointed out. "I'd like to talk it over with Cousin Catherine and Helen Lyons. They may have some insight into this as they're older and may have even known some of the women involved. I also think we should touch base with Sheila Whalen."

"Maeve, maybe the reason we're having such trouble identifying the killer is that Deirdre was murdered in retribution for her past. Maybe we've been looking in the wrong direction."

"We're going to have to involve the authorities, too."

"We will, Maeve, but let's put together a coherent story first. For that, we need more proof. Plus, we don't know what happened with the Delaneys today. I just hope that something they've said makes the Gardaí look away from Rory Connors."

The miles passed, and we listened to the radio. At times, we laughed about Mom almost buying out the McCarthy Woolen

Mills. We even discussed taking Henry on a tour of Trinity College. On the whole, though, our hearts were heavy.

After a few hours, we turned off the highway towards Ballymoor. On our way through the village to the inn, I cried out, "Meg, stop! Stop the car. Pull over."

"What's wrong? Aren't you feeling well?"

"I'm fine. But I just saw Rob Larson in front of Saint Columbkille's, reading the weekly parish bulletin. Why is that guy in Ballymoor all the time? He's definitely not attending a conference in Dublin."

Meg quickly pulled into the nearest parking space. I jumped out of the car and started a fast walk toward the church but slowed down as I crossed the street. I didn't want to scare Rob Larson away. I needed to confront him without putting him off. When I came to the church, I walked over to the main sign as if I were checking out the times of the weekly masses. Rob Larson was intently reading the bulletin, so I took a few steps closer to him and coughed. He turned. When he saw me, he gave an involuntary shudder, and his complexion turned a dull red.

"Hello again," I said. "So nice to see you."

"Yes, yes," he responded. "Nice to see you, too. It's Mary, right?"

"Maeve."

"That's a great Irish name."

"You seem to like Ballymoor."

"I do. I'm doing some sightseeing today. It's such a nice village. I thought I might extend my stay after my conference."

Interesting. I doubted he was at a work event. I believed he was staying close to Ballymoor since I had seen him at the funeral and at various locations in the village. What was his fascination with this town?

"That's great that your time is so flexible," was all I said.

"Yes," he mumbled, looking at his watch. "I have to run. I hope you have a wonderful visit."

My eyes followed his dark brown sportscoat as he disappeared down the busy street.

Could he be the killer, or was he truly an innocent tourist?

Without any answers, I got back in the car and told Meg what Rob Larson had said.

"Well, you were right to put him on the suspect list. I'll try to google 'Rob Larson' again later."

My phone chirped with an incoming text.

"It's from Sheila Whalen. She wants us to stop by today if we have time."

"I'm game if you are. We might as well go now."

We pulled up to *The Ballymoor Times* building and were soon seated in Sheila's office. Meg and I had decided in the car to tell Sheila what Geraldine Shea had suspected about Deirdre Harrington's life. We recognized that we were out of our element in Ireland and knew we would need all the help we could get to solve this crime.

Meg took the lead and, step-by-step, went over Geraldine's conversation. Sheila did not look surprised at all. Had she suspected this? I could not see how. Or was she so desperate to protect Seamus Burke that she would jump on any possible lead?

When Meg finished, Sheila put both hands flat on her desk and gave us a big smile. She looked like the cat who had swallowed the canary.

"It's always so interesting how information comes to you in this business. Today, I had a visit from a former nun. She had read Deirdre Harrington's obituary online, and when she saw her photo, she immediately recognized her as a social worker for the laundries. As you can imagine, the ex-sister wants to remain anonymous about her time in religious life. She was assigned to the laundries for years and feels a lot of guilt about what happened there. She said that Deirdre did arrange a good many of the adoptions. She believes it was a very lucrative business. In fact, she once saw Deirdre Harrington with a brown bag filled with cash after a baby had been adopted."

I sat back in my chair and found myself wrapping my hands around my abdomen. I felt as if someone had kicked me.

"What are you going to do, Sheila? Are you going to publish this story?" Meg asked.

"I already have a rough draft written up for tomorrow's paper. The laundries were a terrible stain on this nation. Maybe if more women see this story, they will come forward. Who knows, maybe children can be reunited with their mothers. When people see Deirdre Harrington's photo, it may ring a bell."

"Please be sure to omit Geraldine Shea's name from the newspaper," Meg said.

"Of course—I will say that an anonymous source in Dublin suspected that Deirdre Harrington was responsible for placing babies from the laundries overseas for adoption."

Sheila paused and a look of sadness filled her eyes.

She let out a sigh and continued, "Many towns in Ireland still get people of a certain age who come to search. Most are in their fifties or older. They are looking for their mothers and their birth family. They rarely have much information, and sadly, many women forced into the laundries have passed on. So, there's no way to reunite these adoptees with their birth families."

Pausing fleetingly, she got a look of determination and said, "Deirdre Harrington's story will be in *The Ballymoor Times* tomorrow. I do expect there will be an uproar in the town. I also imagine some of the groups formed to help the women in the laundries will come to Ballymoor looking for answers."

"Have you shared this information with the Gardaí, Sheila?" I asked.

Suddenly, Sheila looked a bit guilty. "Yes, I did. I need to fill you in on how the Delaneys' interview went down at the station."

Sheila yawned and fidgeted in her chair. By her body language, Meg and I could tell that she was very uncomfortable.

"I spoke to Lindsay and Cillian Delaney, and actually, uh, I already knew most of the story."

Well, wasn't this interesting? She clearly hadn't let Meg and me in on what she knew.

"Usually, after the town council meetings, Delaney's Pub was where everyone gathered to discuss what had happened. The night that Deirdre was killed, the pub was full of locals after the meeting. Tempers were high, and things got a bit out of hand."

Sheila looked as if she had something very distasteful in her mouth. Meg and I waited for her to continue.

"Seamus Burke had too much to drink and confronted Deirdre. She did not like what he had to say and slapped him across the face."

The scratch marks! So, that's where Seamus Burke got his injury.

"Cillian Delaney had Seamus leave. Deirdre was in a rage and told the Delaneys that she would report the pub as unsafe. When Gracie Delaney told Cillian and Lindsay that the knife was in the kitchen after Rory left, they forbade her from saying anything. They were terrified that the Ballymoor Garda Station would issue injunctions against their establishment because of the altercation. Remember, Deirdre Harrington had already lodged numerous complaints against them. They apparently have a considerable loan outstanding from their recent redecorating. They are painfully aware that if they were closed for any amount of time, they could lose the business. Of course, now they are very sorry they didn't come to Rory's defense."

I felt another gut punch. It reminded me that you never knew how people would react when their backs were against the wall. Sometimes loyalty didn't mean anything. Or maybe Lindsay Delaney had decided to take the situation into her own hands.

Sheila looked weary as she said, "Based on their interview, the charges against Rory have been dropped. He, of course, can't leave town, but for now is home with his wife and daughter."

So, Rory might be cleared but what about Lindsay Delaney? When did the knife disappear? Did Lindsay try to throw Rory under the bus to protect her family's interests?

Meg and I bade farewell to Sheila and got back in the car. Neither of us spoke. Instead of driving back to the cottage, Meg pulled into a parking lot in front of Ballymoor Bay. Water was always our place to debrief. We might be across the pond from Langford, but suddenly, the bay felt like home.

Meg passed me a milk chocolate bar and, looking out at the choppy water, finally said, "There are so many possibilities with this case and all of them are bad. We have too many loose ends and no forward direction. This could be the straw that breaks the M&M's backs."

CHAPTER THIRTY-SEVEN

It is estimated that at least 30,000 Irish women were confined to the Magdalene Laundries.

The candy bar sat unopened on my lap. Meg looked over at me and stopped eating hers.

"What? I know that was hard to hear, but have you lost your appetite?"

"Rowan," my voice squeaked. "My sweet, sweet Rowan."

Will and I adopted Rowan Margaret soon after her birth. We had wanted an open adoption, and, luckily, that was exactly what her mother desired. I knew the name of her birth father but had never met him in person. Her birth parents had a very brief relationship when they were freshmen in college and ultimately decided the best thing for Rowan was to place her with a loving family. I sent photos a few times a year to Rowan's birth mother, and although she had never asked to visit, she kept her address current with me and always thanked me for the correspondence. She was still in college on a pre-med path and doing well. Will and I would share information with Rowan when she was old enough and wanted to know more about the circumstances of her birth.

"Meg, this connection to the laundries is so difficult for me to wrap my head around, not just as an adoptive mother, but also as a birth mother and a midwife. To know that women were forced to place their children with unsuspecting parents a continent away is soul-crushing. I'm sure that the adoptive parents assumed that the birth mother willingly decided on her child's placement."

"I hear you, Maeve. Sheila was exactly right. The era of the laundries was a very dark time in the history of the Catholic Church and Ireland."

"I can't help but think about those mothers longing to see their babies and desperate to find out what happened to them. And what about the children? You heard Sheila say that many of them have traveled to Ireland searching for their mothers. Just so much trauma."

Meg reached over and hugged me.

After a few deep breaths, I continued, "I remember how I longed for a baby. I'm so fortunate that adoption is different now and that Rowan will always know she was adopted and who her birth parents are."

Meg was very quiet, which was unusual for her. Finally, she said, "It's all about women's rights. I know things have radically changed in the past few decades, but we must never forget and never let that happen again. I think about your girls, Rowan and Sloane. Their futures have to be protected."

For a long while, we sat and looked out at the bay. Our hearts were heavy, but I believe we'd both found an even more profound conviction to find the killer. This was a chapter in Ballymoor's history that needed to be closed.

The following day, as Meg and I entered the breakfast room, we could hear Molly Farrell on the phone line informing someone that both the guesthouse and cottage were fully booked. We saw Mom, the ladies, Catherine, and Helen Lyons chattering at a large table. A few copies of *The Ballymoor Times* were spread out among the plates. Glancing at the front page, I saw a photo of Deirdre Harrington and a headline about the laundries.

"Good morning, Meg and Maeve," Mom said. "I assume you contributed to this story. Tell us everything you uncovered on your prolonged stay in Dublin."

Mom probably imagined Meg and I running around Dublin with a myriad of disguises.

Before we could say anything, Helen piped up, "Thank goodness Rory was released. Now the true killer needs to be named."

"Are Rory, Annie, and the baby still living with you?" I asked.

Helen's brow unfurled and her eyes brightened. "I have plenty of room, and I'm happy for the company. They have the whole upstairs. I hope they stay for a long while."

Catherine poured her more tea. Helen looked at the cup and then looked directly at Meg and me. "*Someone* took that knife out of Delaney's Pub after Rory left," she said exasperatedly.

"I'm sure the Gardaí are checking out all leads," Catherine replied.

Mom had a look of outrage on her face. She was small but oh-so-ferocious when someone was wronged. "Deirdre Harrington was a horrible woman, and everyone involved in the management of the laundries was vile. No more innocent lives should be destroyed because of them. Meg and Maeve, you need to find out who killed her."

Helen went very still. Her hand went to her neck and clutched the necklace with the five tiny silver hearts she constantly wore. I knew that she had four sons, and Catherine had said that Helen had lost a son. I'd wondered if he died in childbirth, but now…

"I have something to tell you all," Helen said with a confident voice.

Catherine leaned over and touched her shoulder gently. "Helen, are you sure?"

"I'm sure, Catherine. Surer than I ever was in my life."

Helen met our eyes, one by one. I felt Meg's shoe lightly touch my toe. I think we both knew where this story was headed.

With clear eyes, she began. "I was a laundry girl. I was one of the fallen women, as they called us."

I clenched my hands. Although I had guessed what was coming, it was still difficult to hear.

She began to speak at a low volume, but her tone strengthened as she continued her story. No one at the table moved. Mom and the ladies gave her their rapt attention.

"When I was sixteen, I had a boyfriend. His name was John O'Malley. I thought I was in love, but now I know I was in love with love. He was tall and handsome, and I had stars in my eyes. I knew nothing about my body. I knew nothing about how one got pregnant. It might sound silly to say now, but that was a time when such things were considered too sinful to even talk about. So, I was totally in the dark. And it didn't help that John was older than me and full of sweet words and promises. Within a few months, however, he was off to another girl while I was sick to my stomach every morning and wondering what type of illness I had."

As I looked around the table, I saw every eye wet with tears.

Helen continued, "My parents were strong churchgoers. That meant there was only the law of black and white in my home. Plus, I was the oldest in the family and supposedly the most responsible. So, when I was about five months pregnant, and my mother guessed what was happening to me, my parents were greatly disappointed, to put it mildly. After a trip to the local GP, I finally came to grips with the fact that I, indeed, was expecting. And the one thing I knew then was that, even though John had left me high and dry, I desperately wanted to have my baby."

Helen took a deep breath and stopped speaking. She still held her necklace in a death grip.

"My father, who was very strict, said I could not tell my sisters what had happened. He said I would shame the Gallagher family name, and the only thing I could do now was to go to a school—yes, that's what he called it, a convent school—and have my baby."

I could picture Helen preparing to go to what she thought was a safe place to be pregnant and have her little one.

"I was completely in the dark. I thought that the nuns would take care of me, and I would have my baby and then come home and raise it. Of course, once I got to the laundry, I saw that it was a far cry from any convent school. And the nuns disabused me quickly of the notion that I would be leaving with my child." Helen gave an involuntary shudder as she relived these painful memories of her past.

She finally released her necklace and fiddled with the pale blue napkin at her place setting. "There were so many girls there, and we were all, as they called it, in the family way. We worked long hours in the laundry. It truly was backbreaking. My hands blistered immediately, but there was no lotion for them. There was no school, no books, and the message that constantly came across was that we needed to work to atone for our sins."

She looked out to the garden as a single tear trailed down her cheek.

"Girls would have their babies and sometimes even care for them for a few months. That was when we would all get our hopes up, but usually, by six months of age, the babies were gone in the night. The next morning, we would all try to console the heartbroken girl."

Turning back to us, she gave a brief, sad smile.

"And then my time came. There were no childbirth classes, so we just learned what labor would be like from each other. I remember waking up in the middle of the night in pain, but I stayed in my bed because I didn't want to have the baby. I didn't want my baby to leave me. Finally, in the morning, when it was time to get up for work, one of the sisters saw that I was in active labor, so I was sent to hospital."

Catherine moved her chair closer and put her arm around Helen's shoulder.

"I do remember there was a lovely nurse there. I don't know her name, but she was very kind to me. At that time, there was no pain medication or anesthesia. I remember it was hectic, but she still tried to come and see me as often as she could. She would give me a warm cloth for my face and rub my back."

While Helen was telling her story, I thought of all the labors I had attended. I knew how women could be comforted by a touch or a kind word, and I often thought back to something the magnificent Maya Angelou wrote. She said a patient may not remember a caregiver's name but would never forget how they made them feel. The nurse who was with Helen during labor showed her kindness, and that act is still remembered these many years later.

"The doctor must have been very busy that night because I had barely begun to push when he applied forceps, and my baby was born. The nurses wrapped him in a blanket, and I could only see his face for a second before they whisked him to the nursery. He was a beautiful baby. He was bald, and his eyes were shut tight. I named him Michael. I always loved that name. It means gift from God."

Helen took a long sip of tea and wiped her eyes.

"It's funny what you remember. I had a lot of stitches and was very sore, but I was discharged the next day with the baby. At the laundries, the newborns were kept in a special nursery. I had to report for work a few days later. None of us were allowed to breastfeed, but I was allowed to bottle feed my Michael once a day. I wrote so many letters to my mother begging her to let me keep him, but she never answered. Then, one day, the mother superior brought me to her office and told me I had to sign papers relinquishing my baby. She said there was no other way. I cried and screamed, but eventually, signed my name to the document. I saw Michael every day until he was three months old. Then, one Thursday morning, when I went to the nursery, he was gone. I felt like my whole world was ripped apart. My baby was gone, and I had no idea where."

Catherine rubbed Helen's back slowly.

"The other girls became my family. We all tried to comfort each other as much as we could. I had to stay on for another year because the nuns said I had to work to pay for the care I had received. When it was time to leave, I was eighteen and had nowhere else to go but home. I came back to Ballymoor and worked on the farm. My younger sisters never asked where I had been. When I was twenty-four, I married my Jackie. He was such a wonderful man. When I told him what had happened to me, he said he didn't care. He always loved me and would bring me flowers every year on Michael's birthday. I tried for a long time to find out where my baby had gone, but I never could. That's why I wear this necklace with the five hearts. My Jackie gave it to me. I have my four boys here with me now, but I know the fifth, my Michael, is someplace in the United States."

Tears were now streaming down Helen's face.

"Maybe that's why I took such a liking to Rory Connors. He didn't have a mother, and his father was not much good. I felt that he was alone in the world."

The table was so quiet you could hear a pin drop. We were all so bereft at what Helen had gone through.

Then Helen looked rueful. "I truly had no idea that Deirdre placed babies for adoption from the laundries. She probably even placed my son. I wish I could have had a chat with her about it. When I called my four boys and told them this story last night, they were all very supportive and said they would love to meet their brother."

No one moved. Everyone had their eyes downcast. We were all contemplating what Helen had gone through.

I had never heard a first-hand account of the laundries. I felt emotionally drained. How had Helen gone on? How had any of the women survived?

Just then, Molly walked into the dining room and approached our table with fresh coffee. "Our phone has been ringing off the hook since the story broke. Many women's groups are coming to town to see if any records exist about the adoptions. Ballymoor is going to be bursting at the seams soon."

CHAPTER THIRTY-EIGHT

——

The Magdalene laundries were named after Mary Magdalene, a biblical figure.

As I digested this information, I saw Elisabeth speaking to Meg.

No one desired any more breakfast, and one by one, the ladies left to get ready for their various activities. I said goodbye to Catherine and gave Helen a long embrace as she was leaving. Finally, Meg and I were the last two at the table.

"Well, that was heart-wrenching," Meg said. "Helen Lyons always seemed a bit melancholy to me, but I had no idea that was her story."

I shook my head sadly. "Thank goodness those days are behind us."

"Maeve, Elisabeth has an appointment at Deirdre Harrington's farmhouse today. She wants to put an offer in soon and wants me to walk through it with her. I'd love you to come."

"I'll be very interested in seeing her house."

"Great. I guess Martin Ryan is going to meet us there, too. He's going to help Elisabeth and James arrange a mortgage, and he wants to get in and see the house."

"He wants to see her house? I thought he visited Deirdre off and on about her will. He must know what it looks like inside."

"Who knows? Maybe he wants to take another gander now that he's going to help them obtain financing."

We went back to Briar Cottage to get light jackets.

"Gosh, Meg, Helen's story was just so difficult to hear. And now it seems that our suspect list may have tripled. Will we ever unravel this mystery?"

"We need to keep trying, Maeve. Let's see what we find at the house. Maybe there'll be some obscure clue to the murder. Remember old photos have helped us solve cases in the past."

"I've been going over Sheila Whalen's story about what occurred after the town council meeting. She said the meeting went till about ten. Afterword, many people gathered at Delaney's Pub. According to the coroner, the murder occurred around eleven thirty or later. Rory's fingerprints are on the knife, but that's easily explainable. If he is eliminated as the killer, it seems most likely that someone from Ballymoor killed her."

"We now know that Deirdre Harrington and Seamus Burke had an altercation at Delaney's Pub," Meg said. "Lindsay and Cillian were desperate to keep it quiet. So desperate that they didn't come forward with information that could help free Rory. Lindsay Delaney was alone in the pub doing payroll after everyone else was gone. It would have been easy for her to grab the knife and follow Deirdre. And we know that Brianna and Patsy Shaughnessy are thrilled she's dead, so she can no longer block their B&B."

"Could it be someone we don't even have on the list?" I asked.

"Of course it could be. We're just beginning to realize how many enemies Deirdre Harrington made during her life. However, I think that someone on our list is the murderer. It appears that Deirdre managed to make a clean break from her past when she came to Ballymoor. I believe the killing involved someone local with a grudge."

We pulled up to the farmhouse, which was high on a hill overlooking the town. A late model Mercedes was parked beside Elisabeth and James's Ford Focus.

"Hello," Meg called out as she opened the front door of the house.

"Hello, Meg and Maeve. Thanks so much for coming. James is in the kitchen," Elisabeth said, fixing the Peter Pan collar on her starched white shirt. She had taken great care with her appearance today. I noticed that pearl earrings peeked out from her recently curled hair. Purchasing this house meant so much to Elisabeth and James.

As we wandered through the rooms on our way to the kitchen, I saw that the farmhouse was indeed in prime condition, except for the dining room window, which was now boarded up. The walls were beautifully whitewashed, and the overhead beams were stunning. It was strange looking at dishes drying on the top of the counter, though. It was as if they were waiting for their owner to come back.

Walking into the main bedroom, I saw a long white cotton nightdress. Deirdre must have put it on the bed before she went to the town meeting. A leather bound book on an antique round maple table had a marker minding her place. There were three other neatly made-up bedrooms, awaiting nonexistent friends and family. Nothing seemed to be touched, and I wondered what the burglars had been after.

As I looked in the glass door of the pristine library, I saw Martin pulling books off the shelves and leafing through them. What was he doing? He looked up and grimaced, as though I had caught him with his hand in the cookie jar.

"Good morning. I was just checking to see if Deirdre had any valuable first editions. I feel so responsible since she has no next of kin."

"She has an attorney who will have to come in and put this all to rights," Meg said, entering the library. "I'm sure the archbishop or the parish office has that information."

Martin walked over to the window and looked out at the acres of farmland. "You are right, of course. I was just trying to lend a hand." He paused for an instant before continuing, "I really hope I can assist Elisabeth and James to get this estate under agreement. I'll talk to the bank and see if we can do a quick deal. The Devlins should be in good standing. They're locals and their affairs seem to be in order."

Martin Ryan seemed to be unusually chatty today. He'd obviously been looking for something in the books, or was I just imagining it? He and Deirdre were about the same age. Could they possibly have been an item? Was he trying to retrieve a special gift? A love poem?

Oh, come on, Maeve. This isn't a Lifetime movie.

Meg and I toured the entire house. All the furnishings were included in the sale. Elisabeth would have her hands full, deciding what she wanted to keep. Walking to the barn, we looked in, but it was virtually empty. In the loft, there were a few trunks filled with old, musty quilts, which we didn't bother to unwrap. They would need to be aired out later.

"Well, Elisabeth, what do you think?" Meg asked.

"I love it. It will be grand for us. It's close to my mum and near our jobs. I just hope the sale goes through. Martin Ryan has been so wonderful. He's helped so many families like us over the years. I know he'll put in a good word at the bank."

"It does look like a wonderful place to raise a family," Meg commented.

I continued looking around as Meg, Martin, Elisabeth, and James discussed the price. I knew that Elisabeth and James couldn't have a finer consultant than Meg.

Later, as Meg drove back through the village, we both noticed that there was a lot of traffic.

"Looks like the women have arrived, just as Molly predicted," Meg said.

CHAPTER THIRTY-NINE

———

In 2013, Ireland issued a formal state apology to the Magdalene Laundry women, and compensation was offered.

Within a few days, the village was flooded with various women's groups who had heard about Deirdre Harrington's role in the laundries. Many of the women, or their mothers or aunts, had been in the laundries, and they had come looking for information. They wanted to make things right.

The town council planned a meeting to discuss what was known and what, of course, was not. Meg, Mom, the ladies, Catherine, Helen, and I planned to be there front and center.

The meeting was held in the Ballymoor Town Hall auditorium. It started with Sheila Whalen stating what she had heard from the former nun in as much detail as possible.

Meg and I had been asked to speak, and I gladly let Meg handle that aspect. Rowan's adoption was front and center in my mind, and at times my voice cracked when imagining what the laundry women went through.

As Meg took to the podium, I heard Mom stage-whisper, "That's one of my M&M's."

Looking polished and speaking in a clear, calm voice, Meg relayed what we had discovered in Dublin. Finally, the town manager opened the floor to anyone with questions.

Several older women talked about their experiences and relayed their hopes that a chronicle or some sort of paper trail could be found in the farmhouse. Everyone hoped for information linking birth mothers to babies. It fell to Sheila to explain that a thorough search of the property had turned up nothing. As I surveyed the crowd, my eyes met the Irish Zeena's. She stared at me and nodded slightly. Nan was spot on. We had to care for the babies and, of course, the mothers.

At the end of the night, I saw Rob Larson, the man from the plane, sitting in the last row with his head in his hands. Helen, Catherine, Meg, and I were the last people in the hall. Finn, always on time, had already escorted Mom and the ladies back to the Farrells'.

"Hello, Rob," I said as I saw him.

He looked at me sadly. "Maeve, I think you've had suspicions about me, and you were right. I'm not here for an IT conference in Dublin. I'm staying in the next town over at a B&B."

The four of us pulled up chairs beside him. Suddenly, I had a hunch about what he would tell us.

"My mother was one of the young women in the laundries."

I saw Helen's hand fly up to her necklace.

"Please, don't misunderstand me. I've had a great life. My adoptive mother and father were wonderful, and they were honest about where I came from. However, for years, they believed that my birth mother wanted me to be adopted. But when I heard the stories of the laundries, I began to question my background and even hired a private investigator. He suggested an ancestry test, which I did but it didn't turn up any close relatives. I was told it's used more by younger folks. The PI went through many records and came back to tell me that he believed my mother was in the laundries for a time."

Helen looked at him for a long time as if studying his features.

"Do you have any information on your mother?" Helen asked.

"I know that her name was Fiona. My mother said I came with a white and blue blanket. When I was about four years old, she noticed a name well hidden in the stitches. It was Fiona. She realized it was sewn by my birth mother. I still have it."

"What is your birth date?" Helen asked almost sternly. Her eyes were riveted on Rob's face.

He told Helen, and she immediately began rocking back and forth while holding her necklace tightly. She stared at him but said nothing.

"I have to say I was very bitter after I read all the stories in the paper and realized that my birth mother may have been forced to consent to my adoption."

He paused and looked very weary. "My adoptive mother gave me all the paperwork to aid my search. I knew my parents had met with a social worker from Dublin, and my mother still had a paper with a woman's name on it. It appeared to be altered, but you could see that the name Harrington had been scribbled over. That's how I tracked her down. I tried to talk to Deirdre Harrington the day before she died. I went to her house, but she wouldn't open the door. She just told me to go away."

Again, he paused, and his voice broke. "Please, believe me. I didn't do anything to her. I would never try to harm her. I just wanted to find my birth parents."

As I looked at him, I thought he might have risen a little higher on our suspect list. He was so sad and bitter. Could he have confronted Deirdre again on the night she died? Of course, he could have. Did he know Delaney's Pub had an unguarded kitchen knife for the taking? Very possibly. There were still so many unanswered questions.

Helen was staring, open-mouthed, at Rob. She finally leaned over and asked, "Could you please raise your right pant leg so I can see your calf?"

We all looked at her incredulously. Had Helen lost her mind?

Rob didn't move.

"Just pull up your pant leg," Helen repeated with a slight air of impatience. "I need to see your right calf."

We all watched as Rob extended his leg and lifted his khaki pant to his knee. There was a small brown and reddish birthmark that looked like a tiny rainbow on his calf.

Helen gasped. Rob looked at her with confusion on his face. "What is it?"

In a very shaky voice, Helen said, "I may know who your mother is."

Rob put his hands on his knees and looked at Helen with his mouth agape.

She gently reached over, touched his arm, and said, "I could be wrong. I could be very wrong. But you look a lot like a Fiona I know. I remember your birth date because I, too, was in the laundries. You were born six weeks before my Michael. Fiona remarked on the tiny rainbow on your leg. She has one exactly like it on her shoulder. Fiona always said that's how she'd know her Andrew one day."

Rob looked at her as if in a trance. He was incapable of speaking.

"She knitted you that blanket. I'm surprised they let it go with you, but I'm not surprised they overlooked that she had stitched her name in it. It was well hidden."

"Please tell me she's alive," Rob said pleadingly.

"Oh, she's very much alive. She lives right here in Ballymoor. If you have your car, we can go see her."

"But it's late. Should we call her first? Maybe we should wait until tomorrow," Rob said.

"I'll call her to tell her we're on our way. I don't want to give her a heart attack when we knock on the door," Helen said. "She lives alone in Ballymoor's senior housing."

Helen stepped out into the foyer to make the call. Catherine, Meg, and I stayed with Rob. I think we were all in shock at what had just transpired.

In a few moments, Helen came back with tears in her eyes.

"Does she want to see me?" Rob asked.

"She said she's been waiting a lifetime for you to come home."

We watched them go with a feeling of happiness tinged with disbelief.

"Imagine. He has been looking all this time, and now he just happens to meet Helen. It's a miracle," Catherine said.

"It's wonderful," Meg said.

"I hope Helen is right, but I know she wouldn't have said anything unless she felt certain," Catherine said.

"Did you always know Helen's story?" I asked.

"Yes," said Catherine, with a somewhat reluctant smile. "She told it to me many years ago." Tears filled her eyes. "She hopes that one day she can find her son."

When we returned to the cottage, Meg made us a cup of tea with a generous helping of Jameson Irish Whiskey.

"What a holiday this is turning out to be. I mean, it's been all about murder, meeting distant relatives, reuniting families, and ending up on the front page of the local newspaper. There's just never a dull moment with you, Maeve."

"I would say we're sharing equally in this adventure."

I sat back, drinking Meg's delicious potion. So many secrets had been uncovered, but a cold-blooded killer was still on the loose.

CHAPTER FORTY

In 2022, a monument at Saint Stephen's Green in Dublin was dedicated to the women sent to the Magdalene Laundries.

Martin Ryan and Meg worked their magic, and Elisabeth and James's offer for the farmhouse was accepted. As promised, the property was sold fully furnished. Catherine, Mom, the Ladies of the Lobby, Meg, and I promised to help sort out the furnishings. We needed to get this done as the rest of the family would arrive at the end of the week. I missed Will and my sweet girls so much.

The archdiocese decided to participate in a town meeting to discuss what would happen with the rest of Deirdre Harrington's land. Martin Ryan gave a persuasive talk about why it should be developed for the townspeople. He spoke against a neighborhood of holiday homes that tourists would use only a few months a year. The need for tourism was acknowledged, but Martin gave a compelling argument for keeping Ballymoor's identity intact. He warned about ending up like other villages that had lost their community spirit. Archbishop Flaherty said nothing but listened intently. Young Father Leahy spoke and seconded Martin Ryan's opinion..

The meeting lasted about two hours, and at the end, the archbishop got up and addressed the crowd. "Thank you all so much for coming. I wanted to hear everyone's views on the subject. The town of Ballymoor and Saint Columbkille's parish have a long and beneficial history together. After listening to tonight's presentations, I am happy to announce that I have decided to seek bids from a developer to create homes for the residents of Ballymoor."

Loud cheers and sustained clapping rang out.

As the room began to empty, several people stood in line to shake Martin Ryan's hand. They knew how instrumental he was in convincing the archbishop to go down this path.

"Amazing timing," Meg said, turning to me.

I looked at her expectantly.

"Think about it, Maeve. All these women's groups are in town to talk about what happened to them or their loved ones in the laundries. Deirdre Harrington was deeply involved in setting up adoptions. It's her land that's at the center of the Ballymoor controversy. That property must have been purchased with money she was paid by families who adopted the babies. Talk about a little pressure? I'm sure all these factors more than tipped the archbishop's hand in favor of the citizens."

As usual, Meg was right on target.

Over the next few days, visitors to the town began to disperse. Many women realized there was nothing else to find in Ballymoor. Deirdre Harrington apparently had kept no records and the ex-nun who had anonymously come forward was not interested in any more publicity. For the church's part, Saint Columbkille and Archbishop Flaherty denied any knowledge of the laundries' operation under their jurisdiction. With the potential leads in Ballymoor dried up, many groups headed to Dublin to see if they could find more information. It seemed quite hopeless because everything had been kept so secretive.

Meg and I were at an impasse in our investigation. We just didn't have a good handle on what happened the night of the town council meeting when Deirdre Harrington was killed. We didn't have solid evidence linking any of our suspects to the murder. The Ballymoor Gardaí also seemed to be at a loss. They held no new press conferences and, according to Sheila Whalen, were not currently interviewing any further suspects.

"We are overlooking something," I said to Meg.

"Let's keep our ears open, but I'm not optimistic," Meg replied.

The following day, we went to assist Elisabeth and James at their new home. As I looked around the farmhouse, I was again struck by the complete renovation. One could see by the way her many belongings were kept that Deirdre Harrington was organized and very particular. This impression was reinforced by the fact that the main house was in top-notch repair.

By the end of an exhausting day, the sorting and packing were pretty much in order. Stretching, I said, "Meg, I don't think there's much left for us to do in the house. Why don't we have a look in the barn?"

"Ugh. I'll go with you, but if there are a lot of spiders, I'm history. And you don't need any musty linens," Meg said as she marched out the front door.

Meg knew that I loved antique bedding. Hopefully, she would be patient while I checked out the quilts I had spotted on our last visit.

We climbed up to the loft and found four identical wooden trunks. As I opened the first one, a cloud of dust flew up, and we both started sneezing.

"Seriously, Maeve?"

I ignored her and pulled out the first quilt, which was magnificently designed in shades of ivory and rose.

"These need to be aired out. We can carry them down and hang them on the clothesline behind the house." I unfolded the first one and looked at it in the light. "Meg, this one is stunning. Are you aware how much time it takes to hand quilt?"

"I'm not one for vintage. All I can think about is dust mites. But I do have to admit that it's a work of art."

"I've never seen a quilt done like this before. Each square has a unique flower, and the border has tiny butterflies."

I took the king-size quilt down to the bottom floor of the barn and spread it out on a tarp. As I smoothed it with my hand, I could feel crinkling. What an odd sensation. The squares had obviously been stuffed with some type of batting. Why would it make that sound? Was the material they used very stiff?

I turned the quilt over and saw loose basting stitches around each square. This was as odd as the noise they made. Why would someone sew every square shut? I felt the quilt again and realized that the crinkling was specifically contained in the squares.

"Meg, do you have your manicure set with you?"

"Of course. You never know when a nail might break."

That was my sister—Girl Scout of fashion.

"Let me see the scissors."

Carefully, I snipped the basting stitches in an upper square and slipped my fingers inside. I felt around and then carefully withdrew a yellowed piece of paper.

I saw there was elegant cursive script, and as I read, my hands began to shake.

Mary O'Sullivan – boy born 22/12/71 – Mr. and Mrs. Keith Preston, Atlanta, Georgia, 13/04/72 – USA/CACC

I couldn't breathe.

I quickly opened the next square. There was another piece of yellowed paper with the same handwriting.

Phyllis Flynn – girl born 01/05/68 – Mr. and Mrs. Clinton Smith, Boston, MA, 24/07/68 – USA/CACC

"Meg," I called out in a tremulous voice.

"What is it? If those quilts are covered with bugs, we must burn them, Maeve," she said, looking up from her phone.

"Meg."

"Maeve, what's wrong? You look like you've seen a ghost!"

I couldn't speak, so I held up the two pieces of paper for her to read. As she did, her jaw dropped.

"Oh, my word. Deirdre Harrington must have hidden all the adoption records here. I can't believe she sewed detailed information into the back of these quilts. Why did she keep them? One would think she would have wanted to destroy all the evidence."

I was beginning to calm down. A plan was formulating in my mind.

"Who knows? Perhaps she just wanted a record. Or maybe she came to regret that she had participated in this and wanted to safeguard the information about where the babies went. Meg, let's open all of these squares so we can keep this information secure."

"I saw a small wooden box up in the loft. I'll get it, and we can put the pieces of paper there."

Meg was up the ladder staircase like a shot. Now it was the spiders' turn to look out. My sister was on a mission.

Meg and I carefully collected all the papers from various quilts and put them into the small pine box she had found. When we were done, we looked at each other as if suddenly realizing the weight of what we had uncovered.

"Meg, let's make copies of these scraps of paper. They're so tiny, we could lose one."

"Will do. We must guard this information. I could not bear for even one of them to be misplaced."

"We need to find a copier quickly, Maeve."

Meg was so right. We held many, many lives in our hands.

CHAPTER FORTY-ONE

———

About seven million Americans are adoptees.

Meg and I double-checked to ensure we hadn't missed any papers. Then we folded all the quilts and placed them back in the trunks, knowing that others would come after us to do their own search.

Every one of these paper slips was so precious and irreplaceable. I held the box securely as we went to the farmhouse, determined not to let go of it until we had duplicated all the information.

"So, how did things look in the barn?" Elisabeth asked, brushing an errant lock of hair from her face. She had been working hard all day to ready her new home.

"Everything looks great. There are a few old quilts but nothing else," Meg replied.

My sister and I understood the sensitive nature of our find. Without exchanging a word, we were in full agreement to protect the mothers and babies. "Find the babies," reverberated through my thoughts. *We're trying, Irish Zeena, we're trying.*

"I did find this cute little box," I said, showing it to Elisabeth. "I'll wash it and bring it back."

"Please keep it. There's so much stuff in this house already. We don't need anything else."

James came into the kitchen with a handful of papers. "Honey, I'm going to have to put off a run to the shops. I need to get these to Martin Ryan."

"Is it just a drop-off?" Meg asked.

"Yes. They're just some tax papers, but Martin said he needed them by tonight."

"We'll take them," Meg volunteered. "Maeve and I have to do a few errands, anyway. We'll be happy to drop by Martin's."

"Thank you so much. You don't know how much I appreciate it. I want to get to the hardware store so I can fix the back door," James said.

He handed Meg a file. We said our goodbyes and were off.

As we drove along the rural road, I was still in disbelief at what we found. What should we do next? Telling the detectives would be high on our agenda.

"Meg, I'm not sure I want to get out at Martin's house. I'm afraid to leave this box in the car. What if something happened to it?"

"I understand, Maeve. Don't worry, I'll just pop in and pass him the file, and we'll be on our way."

About three miles down the road, we pulled into a drive surrounded by tall hedges and a white brick wall. A gold plaque embedded near the top read, *Cry of the Heart*.

"Well, that's certainly an interesting name," Meg said.

We came to a very impressive manor house at the end of the paved driveway. Martin Ryan had spared no expense.

"He certainly must have done very well in banking," I said.

"I'd say so," Meg agreed. I knew she was tallying up a guesstimate of the estate's valuation.

She was about to get out of the car when Martin came around the side of the house. He was dressed in gardening clothes and green rubber clogs. Meg lowered the window to greet him.

"Well, good day, Meg and Maeve. What a nice surprise. To what do I owe the honor?"

"Hello, Martin. We're just dropping off some papers from James Devlin," Meg said, passing the file out the window to him.

"Great. Thank you so much. How are things going at the farmhouse?" Martin asked, casually brushing some dirt off his shirt cuff.

"Elisabeth and James are doing well. They should be ready to fully move in tomorrow."

"That's grand. I'm happy that a local family will live in this house."

"I know they're very grateful for your help, Martin," I said.

Martin gave a tiny nod of his head. "Would you like to see my gardens?" he asked hopefully.

"Maybe another time. We have a few pressing errands." Meg's voice was a bit taut, but I was certain that only I could detect her tension.

"Fine then, I won't hold you up. By the way, how long are you two here for?"

"Our family arrives next weekend. We'll do a bit more traveling, then," Meg replied, starting the ignition.

"All right then. Safe travels," Martin said as he lightly tapped the roof of our SUV.

Meg got us back on the route to Ballymoor. We had to get these records copied as soon as possible.

"I bet there's a copier at the Ballymoor Library, and right now, it should be pretty empty," I said.

"I should know better than to go into a library at closing time and use a copy machine with you, Maeve. Let's just hope we don't find any more dead bodies."

"Meg, you know that only happened once, and it was in Langford. Please have mercy," I said, laughing.

We parked behind the Ballymoor Library and carefully divided the paper strips into two stacks. We each took one and placed them in our purses. We figured we would draw attention to ourselves if we walked into the library carrying a box.

We worked efficiently and speedily, placing eight pieces of paper on the copier at a time. When our task was complete, we gathered all the papers, carefully checking that nothing was left on the top of the machine or in the tray. I still had bad memories of my untoward adventure at Langford Library.

As we walked back to the SUV, I could feel a bit of tension leave my shoulders.

"Okay, what should we do next?"

Meg pulled out a Fruit and Nut Cadbury, handing me a hefty chunk.

"We need to report this, but it must be handled with strict discretion. What about calling Aisling's husband, Thomas Doyle? We know him now, and he's already involved in this case. I think we could trust him to be discreet with this information."

"That's probably our best option." I sat very still for a few seconds. "There is something else we have to do first."

Meg stopped chewing for a minute and looked at me. She raised an eyebrow but didn't say a word.

I pulled a crinkled piece of paper out of my shirt pocket and read:

Helen Gallagher – boy born 12/4/66 – Dr. and Mrs. Charles Leighton, Chicago, IL, 14/07/66 – USA/CACC

"Is that Helen Lyon's record?" Meg asked with her voice shaking.

"I believe it is. That's her maiden name and the dates match up to when Rob Larson was born. We know she was in the laundries at the same time as his mother. We also know that she had a son. I think we owe it to Helen to have her see this record in private. And if this isn't hers, I want Helen to look through the rest of the stash to see if she can find her information."

"Let's go." Meg already had the car keys in her hand.

On the drive to Helen's house, I called Thomas Doyle and arranged to meet him at the station later.

As Meg pulled into Helen's driveway, I whispered a silent prayer, hoping we had found the answer to her dreams.

CHAPTER FORTY-TWO

After a 2005 amendment to the Irish constitution,
citizenship by birth is no longer automatic.

Helen's home was painted white and had Nordic blue shutters. There was a flower garden to the right and a vegetable garden beyond that. Because of its position on the bend of the road, you could glimpse Ballymoor Bay in the distance.

I made sure that Meg securely locked the car and only then went to knock on the front door. I knew I would worry about the adoption records right up until they were safely stored.

Helen saw us approaching through a large bay window. She came to the front door with a look of surprise.

"Hello, Maeve and Meg. It's so nice to see you." Although she was clearly puzzled as to why we were there, she would never say that.

"Can we come in for a minute, Helen? Are you alone?" I asked.

"Yes, I am." She looked puzzled but said, "Can I get you some tea?"

"No, we're fine. Thank you, though."

Helen sat facing us on a brown tweed sofa in the front parlor. I began to get cold feet. What if I was wrong? This woman had already been through so much in her life.

Meg and Helen both looked at me. Swallowing hard, I began. "Helen, Meg and I cleaned Deirdre Harrington's barn today."

Helen suddenly sat bolt upright but did not say a word.

"We found some papers. But before I show one of them to you, I want you to know that it might not be yours. I may be wrong and don't want to upset you."

Helen's eyes grew wider and wider.

"We found some papers sewn into the back of old quilts. We'll bring them to the Gardaí to look at, but first, I want you to look at one."

I took the yellowed, crinkled piece of paper and handed it to Helen. She held on to it very tightly as she stared at it. I could see her mouthing the words as she read. After a very long minute, she looked up at me and gently swayed from side to side.

"It's me," she said in a very, very small voice. "It's me."

Helen's right hand immediately went to her silver heart necklace.

Meg reached over and patted her back. I felt tears running down my face.

"My boy, my Michael, he went to Chicago," she said, smiling. "All this time, he's been in Chicago."

"Can we call anyone?" Meg asked.

"No, thank you," Helen said. "Tell me again where you found this."

"It was in the barn. She had an old trunk filled with quilts. It sounds crazy, but these records were sewn into the back of the quilted squares. When I spread one out, something didn't feel right. When I turned it over, I saw basting stitches on the back. Every square held a piece of paper with names, a birth date, and an apparent adoption date. I don't know what the initials 'CACC' mean at the end."

Helen shut her eyes. It was as if she had been transported back in time. I was sure she was trying to remember everything about her son's birth and signing his adoption papers.

"I'll never forget these dates. My Michael was born on Tuesday, April 12th, and was gone on Thursday, July 14th. Strangely, I don't remember much about signing the papers and the mother superior's office, but I remember seeing the initials CACC on the line beside my name. Over the years, I've thought about it many times. Maybe it had something to do with the church or perhaps a law firm." She looked off in the distance. "Perhaps I'll never know."

Helen reached out and touched both my hand and Meg's. "You cannot know what this means to me. I realize that my son may not want to know me. I realize Michael might not even be alive. But I will do everything in my power to try to locate him. I can never thank you enough."

"I think thanks are also due to Martin Ryan. If Elisabeth and James Devlin were not able to buy that house, we may never have found these records," I said solemnly.

"Also," Meg said with a smile, "if my sister was not so enamored of old quilts, they might have been quickly discarded."

"Yes, Martin Ryan has done a lot for this town," Helen said.

"And it's a lovely house that he has," Meg commented. I knew she was still thinking about Martin's expansive grounds.

"Cry of the Heart," Helen said. "I've never been in it, but I hear it's very grand."

She paused and looked down again at the piece of paper, lightly touching it with her fingers.

"Did you show these records to anyone else?"

"You are the first to see any of them, Helen," I said.

"Maeve has an appointment with Aisling's husband, Thomas Doyle. You know he's a Garda Inspector. Maeve and I have found him to be very discreet. We are going to show him the records now."

We stood up to leave, but not before Helen embraced us for a long time.

As we collected ourselves and drove off, I said, "At some point, we're going to have to tell Elisabeth and James what we found in their barn."

"I hear you. And best before it's on the front page of *The Ballymoor Times*."

Thomas Doyle had us come into a private conference room at the station. He carefully opened the box with the originals and leafed through them. I found myself tightly clutching my hands. I was thinking of the hundreds of lives contained within the box. Thomas seemed surprised at what we had found but thanked us immensely. Although I trusted him, the copies were staying with Meg and me for now.

"May I ask how Deirdre Harrington's murder investigation is going?" Meg inquired.

"It's at a bit of a standstill. So much information has come to light that we may have to open it up to a wider field. She may have had many enemies."

"What about Rory Connors?" I asked.

"I'm not allowed to speak about ongoing official matters," Thomas said. "But I recognize that you two have been extremely helpful. I will say that Rory is no longer on our active list. As you helped me discover, the knife was at Delaney's Pub after he left."

It certainly was good to hear that the cloud surrounding Rory Connors was beginning to clear.

Thomas told us that his staff would have a meeting about when and how to release the records. He said it would be done as soon as possible, and they would probably have a news conference in the morning.

Meg suggested that we grab a quick bite at Delaney's Pub. This sounded great to me. As we entered, we saw that the restaurant was quiet because it was between mealtimes. Lindsay and Cillian were nowhere to be seen, but Gracie Delaney welcomed us with a big smile and led us to a booth in the corner. We both ordered the pub lunch special: a bowl of fish stew, delicious slices of thick cheddar cheese, and, of course, a platter of brown bread.

"It looks like we came at a good time," Meg said to Gracie.

"Yes, the town has quieted a bit now that most of the women's groups have left. Mum and Dad took a trip to Dublin today for a much-needed break."

"That's nice. I'm sure they'll enjoy a nice getaway," Meg said.

Gracie poured us water and then looked at me. "Maeve, thank you for keeping my name out of the investigation."

"Of course, Gracie. And thank you for trusting me."

Meg was studying the menu but stopped and asked, "Rory still works here, right, Gracie?"

"Oh yes, he most certainly does. And it's great that he does late nights. That gives my parents a break."

"Do you get a lot of customers late at night?" Meg inquired.

"Well, we certainly have our regulars. The hospital workers who are getting off shift always stop by for a quick bite. We get a few customers after the weekly Ballymoor poker tournament, and a few lads after late evening soccer practice." She stopped and chuckled. "And, of course, there's Martin Ryan. I don't think that man can sleep unless he eats an éclair. I mean, he's here every single night. He never makes a fuss. He never wants tea, never a plate. He just wants a chocolate éclair on a napkin to take out. Then he walks to the car park."

We finished our delicious meal as a wave of exhaustion overcame me. What a day! I was more than ready for my comfy bed and a nap.

After saying goodbye to Gracie, Meg and I walked back to the SUV. We were just passing Ballymoor Green when I stopped dead in my tracks.

"What's up? Are you having a flashback to the dead body?" Meg asked, a bit sarcastically.

"Actually, I am. The napkin, Meg, the napkin."

"You're not making any sense, Maeve."

"Just before we found Deirdre Harrington's body, I picked up a napkin with the Delaney's Pub logo on it and put it in the trash. It was covered with chocolate sauce."

Meg looked at me, surprised at first but then thoughtfully.

"Maybe Martin Ryan dropped the napkin when he killed her, or maybe he saw something that could help us with the case."

"Why would he want to kill her? He had no motive."

"Maybe not, but he might have seen something," I insisted.

"I know I always call you the litter cleanup crew, but this time, you might help us find a killer. Let's talk to Martin and see what he remembers about that night."

CHAPTER FORTY-THREE

───────

Cnáimhseach means midwife in Irish.

As Meg and I approached Cry of the Heart, we saw an older Toyota parked beside Martin's Mercedes.

"Looks like Martin has company," Meg said.

"Let's knock and see if he's available."

The front door was ajar, and we exchanged curious glances. I leaned into the foyer and glanced around. The house appeared empty, but I heard voices from the back garden. I motioned Meg to go around the side of the house. As we came to the massive hedge, we stopped in our tracks. I gasped in shock. Helen Lyons was pointing a hunting rifle at Martin Ryan.

What in heaven's name was going on? Meg put a finger to her lips as we listened in.

"How could you possibly do that to young, innocent women? And to so many young, innocent women?"

Helen looked very calm, almost too calm. She pointed the rifle directly at Martin Ryan's chest.

"Did the money turn your head, Martin? Did it make you forget about all the pain you caused?"

Martin Ryan stood against a rock wall with his head in his hands.

"I was young, Helen. I was misguided."

"Weren't we all young once, Martin?" Helen waved the rifle back and forth.

I looked at Meg. We had to intervene. We could not let Helen kill Martin. No matter what he had done, it would ruin the rest of her life just when she was so close to finding her son.

Before I could stop her, Meg walked into the yard. A few seconds later, I followed. I wasn't letting my sister step into harm's way without me.

"Meg, what are you doing here?" Helen asked.

"What are you doing here, Helen?" I asked gently, coming to stand beside Meg.

Helen shook her head. "I don't want either of you girls to get hurt. Just go now and let me deal with Martin."

"Think about this long and hard, Helen. If anything happens here, you won't get to meet your Michael," Meg said softly.

Helen kept the rifle pointed at Martin, but it wavered a bit. "But he did so much evil. He needs to be punished."

"Let the Gardaí take care of him, Helen," I pleaded.

Meg walked to the open shed and returned with a roll of gray duct tape. "Helen, I'm going to tie Martin's hands together. His days of hurting people are over."

My sister motioned to Martin to put his arms behind his back and quickly wrapped duct tape tightly around his wrists. I walked over to Helen and, putting my hands on her forearms, helped her point the rifle at the ground. At this, she burst into tears.

I dialed 9-9-9 and said we needed assistance.

Meg led Helen to a chair on the patio after depositing the rifle in the trunk of Helen's car. Then she poured her a glass of water, and the whole story came flooding out.

"Once you two left my house, I studied the piece of paper you gave me. I knew that I had seen the initials CACC before. Remember, I told you that they were on my adoption papers. Then you talked about visiting Martin's home and that it was called Cry of the Heart. Something just clicked in my brain. Cry of the heart in Irish is *caoin an chroí*. I realized that the initials CACC could mean Cry of the Heart Company. In addition to working at the bank, Martin Ryan had a private loan business."

Meg and I were silent. Martin just stared at the ground and said nothing.

"I knew Martin was the only one in Ballymoor who met privately with Deirdre. He always said it was to try to have her sign her property over to the town, but when I heard she was deeply involved in adoptions at the laundries, I figured out it was something else. That's why I came here. I needed closure. I wanted to get him to confess his part in the adoptions. He admitted everything just before you came."

Martin raised his head. "Deirdre Harrington was bleeding me dry. Four years ago, she moved here and began harassing me daily. If I didn't give her money every month she said she would tell everyone my role in the laundries. She said she had written evidence. For years, I had been trying to make up for what I did. I tried to help everyone. I tried to make Ballymoor a better place, but it was all for naught."

"So you killed her?" I asked.

He was silent. Then he looked up and said, "I want to call a barrister."

"Of course you do," Helen said. "Do you now think you can buy your way out of a murder charge?"

Helen and Martin glared at each other.

"If I were a stronger woman, I would have shot you."

"You are a stronger woman, Helen," I said. "You've already proved that a hundred times over. But you, Martin, you were willing to let innocent Rory Connors take the blame in your place. He could have been imprisoned for years."

"I want a barrister," Martin repeated.

"It was you," I said, putting two and two together.

"You took the knife from Delaney's Pub and killed her. I heard you were always there for a late-night treat. Rory Connors was arrested, Martin. How could you let an innocent man take the blame?"

Martin did not respond. I, on the other hand, could not stop talking.

"You were the one who broke into Deirdre's home. And then, I caught you searching her library. You must have been hunting for the adoption records. And you were throwing Ballymoor teenagers under the bus to cover your actions."

"I want a barrister."

Sirens filled the air. When the caravan arrived, Thomas Doyle stepped out of the car first. He briefly stared wide-eyed at Meg and me before getting down to business. He had us give statements, and soon, the entire picture became clear. Martin Ryan, meanwhile, was silent the whole time, except for repeating over and over that he wanted a barrister.

By the time Meg and I got back to the guesthouse, platters of food had already been set on the table. We were greeted by sustained applause and cheering as we walked into the main area to say hello to Mom and the crew.

"I told you all that my M&M's would solve the case," Mom crowed.

"Even in a foreign country," Gaby said proudly.

Molly and Owen Farrell poured champagne, and we all had a quick toast before our much-welcomed meal. I knew the next day would be very hectic, and even though many thoughts raced through my mind, I fell asleep the minute my head hit the pillow.

CHAPTER FORTY-FOUR

———

Midwife means 'with woman.'

The following day, Meg and I joined the group at a very early meal. Catherine and Helen were now regulars at the Farrells'. Catherine immediately assured us that Elisabeth and James were pleased we had taken care of the records we found.

As soon as our tea was poured, the barrage of questions started. Many caustic opinions regarding Deirdre Harrington and Martin Ryan were expressed along with the questions.

In her typical fashion, Mom had a unique view of the situation. "Remember, there is the Church, and then there is the church. Evil people did wrong. That's absolutely true. There were a lot of mistakes made. But you must divorce people issues from your faith. Look at Saint Columbkille's now. There's a new young priest who is very inclusive and wants to make things right. The Church is what happens next. And because of all the pressure from women's groups, the archdiocese has decided to sell to builders who will cater to the people of Ballymoor. Forgive, but never forget, and move forward."

"You are so right, Mary," Catherine said. "And thank you, Meg and Maeve. Think of all the good that has come in a short time. Rob Larson has found his mother, and they could not be happier. My dear Helen will start trying to contact her son Michael today. Many other women have new hope from the records that were found. Martin Ryan will pay for what he did while, thankfully, Rory Connors is fully exonerated. And, God rest her soul, Deirdre Harrington paid for her sins."

Our last few days in Ballymoor were very full. Finally, it was *the* day. The rest of the O'Reilly family would arrive this morning. Finn was there to collect Mom and the ladies, all resplendent in emerald sequin scarves. Meg and I followed in the

SUV. We stopped briefly at a neighboring B&B, where we had booked rooms for the arrivals for tonight. Mom had planned a goodbye dinner at Delaney's Pub, and tomorrow we would bid a fond farewell to Ballymoor.

I had talked to Will several times in the past few days and filled him in on all that had happened. I couldn't wait to see him, Rowan, Sloane, and the rest of the family, of course. Meg and I even had a lengthy chat via Zoom with Patrick. After repeatedly asking if we were fine, he told us how proud he was that we were his sisters.

Yesterday, Meg and I had met with Sheila Whalen and gave her an exclusive interview detailing Martin Ryan's role in the murder. We made sure that Helen Lyons got full credit for figuring out his connection to the adoptions but made no mention of a hunting rifle.

Pulling into the airport car park, I could see that it was nearly full. Our family's flight had just landed. They would be in customs for a while, but we wanted to greet them at the arrivals gate.

I saw one space beside a long, white retaining wall clearly marked for a compact car. Meg headed straight for it.

"Ah Meg, I don't think we'll fit."

"Of course we will."

Meg turned in and pulled as close as she could.

"You have arrived at your destination. The route guidance is complete," Colleen, the GPS voice, stated adamantly.

"Hush, Colleen," Meg said, turning sharply.

Screech.

Ouch, that was the sound of metal hitting concrete.

There was total silence. I was not about to say anything or mention the fact that I could not exit the vehicle.

"Well, that went well," Meg said, and we both broke into gales of laughter.

"Meg, you better back out. I can't get out."

"That's why you have long legs. Climb over the center console and come out my door."

After an acrobatic maneuver worthy of an Olympic medal, I was finally standing beside Meg.

"Not a word to the brothers. I don't want to hear about this all week. I'll say someone must have backed into me in the parking lot. I'll square it with the car agency when I turn it in."

Meg was adopting the Irish "say nothing" policy.

The words "extra auto insurance" would not pass my lips. Every few steps though, I started giggling again, and Meg swatted my elbow as we walked.

Will, Rowan, Sloane! Suddenly I was engulfed in a family bear hug.

"Mama! Ma!" the girls repeated over and over. Aidan, Sebi, their daughters, and Patrick and Olivia and their girls all surrounded Mom, talking and laughing. Looking over, I saw Henry and Meg arm in arm chatting nonstop. Was this heaven? No, this was Ireland.

The day flew by, and soon it was time for our evening meal at Delaney's Pub. Mom had invited Catherine's family, as well as Finn and his girlfriend, Shannon, to join us. After dinner, she made sure that everyone she knew from Ballymoor would congregate here for drinks. Will and I entered the private dining room and saw that Gracie had decorated it with balloons and streamers. It was all in green of course. Olivia and her four girls were in matching brocaded Irish step-dancing dresses. It didn't even surprise me. Everyone wore a bit of green, even Louella.

Before the meal, Cillian Delaney took a myriad of family photos.

"Patrick, will you please say grace?" Mom asked when we were all settled at tables.

"Dear Lord, thank you for bringing us all together to enjoy this amazing trip. Thank you for this bounty of food and for our extended family. Oh, and Lord, once again, thank you for protecting my fierce, Irish sisters. Amen."

Applause and cheers rang out. There were numerous toasts and then praise for the wonderful meal.

After the main course, Henry stood and, raising his water glass, said, "Grandma, you are the best. You made this possible. We'll never forget this trip. We love you so much."

Mom was overcome with emotion and covered her face with her hands. Gaby and Ethel both leaned in and spoke to her softly. Louella patted her hand.

She dried her eyes with her blue flowered hanky and said, "I am so lucky to have all of you. Have dessert now, we still have a long night ahead. I want you to meet all our Ballymoor friends."

When we were done, we joined a crowd in the main room, where traditional music was playing. Mom started a reception line so everyone would meet. Meg gave me a sign that she wanted to talk outside. As I got to the door, she asked, "Up for a last Ballymoor walk?"

"Of course," I responded.

We slowly strolled the main street, both thinking of our Irish adventures. As we passed the Ballymoor Cemetery, Meg had us detour to Deirdre Harrington's grave. There were red and white roses placed against her headstone.

"Looks like Brianna and Patsy Shaughnessy are making amends," Meg said.

"It seems that Gloria Manly saw them writing *EVIL* with flowers on the grave after her funeral and she asked them to let the dead be."

"So that's what they felt guilty about," I said.

We continued walking and took the path that wound along the bay. The water was calm, and the sky was a deepening blue. Off to the left, the sun was setting, and to the distant right was a rainbow. I had seen more rainbows in Ireland in a few short weeks than I had ever seen in my life. For me, no more proof was needed that it was a magical country.

We came to a bench overlooking the marina and sat, each lost in our own thoughts.

"I got you a little something, Maeve," Meg said.

"I got you a little something, too," I responded.

Meg handed me a small package, and I recognized the wrapping paper. It was from the Eire Gold shop. I gave her an identically wrapped package, and she immediately started to chuckle.

Together, we opened them and saw, to our delight, that we had bought each other matching Claddagh rings. They were gold, and each held a tiny emerald. I remembered that the Claddagh design was an emblem of love, loyalty, and friendship. That was the essence of my sister. That was my Meg.

Meg turned to me. "Here we are in our homeland."

We looked at each other and in unison repeated the question our dad had routinely asked us.

"Who's got it better than us?"

"Nobody."

RECIPES

Helen Lyon's Colcannon

Serves 6

1 pound Russet potatoes, peeled and cut into chunks
1 pound of cabbage, sliced
2 leeks, thinly sliced
1 cup milk
1 pinch mace
½ cup butter, melted
Salt and pepper to taste

Put potatoes in a pot and cover with water. Bring to a boil. Cook until tender, about 15 to 20 minutes. Drain.

Steam cabbage until tender. Drain and chop. Keep warm.

Put leeks in a small pot and cover with milk. Simmer until soft, about 5 minutes.

Mash potatoes. Add salt, pepper, and mace to potatoes. Stir in leeks and milk. Stir in cabbage.
Make a well in the center and pour in melted butter. Mix well and serve warm.

Cousin Catherine's Shepherd's Pie

Serves 6

2 pounds Russet potatoes, peeled and cut into chunks
½ cup milk
¼ cup butter
2 tablespoons olive oil
1 large onion, diced
2 cloves garlic, minced
2 large carrots, peeled and diced
2 celery stalks, diced
1 ½ pounds ground beef
1 cup beef broth
1 ½ tablespoons tomato paste
1 tablespoon Worcestershire sauce
1 teaspoon dried rosemary
1 teaspoon dried thyme
1 cup frozen peas
Salt and pepper

Boil potatoes until soft and drain. Add milk, butter, salt, and pepper and mash until creamy.

Preheat oven to 400 degrees. On stovetop, heat oil in a large, oven-proof frying pan on medium heat. Add onion, garlic, carrots, celery, and ground beef. Cook for about ten minutes until meat is browned.

Drain the fat from the pan and add broth, tomato paste, Worcestershire sauce, rosemary, thyme, salt, and pepper.

Simmer for about 8 minutes, until sauce is thickened. Add the frozen peas and stir together.

Flatten the meat filling into a layer. Spread mashed potatoes over the meat layer. Bake for 30 minutes.

Delaney's Pub Brown Bread

Makes 1 Loaf

2 ¾ cups whole wheat flour
¾ cup rolled oats
1 ½ teaspoons salt
1 teaspoon baking soda
3 tablespoons dark brown sugar
½ cup molasses
1 cup Guinness
1 cup buttermilk
3 tablespoons honey
2 tablespoons melted butter
Rolled oats for topping

Preheat oven to 350 degrees. Spray 9-inch loaf pan with nonstick cooking spray.

Blend whole wheat flour, rolled oats, salt, baking soda, and brown sugar. Mix well.

Make a well in the center of the dry ingredients and pour in molasses, Guinness, buttermilk, honey, and melted butter. Mix well by hand.

Spread dough in pan. Cut a line down the middle of the bread. Sprinkle entire top with rolled oats.

Bake for 55 minutes or until a cake tester is clean. Allow to cool before removing from pan.

Delaney's Pub Lamb Stew

Serves 6

2 pounds of lamb cut into 1 ½ inch pieces
2 tablespoons vegetable oil
1 large onion, sliced
4 cups beef broth
3 tablespoons unsalted butter
3 tablespoons flour
1 bottle Guinness
2 bay leaves
3 carrots, peeled and chopped
3 large potatoes, peeled and chopped
1 teaspoon dried thyme
Salt and pepper

Brown lamb in vegetable oil. Remove from pot and put in bowl. Add onions to pot. Cook 5 minutes. Add to lamb.

Add butter and flour to the pot. Cook for one minute over low heat. Add beer and broth slowly, whisking to combine.

Return lamb and onions to the pot. Add bay leaves and simmer mixture for 90 minutes until the lamb is tender.

Add carrots, potatoes, and thyme, and cook for 30 minutes or until the vegetables are tender.

Molly Farrell's Irish Soda Bread

Serves 6

4 cups flour
1 cup sugar
1 teaspoon baking soda
1 teaspoon baking powder
½ teaspoon salt
$^1/_3$ cup unsalted butter, melted and cooled
1 $^1/_3$ cup buttermilk
1 large egg
1 cup golden raisins
2 teaspoons caraway seeds

Preheat oven to 350 degrees. Spray a 9-inch round cake pan with nonstick spray.

Whisk together flour, sugar, baking soda, baking powder, and salt.

Mix the cooled butter, buttermilk, and egg.

Make a well and add the liquid ingredients to the dry. Add the raisins and caraway seeds.

Knead the dough about 10 or 12 times. Shape into ball and put in prepared pan. Make a cross on top of the dough with a sharp knife.

Bake for 1 hour or until a cake tester is clean.

Cousin Catherine's Chocolate Guinness Cake

12 servings

1 cup Guinness
1 stick plus 2 tablespoons unsalted butter
1 cup unsweetened cocoa
2 ¼ cups sugar
¾ cup sour cream
2 large eggs
2 tablespoons vanilla extract
2 cups flour
2 ½ teaspoons baking soda
1 ¼ cup confectioners' sugar
8 ounces cream cheese
½ cup heavy cream

Preheat oven to 350 degrees. Spray 9-inch springform pan with cooking spray.

In a saucepan, heat Guinness and butter until butter melts. Remove from heat and add cocoa and sugar. Mix until blended.

In a separate bowl, combine sour cream, eggs, and vanilla. Add to Guinness mixture. Add flour and baking soda and mix well.

Pour into prepared pan and bake for 45 minutes or until risen and firm.

Cake must cool completely in pan before removing the sides of the pan.

Using a hand mixer, combine confectioners' sugar and cream cheese. Add heavy cream until smooth.

Ice top of the cake.

ABOUT THE AUTHOR

Christine Knapp practiced as a nurse-midwife for many years. A writer of texts and journal articles, she is now thrilled to combine her love of midwifery and mysteries as a debut author. Christine currently narrates books for the visually impaired. A dog lover, she lives near Boston.

To learn more about Christine Knapp, visit her online at: https://www.thoughtfulmidwife.com/

Made in United States
North Haven, CT
09 June 2025

69626344R00141